A House
All Stilled

A House All Stilled

A Novel

A. G. Harmon

The University of Tennessee Press / Knoxville

TENNESSEE BOOK AWARD — PETER TAYLOR PRIZE FOR THE NOVEL

Co-sponsored by the Knoxville Writers' Guild and the University of Tennessee Press, the Peter Taylor Prize for the Novel is named for one of the South's most celebrated writers—the author of acclaimed short stories, plays, and the novels *A Summons to Memphis* and *In the Tennessee Country*. The prize is designed to bring to light works of high literary quality, thereby honoring Peter Taylor's own practice of assisting other writers who cared about the craft of fine fiction.

Library of Congress Cataloging-in-Publication Data

Harmon, A. G., 1962–
A house all stilled : a novel / A.G. Harmon.—1st ed.
    p. cm.
ISBN 1-57233-202-6 (cl.: alk. paper)
1. Assertiveness (Psychology)—Fiction. 2. Fathers and sons—Fiction.
3. Grandfathers—Fiction. 4. Bullies—Fiction. 5. Boys—Fiction.
I. Title.
PS3608.A747 H68 2002
813'.6—dc21   2002005790

For my parents

"One dark night,

fired with love's urgent longings

—ah the sheer grace—

I went out unseen,

my house being now all stilled. . . ."

—John of the Cross

Chapter 1

Late Winter/Early Spring 1975—
Wolfy, Mississippi

Cox decided the kittens were hidden behind a low stack of hay, near the barn loft door. He shuffled close on his knees, turned his head, and put his ear to a crack between the bales. The mother cat—brindled and green-eyed—stood a few feet away, her back high as she watched. He stuck his arm into the crack, up to the shoulder, and felt for fur. One at a time, he drew out the blind, whining things, each small enough to fit inside the palm of his hand. Their mother answered with a stretched call as Cox shoved the kittens inside a burlap sack. When he could find no more, his hand grabbing at straw, he withdrew and tied a knot in the top. He rose to his feet, and the cat dashed past his leg into the hole.

"Now. Get back to business," he said after her. "Catch rats."

With a hand to the small of his back, he arched his spine. Blood rushed back into the taut cords. He walked over to the open loft door and peered down. His height and breadth nearly filled the frame.

Directly below was a fenced lot, which he used to fatten the calves he sold. Several of them, their black hair spotted with dried mud, stood looking up at him. To the right of the lot were the bare backyard and the small, plain brick house; to the left, a field planted with barely sprouted alfalfa. The field reached half a mile, all the way to the base of the first in a series of hills. The landscape was all pines, oaks, and clusters of old, brushy cedars, their bark stripped and scratched as though cats had been after them. The land wasn't very good—too rocky and too much sand in the clay dirt. Although he called it his own, the property really belonged to his father, Tollet, with whom Cox and his son Henry lived. The farm stopped at the end of the field.

The kittens mewed and whined inside the bag. Cox dropped the bag onto the hay at his feet and watched it shift.

Early spring bothered him; the new warmth in the air, the way he heard sounds again—birds, low cattle calls, moving water—the cushioned feel of soft ground beneath his boot. It was like something had come to him after a long forgetting, something he had time and again meant to do, but time and again forgotten. The feeling moved around beneath his skin, like his blood had turned cool, or turned warm— which, he couldn't say. He never liked the way it crept up on him.

Cox shook his head. He had to get to work. He had a new shipment of tractors coming in at the farm store that he managed, and nobody could handle it but him. All of the boys that helped him there were as sorry as could be.

The cat was back now, sniffing at the bag, sending a paw out to touch it. He kicked her away and snatched up the bundle, then headed towards the ladder. As he dropped onto the barn's dirt floor, he thought of all he had to do before he left for town.

First, he had to make sure Tollet was up. If the old man had sat around drunk all morning, Cox would have to wear the same dirty khakis three days in a row. He'd also have to drop by the department store and get him a bag of clean underwear. On top of that, he'd have to bring something home for supper—hamburgers, or chicken, or pizza. It would be better than whatever mess Tollet tried to cook, but it was too expensive.

He cut the lights off in the hall and closed the top doors to the stalls.

He needed to throw hay to the calves too before he left. He had wormed them and wormed them, but they didn't look as good as they should. He stopped at the lot fence, dropped the bag of cats, and leaned over to inspect his stock. The calves stared at him, dead-eyed, sallow.

Cox banged his hand on the planks to make the calves move. They shuffled from foot to foot, but that was all; too tired to care, too sick to care; not afraid of him enough.

It had set him back, having the two calves in the barn with the pinkeye. And seeing as they were the product of his bull breaking over the neighbor's fence and getting in with the man's milk cows, they were an expensive mistake. Cox had had to pay for the vet to doctor the cows, then, to avoid a lawsuit, had to buy the two calves that hadn't been aborted. It had set him back, and he didn't need setting back. Things were hard enough, with having to pay child support to his ex-wife, and having to run the farm on top of running a business with no help to speak of. An old sot for a father, and three children, all of them strange, just about topped things off.

Cox swallowed. He was about to pick up a rock and throw at one of the calves, just to make himself feel better, when a slight wind set up. It brushed against his throbbing temples, like the tips of cool fingers. It brought the smell of young grass and juice from new leaves. He looked about, his eyes casting at something; he remembered, in spite of himself.

This is where he had grown up. His mother had planted bearded, white irises over there, next to the pump house. The sun had burned like a brand through white sheets, hanging.

And someone had sung.

━━━━━━

Henry's face stung from the open wound at the corner of his left eye. The pain licked down the swell of his cheek and hung in the side of his mouth. He wasn't above crying yet, but if he did, the salt water would roll down into the wound and make it sting. He sat still on the kitchen table, his sullen face peeping out from the space between the roll of his stocking cap and the collar of his down coat. Cox had used a sledgehammer to take out the wall between the sitting room and the kitchen, so Henry could watch his grandfather struggling to get the shade off of a lamp.

"Hold on," said Tollet. "Let me bring the light over to your face."

Henry dreaded the doctoring he was about to get: shaky hands, quivering and tugging at his gash—hot, sour whisky breath in his face.

Tollet paid out the lamp's extension cord like fishing line, looping it around the sofa and chair. His house shoes scraped at the floor as though it were covered with sand as he scuffled over to the boy. The naked bulb came close to Henry's head; the wound flushed brightly, like a flower forced to bud.

"Unh," grunted Tollet. "Unh-unh-unh."

Henry stared at a corner of the ceiling where the stove exhaust had blown soot. Though Tollet's breath was as bad as he'd imagined, he hadn't touched him yet. Henry glanced to see what he meant by the grunts, his eyes watering as he looked into the old man's thin face. It was absorbed, head back and eyes narrowed, as if he were trying to see something at the bottom of a dark hole. Only the thinnest, grayest strands remained on Tollet's scalp, but a patch of whiskers showed the hair was once coal black, like Henry's, and his father's.

"Why didn't you move out'a the way?" asked Tollet. He stood back.

"I didn't see it," said Henry. "I wasn't looking."

Tollet bunched his mouth together and shook his head. "You shoulda been."

Tollet set the lamp down. He clutched Henry at the base of the skull with one hand and the tip of the chin with the other. He turned his face this way and that, like a mirror bouncing reflections.

It was the truth. He hadn't seen it. He hadn't even realized he had been clouted until he saw the branch fall from the other boy's hand. By the time the stars had cleared, he'd been kicked over, stomped, and left.

Tollet scuffled to the sink to wet a rag. The water scoured and sloshed against the basin as he ran his hand beneath the spigot to test the temperature.

The blood felt as though it were rushing to the surface of his skin, then back down again, like people running upstairs and down. It was the second time he'd been beaten, but the first time he'd told about it. If Cox knew he'd been beaten before, and by the same boy, he'd catch hell. He'd have made up some lie about this time too, but the woman who lived at the base of the hill had seen it all. She'd run out of her trailer, dressed in blue jeans and a bathrobe. After picking him off the ground and turning him towards home, she'd scampered back to her tin box and slammed the door shut, like a cuckoo bird whose job was done. He'd forgotten to go on to the bus stop, so he'd dragged himself home.

"Do I need to go to the doctor?" He peered at Tollet's preparations on the counter: a hot, wet rag, a bottle of green dish-washing liquid, some rubbing alcohol, a crusted brown bottle of Merthiolate without a label, and five Band-Aids: two pinky-sized, one patch size, and a round one.

"I can fix it," said Tollet. He swept the lot across the counter and collected it against his stomach, then shuffled back to the table.

Henry closed his eyes and presented his cheek. He took a long, bolstering breath, but before the old man could start, the front door swept open with a blast of chilled air. Henry raised his lids slowly, as though they were gummed together.

Cox stood in the entry, his breath cold and smoky, his hands dripping water. Tollet turned to look.

"Nothin' to worry about," jittered Tollet. "He just got in a scrap with somebody. That's all. I can fix it." He bobbed his head in a series of nods. "Did ya' get rid of them cats?"

Cox buried his gaze into Henry's cut. The boy could never stand to look straight on at his father for too long. Cox's head was boxy and covered with cropped, black bristles. His features were cut so sharp they might have been blasted out. For the most part, Henry thought they looked alike—all except for the eyes. They were the same color, blue, but when he talked, Cox used them like a pair of hands that held you by the shoulders. Henry's eyes wouldn't do that, though he'd tried often. And also, looking at him for very long reminded the boy that he hadn't gotten his father's size. Though he thought he might eventually get Cox's muscles, he was very short for twelve. If things didn't change soon, he'd never match him. The bulky clothes Cox wore made him look even bigger.

"Who did that?" asked Cox. He rolled a shoulder at Henry.

The boy's mouth dropped open. He wondered whether he should invent two boys, so he would sound out-numbered.

"Don't know his name," said Tollet. "Some l'il bastard popped him up side the head with a stick. Back 'round Shreva's house. She sent him down here to—"

"Let *him* tell it."

"That's what happened!" Henry said, and nodded briskly. It would do.

"I was walking to the bus along the creek back there, minding my own business, and next thing you know, I heard somebody running up behind me. So I just kinda turned around—to see who it was. And here comes this big ole stick and catches me up side the head."

Cox gathered breath. He wiped his wet hands on his pants. The oak floor gave under his step, popping like hammer strikes. An envelope of cold air grew around Henry.

"Why?" asked Cox. He stared hard at the wound, which was beginning to seal again. His breath blew into the cut; Henry flinched.

"Musta been after some money," offered Tollet.

Henry nodded. He always had a little money on him. Cox wasn't stingy that way. And the first time it had happened, he had been like Tollet, sure the boy was after his Indian-bead billfold. But after it was all over, he had found the billfold still in his pocket. It was the same today.

Cox thumped him hard on the chest with his index finger. Henry looked up.

"Did you know him?" he asked. "Wasn't one of Shreva's boys?"

"Never seen him before in my life," said Henry. "Musta been from Camille, or even further back than that."

Henry gauged his father's expression. For Cox, the world's problems started with the scatter of trashy families who still lived in the hills behind his farm. Laying the blame there was a good idea. Cox eyed him for a moment, then looked to Tollet.

"Can you fix him?" he asked. "Looks like he needs stitches."

"Naaawww!" scoffed Tollet. "It's just bloody. It ain't deep." He took a firm hold on Henry's chin, then picked up the rag.

"Hold that table," Tollet warned. "Don't be jumping back. It scares me when you do that."

Henry shut his eyes and clutched the table's edge.

The first dab of the rag was the worst. It sent a shiver across his shoulder blades and into the joints of his elbows. He gritted his teeth against the strokes, surprised he could still smell Tollet's breath over such a pain. And above it all, he heard his father rummaging through the front closet.

"What you lookin' for?" asked Tollet. A moment passed before Cox answered.

"I'll know it when I see it."

Henry opened his eyes. Cox was squatting at the closet door, surrounded by mud-caked boots, empty gun covers, a broken tackle box, and some car tools. Tollet reached for the soap. Henry clutched the table.

"Don't jump," warned the old man. Henry nodded.

"What 'bout them cats?" called Tollet. "You get rid of 'em?" Again there was a long, rummaging moment before Cox answered.

"Unh-hunh."

"Where'd you find 'em?" asked Tollet.

"In the loft."

Tollet nodded, as if he'd known it all along. "What'd you do?"

Cox shoved aside an old lawn mower motor and began to pick through a bundle of pipes.

"Drowned 'em in the trough."

He lifted one pipe, then the next, tossing them up and down to feel their weight.

"She'll get back to business now. Can't afford rats to get my sweet feed while she's lazing 'round being a milk titty."

"I know it!" answered Tollet, as if he'd been mistaken for siding with the cat. "Can't 'ford it!" He doused a dry corner of the rag with water, then blotted it on Henry's face. The water was sharp, but it didn't sting as much as Henry thought it would.

"I gotta throw hay to the calves before I go on to work," said Cox, more to himself than Tollet. A crash sounded against the hardwood floor, and Henry peeked again. Cox slung a bundle of corrugated pipes against the back of the closet.

"I think we can take two to the stockyards," called Cox. "They're fat enough."

"That'll leave just two to feed," Tollet allowed.

Henry was amazed whenever Tollet knew about the farm business since he hardly ever went to the barn; in fact, he hardly went anywhere anymore, except down the road to his cousin Felix's every afternoon. Felix was bad to drink, too; plus, he sold Tollet what liquor he needed since the old man didn't drive anymore.

Henry shut his eyes once more as Tollet swabbed some brownish Merthiolate onto the third corner of the rag.

Two calves to feed and two to slaughter, he thought. His stomach went soft on him, imagining the two who were left: the two steers, with pinkeye. The ones in the dark barn stall, healing up, so they could be sold and slaughtered.

"You hafta take them girls to their dance lessons this afternoon," reminded Tollet.

"Shit!" Cox stopped his rambling. "There's a shipment this afternoon. I'll be late for sure."

Henry opened his eyes. All three of them locked gazes for a moment.

If Cox didn't deliver Henry's little sisters to their tap lessons at 3:30 P.M. sharp, his mother would scorch the earth. As part of their divorce, Cox got Henry, while the two girls stayed with their mother, an arrangement that suited everybody. But part of Cox's court-decreed responsibility was to cart the girls around to their meetings. Martha had—for spite, Cox said—signed them up for painting, tap dance, and violin lessons, all on consecutive afternoons.

"Late," said Tollet, grim as the moment required. "That'll be hell to pay."

Cox swiped the junk back inside the closet with his boot. As the door slammed to, Tollet put the rag on Henry's face. He gasped and jerked, which sent the old man jumping backwards.

"Don't do that!" yelled Tollet, his face trembling. "I toldja that scares me!"

Tears glutted Henry's eyes. He ground his molars and knitted his brows until the rage lost its bite. When he could see again, Cox was standing in front of him. In his right hand was a stained, brown stick, a little over a foot long. Henry had seen the thing many times, in various places, but he had never given it much thought. It was one of the unexplained objects that cluttered the house—something that was part of something else, but the part it belonged to was lost or busted. Cox held the stick out and shook it for Henry to take.

"Put that under your coat," ordered Cox. "Right now."

Henry opened his coat and lay the stick against his chest. He didn't see how he was supposed to make it stay.

"Here," said Cox, reaching for him. He opened the boy's coat further, and with a sharp snatch, ripped a little hole in the lining, next to the shoulder. Then he took the club from Henry's hand and dropped it down inside, so that only a grasp-long portion stuck out of the hole.

"Next time you see that bastard," said Cox, "you whip that jack out and lay in to him. And don't you stop 'til you give him back what he gave you."

Henry batted his eyes, his right side sagging under the weight. Cox moved aside and Tollet stepped back in to finish his work.

"Don't come in here with a face looking like that again," Cox ordered. "And in case you're wondering, I'm gonna ask Shreva all about this."

Henry's head bobbed about under Tollet's work, but he managed to bat his eyes once more. For all his lies, he rarely fooled Cox. And now, on top of everything, Cox thought he was a coward.

Henry cursed himself. This is what comes from getting seen, he thought.

"Go wait in the truck while I feed the calves," said Cox, motioning him out the door. "I'll take you on to school myself."

"Hold on a second," Tollet said. The old man stuck his tongue in the corner of his mouth and eyed a place for the round Band-Aid. He studied Henry's face carefully, the skin beneath one eyelid, trembling. With the bandage stuck on his thumb, he leaned in and added it to the pile of gauze and glue. The smell of medicine filled Henry's head all the way to his brain.

"Couldn't have got *that* treatment at the hospital," Tollet said, backing off.

Henry picked up his books and followed Cox out into the yard.

The day was a mix of sun and gray clouds that covered the scene with a glaze of yolk-colored light. Spring hadn't arrived yet. The breeze's sharp teeth crept down the neck of Henry's coat.

The small brick house gave out onto a patchy stretch of grass, which in turn led to the feed lot and barn. The barn was covered with black siding on one end, but only bare, bleached wood on the other. Cox headed for the muddy, winter-coated Angus in the lot while Henry climbed into the truck. He slammed the door and sat still, marking time. At length, he leaned over and pulled the rear view mirror longways to see himself. His face was stickered like a baby's puzzle—squares and rectangles and bright red circles. He shoved the mirror back.

Damn Shreva.

Every week she came out from the hill with eggs to sell. She had been threatened with the law and dogs and scalding water, but still she came. She sent one of her children when it rained. Whoever didn't buy something from her wound up missing things: tools, buckets, diesel from the tank. Cox had never bought any, and when all the light bulbs turned up missing from the barn, he had run her off with a cattle prod. She had to cross onto the neighbor's land to get to the road since Cox wouldn't let her set a foot on his property. But now he would. Just to find out. Just to find out if Henry was being what he wanted him to be.

If she hadn't seen, he could have handled it his own way. He had gotten good at lying, and he could have come up with all sorts of excuses: "I was balancing on the top of the fence and fell off; "Slid head first into home plate"; "Helped out a boy who's getting the wine kicked out of him."

A lie could've bought him time until the boy left him alone. But now he was forced to do it Cox's way. And he wasn't any good at Cox's way: *Give him back what he gave you.*

The first time he had seen the boy, it was all of a sudden. By way of a shortcut to the bus stop, Henry had taken to cutting across the barn lot, through the field, and then skirting along the base of the hill. A creek curved through the woods towards a bridge at the main road. That was where the school bus picked up the Wolfy community children and carried them to town. Just as he had reached the creek, he saw the boy.

He was older and bigger than Henry—maybe sixteen—but he still looked like a boy. And though he was dressed in dingy clothes— pants and a big, red, cloak-like thing that wasn't exactly a shirt—he wasn't trash, like Shreva's children. Henry could tell that by his face: a grown man's, without the lines. His expression lay on his skull, quiet and anxious, like he was trapped outside a door he wanted to come through. It was as smart and deep a look as Henry had seen, and it made him stop and stare deep. But before Henry could understand it, before he could even move, the boy had picked up a branch, took two steps, and brought the wood down across Henry's left shoulder, at the join of his neck and collarbone. It sent him reeling onto a dank carpet of leaves and moss. Another blow to the back of his neck finished the wound, like the backstroke of a swing blade. Henry clenched his eyes for the next strike—for the rifling of his pockets—but instead all he heard was the easy sweep of leaves as the boy left him.

After awhile, he had picked himself up, achy but amazed, and went on to catch the bus. He had lied to Cox about the mark, saying it was rope burn from a gym class tug-of-war. He had avoided the shortcut for a few weeks, trying to forget what happened. When he failed to see the boy in town or school, he told himself he had just run up on a nut back there. He took up his old route and forgot the beating, for the most part.

Then he appeared again, this morning, a bit past the first place, just in sight of the cedars near Shreva's trailer. He had stepped from behind a tree, surprising Henry so much that he leapt off the path. He was about to bolt away, but the boy's steady, stubborn approach convinced him he would lose the race. Before Henry could muster sense to defend himself, the boy swung a branch over his head in a terrible, circling motion, then crashed it down on his head. Once Henry was on the ground, he kicked him over and stomped his stomach with the flat of his foot. Then he left.

a house all stilled

As a soft, robbing stillness swept through the place, one that kept even the cedars quiet, he came back to himself. There was a point when Henry thought something else was about to happen—the shunted time before a clap of thunder—time sucked clean of sound. But Shreva had spoiled it by exploding out of her trailer door.

And now here he was, beaten and bandaged and shamed. And worst of all, he was supposed to wail hell out of somebody he didn't even know.

He fumbled with the zipper on his jacket. The rod was cold, its top lying against his shoulder cap. He turned around in the seat to see Cox burying a knee into a hay bale, breaking it clear of the twine. The bundle flooded from the rope and spilled onto the hard, cold ground. Then Cox set to scattering it about with his foot, kicking it under the smoky noses of the calves. Henry faced front again, aggravated.

He was too old for this; too old for beating people with clubs. As far as he was concerned, he was too old for everything, had been for a long time. And he wasn't kidding himself, either. His mother had said that he was born old. He had come out wrinkled and scowling like a man of seventy. He hadn't cried at all, and had made the whole delivery room—down to the doctors and nurses who had laughed about it later—swear that they were the youngest in the room, he the oldest.

He liked that. He was proud of that.

Cox yanked the door open. Cold air rushed into the cab, and he slammed it inside with them. For a moment or two, the engine argued and sputtered under Cox's pumping. Finally, it grudged over. As he pulled onto the highway, Cox raked the phlegm from his throat with a fierce, harvesting cough, then rolled down the glass and shot his spit to the pavement. Henry was fascinated by the power of his father's spit, which slugged like bullets from his mouth. His own barely made it past his feet.

"When you see your Mama, tell her I'll be by to get the girls as soon as I can. But there's nothing I can do about it. If I'm more than ten minutes late—" He stopped, and Henry knew he hated the possibility of what he was about to say—"I'll call her."

As far as Henry could tell, his parents had nothing in common, except for being in a bad mood most of the time. He wondered how they could've ever come together in the first place. Even their bad moods were different: Cox was generally unhappy about everything; Martha was more serious than sad. But then, his father had been famous when he was young—at sports—and his mother said she had not been as smart then as she was now.

Henry glanced at his father. The first time, he had told the school nurse that a cow had kicked him into the wall. He couldn't use the gym class tug-of-war with her, as he had done with Cox, since the nurse was also the gym teacher. He stared out the window, trying to think of a new one.

"How does it feel?" Cox asked, slowing the truck for a stoplight.

"Stings some."

"It'll sting less when you make him look like you."

Henry gave him a nod.

Sure it would. Maybe he'd poke his eyes out while he was at it, and smear his forehead and cheeks with the jelly. He turned his face to the window. The truck lurched forward, and Henry felt the club shift against his chest.

He got some satisfaction out of minding Cox since Martha didn't like it.

"Why'd you miss school yesterday," she had asked, when he had first been beaten.

"Because Daddy told me to," he had answered, though that wasn't the truth.

Of course, he wasn't going to mind Cox forever, either. Not after he got bigger and found out what he was supposed to do. Because there was something he was supposed to do. From just looking around, and from reading in *The World Book*, he had decided there was something that pushed or pulled everything—the tractor, the hay bailer, the bush-hog, the house, the car, all the cows—each had its function, its reason. Whenever he asked his father "What for?" about something, he could always get an answer, though questions in general made Cox nervous. This did that, that served this, and so on and so on. There was always something behind everything. It pleased him to know.

He couldn't think what his own purpose was, but that didn't prove anything. He was satisfied there was one, so he wasn't worried.

The only bothersome thing was the possibility that he wouldn't be up to the task; that something about him was, even then, ruining him for it.

For instance, it was true that he couldn't resist being a liar. He was probably a coward too. After all, lying helped him get along better than the truth. It got him out of having to fool with bad situations, which he didn't have the stomach for. But though it worked, deep down he was scared it would spoil him, like whiskey had spoiled Tollet, and like something else—he didn't know what—had spoiled Cox and Martha. He was afraid one day he'd look down and see that he was worthless, and that his lies had made him so. He would have to know when to stop, when to cut himself off.

The truck rolled up to his new school, Cellarsville Junior High. He had done too well on some test Martha had made him take in order to get to stay where he belonged, so he had been skipped ahead, from his old elementary school to this brand new one. Martha was always after him to go to a private school up in Memphis, one for the gifted. But the court had said both Cox and Martha had to agree before he could go. To his relief, Cox wouldn't allow it.

"Go on," said Cox. "Get out."

Henry cranked the door open and slid from the seat. Before he could get away, Cox leaned over, put his hands on his books and stared him to a stop.

"First thing you do after school, or at lunch—wherever you won't get caught—you find that little fucker and you—"

"He doesn't go to school here," Henry rushed to say. "I told you. He's—from Camille. I think. He just hangs around back in there. I guess."

Cox shook his head at every word. "Come the way you left this morning," he ordered. "Take the bus to the Wolfy stop, and come back along the creek. Do it every day 'til you see him again. Hear me? Do it until you see him again. Hear?"

Worse and worse. Cox squinted at him.

"I'm gonna ask Shreva every afternoon," he said, "to check if you've done it. Hear?"

Henry nodded once more.

"And don't forget to tell your Mama about this afternoon. Hear?"

"I won't," said Henry and slammed the door.

He pulled his stocking cap down to his eyebrows and shifted his shoulder blades, so that his coat rode up to his chin. He tramped into his mother's office.

A rough, brown and tan rug lay on the floor. Every surface— chairs, desks, and bookcases—was covered with paper. The only uncluttered space was around the loudspeaker, from which she made her announcements. He found her sitting in a chair beside the inter-com, dressed in a white, scarf-like skirt, a white top, and tassel ear-rings peeping out beneath her brown, jaw-length hair. She was small, not much taller than Henry himself, so he blamed her for his inabil-ity to grow. Eyeglasses dangled from a cord around her neck.

"Daddy said he's got a shipment coming in this afternoon," said Henry, leaning only part way inside the door. "He might be late for Lucy and Betsy. He said he'd call if he was."

He was on his heels and nearly to the door when Martha called him back.

"*What* happened?"

Even when she was upset, her voice was pretty and soothing. Henry liked to hear her read, as long as it wasn't anything she had written herself. She was bad about wanting to write and then read what she wrote to whoever couldn't get away.

He turned and shrugged, careful not to approach.

"I got in a fight this mornin'. Had to teach somebody some manners."

"Come here," said Martha. She pointed to a spot in front of her, insisting on it with her finger. Henry trudged across the rug and grudged her his cheek. Her hands were cold and soft from turning pages all her life. They felt good.

"Who put all this on you?" she asked. "Tollet?"

He nodded. "Daddy said it was all right."

"Well go down to the nurse and have it taken off. Then have it dressed."

He nodded again. Tollet would sulk when he got home.

"Who were you fighting with?"

He thought for a moment. Shreva never crossed paths with Martha.

"A boy from Camille." He paused for emphasis. "Showed up shovin' people 'round."

"Cover your words," she corrected. "There's a *g* on just about everything you say, and you *know* it. You just do that to make me mad."

He enjoyed dropping his grammar a notch when he was around her. He liked for her to think that Cox was ruining him.

"And who told you to handle things in that way?" Martha asked.

He barely let her finish her question; she was talking to him like a teacher would talk.

"Daddy did. I do what he tells me to."

Martha eased back in her chair, her face as ready for him as he was for her. "Would you walk through fire if he said so?"

He cocked his head, grinding his jaw in consideration. Then he nodded. "Yes. If he said so."

"What kind of a reason is that?" she asked. Her eyes flashed. Martha was suspicious of him too, he knew, but of different things than Cox.

"I want there to be the *right* reason," she answered herself.

He nodded, just the way he nodded at Cox, whenever he was teaching him something.

"I don't want to see you in this shape again. Understand?"

His head bounced like a sinker. He had just as soon not be in this shape again himself.

"Go on down to the nurse, then get to class," she ordered. "It's almost lunch time."

She picked up the phone as he left, calling Cox, he was sure.

He made his way down the ammonia-smelling hall to the nurse. She would hurt him in a different way than Tollet, but still hurt him. Both the place on his face and the spot on his shoulder bit with a bright pain, despite the newness of the second wound and the age of the first. Owing to Cox's orders, he would probably suffer a third that afternoon. And he had no idea why.

"Whyyyyy Lawwww! Henry Tolleeeetttt!" hollered the nurse as he came in. "What in the Lord's name happened to *you?*"

She had just finished teaching first period gym class, so she was dressed in sweat clothes. A pasty, pudgy woman, she was forever eating Hostess cupcakes. She circled her lips with her red fingernails to gather chocolate crumbs, then stood to meet him.

Henry took off his stocking cap and pulled loose the top snap on his coat. He scrambled onto the vinyl-covered examining table, slumped his shoulders, and stared at the muddy tips of his boots. He began with the bored ease of a master.

"I was standing at the bus stop, minding my own business. . . ."

Chapter 2

"**D**addy?" Cox yelled. The kitchen was empty and the stove, cold. "Daddy? Where's supper?"

No answer came down the hall. Nothing.

"Shit," Cox whispered.

There was a time before his mother had died when Cox retained some lingering respect for Tollet, sot though he was and always had been. But after living with him for four years, he thought of him only as a drunk and a sorry housekeeper. He had nearly driven the farm into the ground by the time Cox moved in and took over. By rights, he would get the place when Tollet's brain finally dissolved. There were no other relatives living, except Felix. And Felix was dissolving at about the same rate as Tollet.

"Daddy?" he called, louder. He walked through the den into the dim hallway. His boots tromped, making echoes. When the carpet had gotten old, he had stripped it out, but never gotten around to replacing it. The floorboards were dark as rum and spackled with drops of years-old paint—rust and white and bits of blue. Cox closed his eyes when he reached Tollet's door, took a breath, and turned the knob.

The old man sat in his corner chair, struggling his pants onto pale, withered legs. A grape jelly glass of nearly drained whiskey sat next to him on the floor. Cox glanced at his watch. Half past four.

"Fa—Sol—La—Mi—"

"What's the matter with you?" Cox asked, agitated.

Tollet turned his face up and blinked. His eyes were murky from an hour's worth of liquor, but he was more sober than not.

"I—lost track," he said, clearing his voice. "Slept too long. I'm getting up now, though."

The old man fumbled with his pants zipper. Notes, near whispers, hummed from his throat. Tollet loved the depth of his own voice; he said, often, that it tolled like a big black bell.

"Mi—Fa—Sol—"

"Quit that. Quit that singing."

Tollet pretended he hadn't heard him. Cox spoke up; his voice shook the windowpanes.

"If you're gonna sing that shit, use the goddamn words at least. Don't show yourself to be as ignorant as all that."

Tollet bunched his mouth. "I ain't ignorant."

"Then use the words."

Nothing irked Cox more than to hear Tollet drooling off some old song, using shape notes instead of words, the way country churches used to. But though Tollet cowed about and caved in to Cox on everything else, he insisted on singing his way. It was the only thing he would fight about anymore. His bottom lip pushed out slightly.

"You don't use words when you sing sacred harp—'least not for the first line. Everybody knows that. Everybody does."

"It's ignorant," said Cox, his eyes flashing. "They used it for bastards who couldn't read."

Tollet dropped his hands from his pants waist, leveled his eyes at Cox.

"That's how it started! But even when they learned how, they kept singin' the shapes. You just got to listen to the way it sounds. In Camille—"

Cox shook his head. "Shut up. Shut up—"

"—where my people—and *yours*—were from," Tollet continued. "I used to sing it—"

"Don't start that," said Cox, jerking his head. He couldn't stand a bunch of drunk lies tonight. He was too tired.

Tollet closed his mouth, stared at his chalky, bluish feet.

"Felix likes my singing," he muttered.

He looked away, grinding his teeth against the flesh of his cheek.

It was Tollet's one last threat. To leave everything—the house and barn and fields that Cox had saved—to his sorry cousin down the road. He held the deed on Cox like it was a gun, and Cox had to be careful, just in case.

"Thaw out some stew," he said, turning. "I'll go out and work 'til it's ready."

Gray clouds stretched across the sky, shattering apart at the horizon like bits of mercury. In the sliver of blue between the cloud bank and the tree tops, the sun shot its last light over the farm. The glare was bright enough to make Cox squint at the barbed-wire he was wrapping around a receiving post. Cox didn't believe in gloves, so from time to time he had to swipe his hand across his pants leg to clean them. The wire's end danced and coiled about in the mud, like a snake whose head was caught.

He wanted to go see Lois. The thought of her pawed at his groin, succeeding itself in jeering little taunts. But the best he could do—because he couldn't stop and drive into town just then—was to work faster, hoping the speed would take his attention. For no matter what he did, even if he were to gash his wrist with the rusty wire, the relief wouldn't last. Once he got hungry for something, there was no real distracting him.

It wasn't so much Tollet as Martha that had set him off. His desire was greatest when he'd just met with aggravation, and nobody could aggravate him more than she could. She had called him twice at work, once in the morning to tell him he better not let the girls down, and another time in the afternoon to see if he remembered what she had said. Their phone conversations started in the middle of a locked-horn battle. The receiver hadn't settled on his ear before he heard:

" . . . I don't guess it matters much to you, but these girls are trying to learn something—to help them get the hell out of here one day. The least you can do—if you can spare the twenty-five cents on gas—is take them to their lessons. And since you're only concerned with the least—the very least—you can do, this prospect should be fascinating. . . ."

To which he would stammer out "hold on," "wait just a goddamn minute," "if you'd shut up for a second, I'll tell you," and other statements that ended with him wanting to strangle her.

This afternoon had been no different. Despite the fact that the John Deere deliveries had just arrived, and fifteen minutes late too, he'd had to leave an idiot in charge of squaring away the business—a boy who couldn't find his ass with both hands if every finger was a flash-light. He'd left to drive across town to pick up the girls in tap shoes, who had come out of the house like two released pigeons, stuttering along the sidewalk and into the truck, then back across town to let them out in front of the split-level house of a woman who probably knew as much about dancing as the idiot knew about tractors. What in the hell was she doing here—in Cellarsville, in a subdivision—if she knew so much? Nothing but playing bad music on a record player while children all around town made fools of their parents every week—tippety-tapping a check over to her for the price of being a sucker.

He sighed at the mess. He wouldn't be out of it any time soon, either. His boss at the store, Mr. Porter, was a big Baptist. He wasn't happy with Cox being divorced and asked after his children on a reg-ular basis. He always wanted to know how often he saw them. The girls' taxi service did him some good: *"Took them to piano just yester-day,"* he would say, smiling, winning one in return from Mr. Porter. *"Fiddle lessons tomorrow."*

He caught his shirt pocket on one of the barbs and started plucking at it with his fingers. The point ripped a hole in the denim anyway. He was about to punish the wire, striking it against a post, when he heard the cat mewing around at the loft door. She stood there, appraising him, her face as round and still as a moon. Cox scooped up a handful of gravel and scattered it against the barn wall. The cat disappeared.

He had come to the end of the strand, so he would have to find something else to occupy him, at least until it was time for supper. When Tollet had done all he could to the food, he would call in Cox and Henry, then sit down to watch them, his face still impressed with the ribs of the bedspread. It was beyond Cox how Tollet lived. He ate only fists full of cereal he scrounged straight out of the box and maybe a spoon or two of leftovers—always taken at odd hours and always while standing up, in front of an open refrigerator. Food was the sponge Tollet used to mop up the liquor in his stomach.

a house all stilled

When Cox had wound the tail of the wire around the post, he set it against the barn. He had already fed the calves and watered the mares, so he couldn't do that now. After a moment, he remembered the fence. He nodded to it, as if it were a customer, then went for his paint. He had started to cover it with a new coat two weekends ago after Martha had bit his head off for being late to pick up Henry, but that had made him so mad he'd had to stop before he was done and run in to see Lois. The good thing about Lois was, no matter how busy it was at her gas station, for twenty-five dollars, she would drop everything and lean back against the office wall for him. And she took checks too. She would even let him have a free pack of Nabs crackers on his way out.

At the fence again, he realized he had to smooth the surface before he started to paint. So he centered a ten-penny nail and hammered it in. He was careful to pull his arm so as not to bend the nail or split the wood.

He hoped Martha had seen him when he'd come to get the girls. He always tried to make a point of getting out of the truck, just in case she was watching from behind the curtains. He knew she liked the way he looked, and he—for some reason—liked the way she did. Together—from the very first time even up to the very last, when they seemed to hate each other enough to kill—they could make the house frame rattle beneath their bed. That was what had got them together in the first place, had kept them together for so long. It even made his times with Lois better, remembering it. So let Martha scream and holler and pitch a fit all she wanted; he had the ace.

A smile passed over Cox's face. He pounded in two more nails, moved to the next post.

The sun had fallen behind the hilltop, so that its light skimmed the surface of the ground like a rock skipping over pond water. There was a slight rustle in the barn from the cows chewing their cud. Occasionally, he heard Tollet in the house, screaming and cussing. Cox was used to that; the old man burned himself a lot.

He took a nail from between his lips and centered it on the plank. But before he could hammer it in, his nose caught the close, fetid smell of feathers. He raised his gaze from the fence to squint across the field.

A woman's slouched figure was crossing through the neighbor's pasture. Dressed in a man's gray overcoat and a pair of rubber-toed hunting boots, she carried a large cardboard box, crumpled at the top, which rested against her hip. Trailing her was a brood of mismatched boys, passing a cigarette between them. Their long, dagger-shaped shadows weaved and parted beside them as they came.

Cox climbed over the fence and walked towards her. The boys, spotting him first, scowled as he came. They had mean, rats' faces, threatened too much in their lives to be really scared of anything. Their eyes were always darting back and forth, looking for a way to get around or out.

"Go to hell," yelled Shreva, her eyes wide. She rocked back a step. "I'm just crossin' through. I ain't even on your land."

"Wait a minute," said Cox. He walked to the fence and rested his hands on the page wire. "I've got something to ask you."

She took on a boxer's stance, one foot in front of the other. Her bony cheeks showed through her drawn, yellowed skin. Her shorn hair was the color of dead moss. Older than Cox by ten years or more, she looked closer to Tollet's age than his.

"I hadn't got nothin' to say to you," she said.

"Wait a fuckin' minute," Cox bit back.

He took a minute to compose himself. He couldn't afford to run her off, no matter how much he wanted to.

"I'm—I'm gonna," he took a breath, "buy some eggs."

She squinted at him, clutching the box to her chest, like it was a child he might snatch away. "The hell you say. How come?"

"Never mind. Come here and let me look."

When she was at the fence, he peeked in at the mottled eggs and shrugged. There were layers of them, nested among wads of toilet paper. "This much," he said, holding out a dollar bill.

Shreva glared at the money.

"You'll get a discount if you buy two dollars' worth," she said. "I'm runnin' a special."

Cox cut his eyes at her. He rifled around and pulled out some change. Grinning, she squatted to set her box down.

As she sorted eggs into what looked like a used carton, Cox sized up her boys. He wondered if even Shreva knew who had sired which. Except for the wiry, electrocuted hair they got from her, no two of them looked alike. And no matter how much time passed, it seemed they never grew up. They all behaved the same, climbing over everything, like cockroaches in the dark. As he waited, two walked along the fence top, and one swung on the cattle creep. Cox was afraid that if he stood still too long, they'd start up his leg.

The story was that Shreva's second husband was an old man who owned a sliver of rocky, cedar-covered land in the hills behind Cox's. He had either died or disappeared, but somehow Shreva had gotten his deed and a government check for being a veteran's widow. She had had her next man haul a used trailer back there, then kicked him out of it. She had talked another one—a fool who had once worked for Cox at the store—into building some chicken houses and stocking them with laying hens, so as to supplement her welfare check. Then she'd turned him in to the law for running a numbers game. From these men, and others, came all these boys. There were more too, but the youngest stayed back at the trailer.

"Now!" said Shreva. She rose to her feet with her hands out, one holding the carton and one ready to receive the money.

Cox took the carton and set it on top of a fence post. "What's the special then?"

"Them's double yokes, every one. I feed the chickens songbird feed. Does it every time."

Cox rolled his eyes; he didn't have time to argue.

"You seen Henry?" he asked.

"Who?"

"My boy. Henry. You seen him?" He took out his knife and set to cleaning his fingernails with the tip. Curves of brown grit spiraled into shavings and fell away.

Shreva hoisted the box and set it gracelessly on her hip, as though its heaviness was beginning to tell itself. Her eyes searched the fence line for a moment.

"This mornin'," she nodded. "Saw him get a whippin'."

Cox flinched. "Yeah, but what about this afternoon?"

She moved her stare from the fence to Cox, then back again. "Naw. Unh-unh."

He switched his knife to the other hand.

"Well, from now on, I want you to start looking for him every day—in the morning, when he heads for the bus—'round seven thirty. Then again every evening, 'round time the school bus lets out. Then tell me what you saw when you—" He nearly gagged on the words. "When you come around with the eggs. I told him to go by your place every day, so you won't miss him."

She shifted the box to the other hip, then licked her bottom lip. "I cain't be waitin' for him every afternoon. I got rounds to make."

Cox folded the blade of his knife against his thigh and thrust it into his pocket.

"I'll make it worth your while. I'll buy two dollars worth every day you come."

Shreva shook her head. "That's my special anyhow."

"Three, then," said Cox. She was a black-hearted boil on the earth's ass, but if he paid her enough, she would live up to her end. Shreva set her gaze loose—bouncing it along the fence, the barn, the house behind him.

"How long is this good for?" she asked, her voice rising.

Cox waved her down. "I'll *guarantee* you two weeks worth. You know what that means, don't you? 'Guarantee'?"

"I know what it means! Ain't I the one with the special?" she snapped. Her sneer cut ridges into her cheeks. "What you 'spect me to see?"

Cox blushed and glanced to the ground.

"I wanta hear if he runs up on that boy again. I gave him a blackjack. Told him to find that boy and lay his head open. I wanta see if he—"

He stopped in mid-sentence as Shreva shook her head. Her gaze was working over something, considering it.

"You're scared your boy's sorry," she said. It was a flat statement, as if there were no question about the truth of it. "You're scared your boy's no good."

Cox shook his head. "I don't want him taking the long way 'round. Not for anybody. He's gonna find that boy."

"It wasn't no *boy*," she said, and hoisted the box against her hip-bone. "He's a grown man. Has long, stringy ole hair. Hippie, I betcha." She nodded slowly, enjoying it. "He beat the wine outa your boy. Then come over and stomped on him."

Cox's eyes flashed. "Stomped on him?" he moaned.

"With the flat-a-his-foot." She backed up a step, then bobbed her head. "You oughta thank me. I run out the trailer soon as I saw it. Set 'im up straight again. Turned him towards your house so he wouldn't go wrong, bloody-eyed as he was."

She narrowed her eyes into slits. "You oughta thank me."

Henry had been stomped, not just beaten. Cox swallowed. It was the kind of thing he himself would do in a fight.

"I'll go up to four dollars even," he said. "And that's for doing nothing but poking your sorry head out your sorry window twice a day. Take it or leave it!"

"I'll take it," said Shreva. She sent her thin, plum-colored tongue across her lips.

Cox took the egg carton from the fence post, then turned to walk around the lot to the yard. "I'll be expecting you."

After he'd come inside and turned to shut the door, he saw her crossing to meet her ride at the end of the road. A nine-year-old girl, one of hers, drove her around in a car with cellophane windows.

Then he noticed Henry crossing through the unmown Johnson grass. When he got closer, Cox saw that the boy's step was bouncy. A neat, flesh-colored patch had replaced Tollet's Band-Aids. Henry hadn't seen him yet, so he didn't have time to change the relieved, delivered-from-hell look on his face.

"I guess you didn't see him then?" jeered Cox from the door. Henry's head snapped up, his face unstrung. He came onto the porch and stopped in front of Cox, moving from side to side, as though the wind were unbalancing him. He hoisted one shoulder.

"I did just like you said. I got off the bus and walked all 'long the creek—twice—up and down both sides. But I didn't see him. I had my stick out too, just in case. And I called him an S.O.B. too. Out loud."

Cox sized him up. If he was lying, which was a fifty-fifty chance, he would look honest. His eyes wouldn't flinch, and he wouldn't squirm. But if he was telling the truth, he'd look like he was sitting on the stove. Cox eased his head to an angle. The boy's eyes were steady, but he was swaying and rocking on the porch boards.

"I thought you said he hung around back in there?"

"That's just a guess," Henry blurted out.

Cox moved his head further back, so that his chin thrust out. "Then how come you said he was from Camille this morning?"

"'Cause he looked the type. You said they were greasy-grimy and starved-looking."

"He was greasy?"

"—grimy and starved-looking."

Cox couldn't let himself get distracted. He meant to skin Henry of his lying and—worse—his gutlessness. It would be tough. Martha had done her damndest to ruin him—skipping him grades, getting special teachers for him, and making him read too much. But Cox meant to save him, to give him clear eyes and a chipped-tooth temper. With those, nobody would run over him. They'd stand him in good stead up until he got onto girls, which would fix him once and for all. Life would be better for him then, for a time; it had been for Cox, for a time.

He had even decided to start dropping hints that way. Sometimes, lately, Cox set up his Bell and Howell projector in the den at night, so that Henry could sneak a peek at the mail-order movies. During the time between when the boy brushed his teeth and headed for bed, Cox set the clack-clack-clack of the film going, flickering pictures of huge, bare breasts and naked rumps over the wall: no sound, just pictures. And if Henry didn't go right to bed, if he stood in the hall and peeked around the corner—well, good. The sooner he got onto girls, the sooner all the time he had on his hands—which led to reading and brooding and lying—would have a place to go.

He took a deep breath, but his voice came out in a jeer despite himself. "How come you didn't tell me he stomped you? And don't bother lying. Shreva told me."

Henry blanched.

"Well," smiled Cox. He nodded towards the horizon. "I got good news. If you look yonder, you'll see her crossing the property line. I'm paying her to look out every morning and every afternoon. I expect you'll meet up with him sooner or later, and she'll be there to see it, so I can hear what happened." A revelation lit his brow. He pulled his wallet out and fumbled inside.

"In fact," he said, tugging out two limp five-dollar bills. "Take out your billfold."

The boy struggled the beaded wallet from his pocket.

"Here's two five dollar bills. When you go walking around in there—where you 'think' he hangs around—you advertise you got money. Hear? Holler out loud you got something worth stealing. Hear? Tell him to come out, or you're gonna go looking for him."

Henry eyed the money and pushed his bottom lip over his top. Cox saw it, snatched the bills back, and began to study them. Then he took a pen from his pocket and scribbled his name on both.

"There!" he said, throwing his head back. "I've got my name down on 'em. So if he gets 'em, don't be thinking you can get you two more and fool me. I'm gonna check your billfold every night to see. Now I've got me two witnesses. Shreva and this money. Hear?"

He held the money out at Henry, who placed the bills carefully into his wallet. For a moment, Cox watched the boy's face as he searched for a way out. Pleased, Cox moved aside. He held the screen door open and let Henry pass first.

"Daddy?" called Cox from the doorway. "Supper ready yet?"

"Uhhhhh—Unn-unh," garbled Tollet. "Not ezactly."

Cox shut the door and came around the corner. Tollet stood over a mess of stew splattered across the linoleum. A saturated mop lay on the floor beside him, drowned and defeated. For the most part, the flood had been stopped with a roll of paper towels, pieces of which lay in soggy wads at the borders. Still, some had found a route across the tile and onto the sitting room carpet.

"Awww, Daddy," said Cox.

Tollet's eyes looked like ice cubes melting in muddy water. His T-shirt, khakis, and house shoes were sprayed red with the stew's back-splash. Holding the empty tube in one hand, and the last of the towels in the other, he mustered a feeble smile.

"I ain't gonna eat that," said Henry. He was looking at the pot on the floor. "Look's like he's been squeezing it outa the mop and back into the—"

"No I hadn't!" yelled Tollet.

Cox glanced at the old man's stained, wet hands. It would be just like Tollet. Cox stooped to pick up the sopping wad of towels, walked to the pot, and dropped them in with a slosh.

"Hey!" the old man said. He glared at Henry with kindled inter-est. "Who's been messin' with my bandages? A *doctor*?"

Henry shook his head. "They did it at school."

"You shouldn'ta let 'em! I wasted all them Band-Aids—"

"Never mind that," said Cox. "How'd this happen?"

Tollet, glaring at Henry, rolled his shoulders. "Burnt myself." He lifted the back of his seared hand to show them.

"Clean this up, Henry," said Cox, "then go call the chicken place. For the second goddamn time this week, call the chicken place."

Cox slammed the screen as he went back outside. He stood on the porch, his anger building. Now he had to spend another twenty dollars on take-out food. Cat's claws scratched at his stomach. He was starving hungry, and the chicken wouldn't be ready to pick up for at least an hour. It was too much; he had to do something. He drove his hand into his pocket, pulled out his keys, and stepped off the porch. He heard Tollet's bedroom door slam. Henry had the water going in the sink.

"I've gotta go up town," Cox yelled over his shoulder. Nobody answered him. Nobody ever did. "I'll pick up the chicken when it's ready."

In a few years, he thought, I'll be taking Henry with me. Lois has a girl his age.

Chapter 3

For a while, Henry leaned over the kitchen table, reading a comic book. Then he dialed the restaurant's number from memory.

"This is Henry Tollet. We want a bucket of chicken, rolls, coleslaw, baked beans, and mashed potatoes." Half of the order was for Cox, who would come back starving from his trip to town.

He sat the phone back into the cradle, then looked down the hall at Tollet's door. He hadn't been completely sober before. In another fifteen or twenty minutes he would be onto a good drunk. Henry sat on the couch, marking time.

Before his drinking took over completely, Tollet's mind tended to teeter around, remembering snatches of odd things. It was what Cox said disgusted him most, and Henry nodded whenever he said it, as if he agreed; all the same, he liked the stories.

It wouldn't be long now, Henry thought, looking at the clock.

He had learned to open the door to Tollet's room without making it squeak. The old man kept it dark, except for a seashell nightlight that glowed from a wall outlet. His vinyl chair was backed into a corner, away from the window; it sat there like a throne, with Tollet its shrunken, dying, king. Henry tiptoed in and eased onto the floor beside him.

He only noticed the bottles' shapes—round or square and even octagon one time—never the names on them. This particular bottle rested between Tollet's legs, snug against his crotch. The old man's hands, the skin purplish and as loose as drapes, lay around the glass shoulders. His eyelids sagged as his head lowered gradually to his breastbone. At any moment, he would stir, letting out scraps of things in a slobber-choked voice:

"You don't know nothing 'bout this—" he'd say, scornfully. "But one time. . . ."

"You never heard tell a this, but. . . ."

"These folks is all dead now, but. . . ."

And whenever he started like that, Henry felt a sweet soreness in his chest, as if he had been cheated. It was not as though what his grandfather spoke of was particularly interesting. There were better things now than the telephones Tollet had; there were better roads than the ones he had traveled on. Food was better now, in Henry's estimation; more of it and different kinds. There was Coca-Cola now. There was air conditioning. Then again, Tollet never spoke of it as being better then. It had just *been*.

"This right here," he'd garble, "this here, I can count on. I know this. See? I was there, so I know about it." He'd wave his hand vaguely in the air, as if to rest it on the memory closest.

"See? You cain't be sure of what you got—" He'd jab his finger at Henry. "And to hell with what's comin'. But this *here*"—and he set his hand down on what his mind remembered—*This* ain't goin' nowhere. It cain't fool me, 'cause I seen it. I seen what it was. And it'll always be just that. What it was. See? It's done *being* anything else."

There was no use nodding, because Tollet probably didn't know he was there. But Henry could see the sense in what he said. To have something you were sure of; something that couldn't fool you. It didn't matter that Tollet was drunk; he was smarter that way than sober.

Tollet's head rested back against the chair and his mouth opened. A shiny glaze lay across his teeth, a slight shimmer. Henry leaned in close. The old man's eyes eased over.

Now. The story was coming now.

"Me'n Royce," he started. "Me'n Royce? Yeah. Naw. Couldn'ta been. Me'n Marcel—in the bushes—outside a nigger's house."

Royce and Marcel were Tollet's older brothers. Royce had died when he was fourteen, but Tollet liked him better than Marcel, and always forced him into stories when he couldn't have really been there.

"Niggers sittin' up in a house. Been a funeral. Or gonna be one. One or the other. Anyhow. There's a dead man in the box. And them sittin' round 'im, laid out in the box." His eyes danced, happy at the memory. Him and Marcel in the bushes.

Henry could catalog the tales. This one fit into Tollet's joker stage, when he was around sixteen. It was one he'd heard a little of before, but not the whole thing.

"All of 'em left to go outside to the jug, see? Had it out by the well—kept it at the well. Left that'un in the box." He tried to lean forward but fell back again.

"Me'n Marcel come in through the window. Marcel had 'im a sweet potato in one hand. We rasseled that dead man outa the box— set 'im up in the rockin' chair, facin' the door. Stuck the sweet potato in his hand, like he'd just took a big ole bite!"

He blinked, dazed a bit. "Then we heard 'em comin' back. Jumped out the window."

Henry waddled closer. Tollet set into a wheezing, phlegm-choked laugh that made him clutch at his chest. Then his head rolled about on the chair cushion.

"Niggers hollerin'—Ohhhhh Jeeesus—Sweeeeet Jeeeesus— screamed and run off to the road! And us in the bushes—rollin'— scratchin' dirt for breath."

He strained and wheezed again, nearly losing his hold on the bottle. Henry wanted him to go on, but all at once his head slid over to the side. With his eyes closed, his mouth worked at words that wouldn't form, wouldn't take volume and sound. He was worn out, and whatever was left of the story, Tollet would watch behind his eyelids. Henry eased up and left the room.

Sitting a dead man up in a rocking chair. It wasn't the worst story he'd been told. It had taken Henry a while to put all the pieces together, as they had come out at different tellings, but when Tollet was seventeen, he'd taken nightly trips to a girl over in Maben—a girl who was married. He'd done something with her on the back porch, standing up, with her clutching at the eaves for balance. Henry wasn't exactly sure what, but he knew from listening to older boys on the bus that Tollet and the girl were naked when they did it. Tollet had also stolen money from his brother-in-law over at the shirt factory, and once, had been part of a group that beat a boy's left eye clean out of his head.

Bad. All bad. But he had never seen Tollet hurt anybody. He had seen him get angry many times, but it just ended in his pouting and going to his room. It was enough to make Henry wonder if Tollet was taking stories about Marcel and Royce and putting himself in. He could understand his wanting to do that; he sometimes put himself in stories people told him about his father—football and baseball, mostly. But whoever's stories they were, Tollet loved them. In a way, Henry did too.

After supper, Tollet came to the table. His eyes were bleary, and he held his head tipped to the right, as if his ear was weighted. Cox, relaxed and full, sat in his easy chair, watching television, ignoring them both. Grease glistened from his fingertips. Beside him, on a shelf built around the shaft of a floor lamp, lay the empty bucket of chicken. Whenever Cox came back from his trips to town, he was quieter for a while.

Having picked at his food, Henry pretended to read his comic book. The day had been terrible, with Martha, Shreva, and Cox, on top of the beating and the threats. Even what he'd thought would salvage the day, his afternoon escape through the woods, had been ruined.

Scared dead, he had gotten off the school bus and set off just as Cox had ordered. There was a spiked smell to the cedars—shocking, fresh—like a new wooden box, opened suddenly. The ground was spongy beneath his step, and a late afternoon warmth forced buds of sweat at the nape of his neck.

He made his way past Shreva's crumpled trailer. It was surrounded with rain-bleached garbage and a scatter of hen houses, all in a shaken rubble. To the left was the creek, roaring like a river in flood season. He faltered for a while, staring into the thicket, then pushed himself over the border. His eyes danced about the ground, into the treetops.

The boy was somewhere among the limbs and vines. As sure as there was a heart in his chest, he was there. And at any moment he would drop out of a tree on top of him—take him by ambush—drag him off—doomed, kicking. Though he kept up his pace, he cringed inside his coat, too scared to pull out the blackjack. The cut on his face stung with a rippling pain; so did the lashing at his neck. It was as though the places had begun to simmer, like something set upon the eye of a stove. The further he got into the woods, closer to where the boy was hiding, the more they burned with blood and fire. He rushed on, scared his skin would reach a flashpoint; rupture, hemorrhage. Still, the boy himself didn't appear.

Henry drew closer to the edge of the woods, where the hill gave out to the field. Nothing had happened. Nothing was happening. The possibility of deliverance crept over him like a rumor of escape. Then, as he came into the pasture, he mustered a timid insolence. Half for himself, half for Cox, he mumbled: "*Sonuvabitch.*"

He listened. Still nothing but trees, trees, trees.

Now he could tell Cox: *I called him a sonuvabitch—but he still didn't come out!*

The back of his house lay just across the field, staring at him like a promise. The tall weeds swept against his thighs and hips as he tromped along. Nobody, no matter who they were, would jump him in the pasture right behind his own house. His relief was all the greater because the boy had been there—he knew it. He *knew* it— but still he hadn't come out.

He closed his comic book and popped a last bit of chicken skin into his mouth.

Why hadn't he come out? Because he was scared of getting caught? Because Henry hadn't fought before? Was it no longer any fun for him? Whatever it was, it didn't matter. All that mattered was that he had left him alone.

He pushed away from the table.

It would have been all right, but now he had ten more dollars in his wallet. And tomorrow, Shreva would stick her yellow skull out the window to see if he was advertising himself, like Cox told him to. Cox was right to mark the bills. Paying the boy off had shot through

Henry's mind the moment he had laid eyes on the money. So now, it would go on, whatever it was; now, it would continue.

He jumped when the phone rang in its loud, rude jangle. He scrambled over to the receiver.

When it came over the line, Martha's voice often took him by surprise. It was so soothing that several seconds passed before he could put her face to the voice. Sometimes he had to make her repeat what she had said, since he would be listening to how she spoke, not to what she meant.

"I said," Martha repeated, "*are you feeling okay? Did the nurse fix you up?*"

"Oh. I'm okay. She did."

"*Good.*" Martha paused. "*You didn't get into any more trouble, did you?*"

Henry glanced at Cox. He had the edgy, cornered look on his face that he got whenever Martha or her voice was around.

"No. No more trouble."

"*Fine. I expect you to be bigger than that from now on.*" She paused again. "*We're not animals—you and I.*"

Henry nodded, frowning.

"*Are you going to ride home with me tomorrow,*" she asked, "*or is he going to bring you by my house?*"

A surge of hope flooded his chest. Tomorrow was Friday. It was his weekend to stay with his mother. If she took him home with her, his morning walk to the bus would be the last one for three whole days. Maybe the boy would be gone by then. He had to be careful though, or Cox would know.

"*Did you hear me?*"

"Hold on," said Henry. He pressed his hand over the mouthpiece, bit his lip, then spoke.

"She says don't forget to bring me to her house tomorrow afternoon. And don't be late. She says if you gotta get off work early again, that's just the way things—"

Cox shifted in his chair and tossed his head.

"Tell her I am *not* gonna get off work early, either. I did that today. Why can't she take you home? What's wrong with *her* car?"

Henry nodded and let out a long breath.

"He says he can't get off work early again and you'll have to take me with you."

"*I didn't ask him to get off work early,*" she snapped. "*Just wait for me.*"

"Okay," said Henry. He went straight to his room and straight to bed. It was better to quit the day with a success, even a minor one.

After school the next day, Henry sat in Martha's living room. He had lived in this house for the first eight years of his life, but had no attachment to it. It was partly because Martha had changed it so much. Though his memories were foggy, he was sure that there used to be carpets. Now there were only a few scratchy rugs that some Indians had made. The rest was cold, dark-stained hardwood. He also remembered ceiling lights with glass covers. But after Martha went back to school and got another diploma, she had replaced them with mismatched table lamps, too small to read by. What he remembered of the house, Cox had taken with him.

Maybe that was why he had kept running away from here, even at eight years old. When Cox had moved out to the farm, the house had been gutted. All of them, his mother and he and the girls, had slept in the kitchen, in sleeping bags, while painters shellacked the walls. Then Martha added this chair and that picture, took out doors and put up shelves. And at the same time, Cox was adding to the farmhouse the things that were his, Henry's, first and best memories: the white, metal kitchen cabinet with red plastic pulls; the sun-yellow refrigerator; the brass floor lamp, and other things he grew to miss seeing in the places where they had always been. Again and again, Henry had run away, always just at first dark. He hadn't even known the direction, and once had gotten lost close to the highway. Martha had cried when the police brought him back, and Cox had spanked him, but he had run off the very next night again. Martha had given in then—out of fear, she said—and let him stay with Cox for a while. But that was four years now.

The room would have been all right if the furniture had been comfortable. But Martha picked things that held you in an odd way; either you felt as though you were about to fall out of them, or would never escape from them. The sofa was too deep, too plush, and the chairs were like slings—stretchy material draped over wire frames. Henry sank into one, his rear suspended over the floor like a rock in the bottom of a stocking. His knees nearly met his face. It took a minute to struggle out. He would take his chances on the sofa.

Before she had gone to change clothes, Martha had given him some water in a glass, wrapped with a paper napkin. He perched on the cushion's edge and used his knee as a ledge for the glass.

"I'll be there in one more minute," she called from her bedroom. Her voice was stifled, like she was shouting against a drum-cover. There was a faint click and rattle of clothes hangers. At her house, Henry never saw her in anything but blue jeans, sandals, and either a T-shirt or a sweat shirt, depending on the weather. "Why don't you look at that brochure on the sofa from Lockely Hall. It's a new one."

Henry glanced beside him at the pamphlet. The school's stone façade stared back.

It wasn't new. She was lying. He'd seen it before. Inside, it told of all the classes he could take, and the attention he would get. There was a map of Memphis on the back cover. The thought of it made him sick to his stomach. Everything was all right about the idea, except for having to sleep there. If he just didn't have to sleep there.

"Where're *they* at?" he called, peering down the hallway at the girls' door. If his sisters had been around, they'd have led him to their room to show off their weed collection, road gravel, and jars of stinky water swarming with black bugs. Lucy, a few years younger than Henry, had a guinea pig circus with a new guinea pig in it every month or so. She managed to kill them regularly. Betsy, the youngest, was steadier in Henry's opinion, but she had a wild, "backed-up" look to her whenever Martha or Lucy pitched fits, as though they might turn and eat her. She had the ant farm that had to be refilled on nature walks. Like the guinea pig, the ants drowned or starved or suffocated every week or two. Whenever Martha gave Henry rocks and sand to learn about, he'd carry them as far as the Wolfy town sign. There, Cox would roll the truck to a stop and allow him to fling them into a ditch. He would keep the boxes.

"If you mean the girls," answered Martha, who by the sound of her voice was struggling a shirt over her head, "ask 'where are they'—not 'where're they *at*.'"

"Where are they, then?" Henry complied.

She didn't answer. He heard her shuffle on her sandals and run a brush through her hair. Then she came out of the room, her soles slapping the floor.

"They're at the park with Barnes, looking for new ants."

Barnes was Martha's boyfriend, the pharmacist at the new drugstore in the shopping center. He was a quiet, older man who knew how to play the piano and took the time to teach Henry. Cox had no idea about Barnes, let alone the piano. It would make him mad, so Henry didn't tell.

"They'll be gone all afternoon. It'll be just the two of us. I thought we could have a talk this way. In private."

Henry took a gulp of his drink, which made his nose itch.

Martha scooted past him and lowered herself onto the sofa's edge. That she chose to sit there made Henry nervous. He lifted his glass and shuffled towards the other end, but before he could get far, Martha put her hand on his leg.

"No. Stay here," she said. Her voice lay on the air as smoothly as a needle in the grooves of a record. Henry looked down at her hand, then lifted his gaze to her face.

This was the kind of thing that confused him. With her hand on his leg, and speaking nice like that, she was different. The struts on her face even dropped away at times like these, softening so much that she looked like a new person—in fact, like he remembered her being, once. The change was great, but also subtle, like someone had eased a scarf slowly away. She could get the better of him when she acted like this. It was the way she had gotten him to skip ahead to junior high school—a mistake if he had ever made one.

"Don't be afraid. I'm not mad at you. I just want to talk." She tilted her head and sent her bangs skirting across her eyebrows. "How are—things?"

"Fine. Fine. Just fine."

"Really? How're you feeling?" Her gaze meandered to the corner of his face. The bandages were a day older and dirtier.

"Fine. Just fine."

"Does your head hurt?"

Hell yes, thought Henry, it hasn't even had a chance to scab yet. He shook his head no.

She moved closer, so that their knees touched. For some reason, her hand seemed heavy. He tightened his fingers around the glass, which was slipping under his clutch. For a moment, he felt as though the house had shifted.

"Henry," started Martha, an even softer note in her voice, "you said there was a boy you fought with on the bus. A boy from Camille?"

She lowered her chin and looked over her glasses at him.

"Now, I want you to tell me the truth. I won't get mad. Unless you lie." Her voice was softer yet, and her hand heavier.

"There wasn't any boy, was there?"

He shouldn't have been surprised. He nodded his head up and down.

Martha blinked several times, like he had blown air in her face. "What does that mean?"

"That there was too a boy," muttered Henry.

She gave him a flat, pulled smile, like she had only picked the wrong way to skin the cat. She patted his leg for a moment, speaking just before the silence grew awkward.

"If your head doesn't hurt," she started, "how about your neck and shoulder?"

He blushed, adding it all up. The nurse had spotted the blood on his shirt during gym class.

"You'll never get that out," she had said, eyeing his shirt. "It's set in there for good. But try Clorox."

Yesterday's cuts, added to the ones from the "cow-kicking," had sent her to Martha.

"It's healing up fine," he said, acting surprised. He began to shake his head at himself.

"Daddy tells me and tells me not to walk behind number 251, but I don't listen."

Martha's gaze narrowed a bit. Her lips thinned to a tight, red line. "I'd like to see where you got hurt," she said, "if you don't mind."

Henry rolled his shoulders and pulled down his collar. Maybe that would satisfy her.

After a moment, Martha laid her soft hands on him and pulled his collar down further. She inhaled, then leaned over to peak down inside. Her cool palms felt good on the lash, like clean white sheets. All of a sudden, she let go of him and sat up straight. Her face was hard.

"Why didn't you tell me about this?"

"About what?"

"Hush. Tell me the truth. This minute."

His grip on the glass slipped. He cast a nervous glance at it, sure that any minute he would fall into a palsy and let it smash on the floor. He needed to think fast, to figure out what was at stake.

"I did get in a fight yesterday," he said, "so help me God."

Martha flushed to a strange pink. "Don't say that. I suppose you got in a fight with the cow, too?" She pinched his shirtsleeve between her fingers and tugged it sharply. The stripes on his back woke to the gesture, brightening in a rush that made his teeth cold.

"Well? Tell me."

Henry studied her face, judging. He shook his head and stared at his glass.

"I got kicked by the cow two weeks ago," he said. "You can't fight a cow."

Martha lifted her shoulders, mounting to her full, seated height. She whistled air in through her nostrils. Henry glanced sideways at her hands which were clutched tightly now. He waited a long while for her to snap, but nothing came. Eventually, her right hand prized open, and she eased it onto his knee again.

"Don't be afraid," said Martha.

"I'm not."

She batted her eyes in a soothing gesture. "Sometimes—sometimes do you get into trouble with—your father?"

Henry looked down at the glass, squeezing it tight. He shook his head in a firm, controlled negative.

"No, ma'am. Never."

Martha smiled and nodded, as relaxed as a salesman.

She must think he was a fool, he thought. How could she say he was so smart, but give him so little credit?

"Everybody disagrees from time to time, Henry." She drew a circle on his knee with her fingernail. "*We* disagree sometimes, don't we?"

He nodded.

"So you *must* disagree with Cox sometimes."

"Nope," he said, shaking his head. "Never ever."

Martha's forehead tightened. Her voice came out in a flurry.

"Nobody knows him as well as I do. He's mean, and he gets furious at whatever's beyond his depth. Now, what I'm asking is—and I insist on the truth—*insist* on it—did he—"

"What do you think?" asked Henry, jolted. "You ever seen him do a thing like that? Did he ever do a thing like that to you?"

Martha snatched her hand back. "He's done other things to me."

"So he didn't!"

Her eyed flashed. "Don't raise your—"

"If he hadn't, then how come you can even ask—"

Martha held up a hand to still him.

"Henry, hush. Just hush. You don't know what you're talking about."

She eased her words out to him in small doses. "It's my business to understand behavior. I know the signs."

Henry smirked. What she didn't know could fill a silo.

"And on top of what I know about *him*." She lifted her voice like a whip over his head, "I know a lot more about *you*. I know you'd never tell the truth when you could tell a lie. You've gotten to where you lie so much, I doubt you know what the truth is anymore."

Henry smiled, shrugged. "I know what it is. I wouldn't be any good at lying if I didn't."

A clumsy, ugly quiet worked its way between them. Martha made a few, light-fingered strokes on his knee. He glanced at her hand, then to her eyes, which had misted.

"It's not your fault. You tell lies because you're afraid. And God knows you've had every reason to be. You're afraid if you tell the truth, something awful will happen—"

Two silos, thought Henry. Maybe three.

"No it's not," he said squarely into her face. "If I ever tell a lie, it's because I don't wanta get in trouble. Or 'cause I wanta get outa doing something I don't wanta do. But I ain't—"

"—*am not*," interrupted Martha.

"—but I'm not afraid of anything."

She made a noise with her mouth, a moistureless spit. Her head shook at the aggravations that seemed to swarm about her.

"So you're not afraid of Cox, then?"

He sighed. "I didn't say that."

Her head didn't stop shaking.

"You don't know what you mean, and you don't know what you're afraid of, either. But you don't have to be afraid here." She lifted her hands and gestured with her arms, folding in the whole room and house. "You're safe here."

A black cloud clutched at his chest, choking him. No, I'm not, he thought. I'm not, anywhere.

Martha lowered one arm and put it around his shoulder. The display shocked him so much he jostled some of the water onto his pants leg.

"Listen to me. Listen good." Her voice lowered to nearly a whisper, as if it was all a secret, a conspiracy. "You're too bright to let anyone cow you down. Understand? There's no one you have to take orders from, especially not Cox Tollet."

He liked part of what she said, but he didn't like it that he liked it. He wanted to be able to disagree with her completely, but never could. And when she talked like she talked. . . .

"He doesn't do that. Order me around," said Henry, confused now.

But as soon as he spoke, his gaze shifted. Most of the time, that was true. But as of yesterday, he was carrying a stick to school in the mornings, and whose idea was that? Martha looked him over, her face calm, full of pity.

"You're going to have to put a stop to this, Henry." She gave his knee a generous squeeze. "You're a smart boy. If you weren't, I wouldn't have had you skip a grade in school." She cut her eyes at the brochure. "I wouldn't want you to go *there* if you weren't smart. But you *are*."

She winked and smiled. "The more you learn, the more you'll become sure of yourself. But what you can't do is be afraid. You can't be a sheep following orders. That's the only thing you should be afraid of. *You* be the one giving orders."

Somehow, the way she spoke put everything right. After all, it was what he'd suspected about himself, what he knew. She just put it in a different way. The corners of his mouth teased at a smile. All at once, he felt proud.

Martha leaned in, her voice falling to softness. "Cox did this to you, didn't he?"

The glass slipped sideways from his fingers, spilling the water. It splashed onto the bare floor, and they jumped to their feet. Martha ignored it.

"Don't be afraid, Henry. Tell me the truth."

He shook his head in a swag so strong he felt like a horse shuddering flies. She'd stolen the last bit of air in the room.

"Henry, you *have* to tell me the truth."

His shoulders danced forward and back as he shook his head.

"Henry!" Her foot stamped the floor, but he didn't stop. Eventually, she left the room with a clatter of sandals. At some point she returned with a dishrag. In a flourish, she fell down at his feet and mopped up the water. When she was done, she slowly rose. Her face was blank.

"I'll learn it for myself, then. I won't stand for this. I'm going to watch you, very closely. Understand? And the next time this happens—this or anything like it—I'm going to take steps. Understand? So the burden's on you. Either stop it yourself, by telling me the truth, or have me stop it for you. Think that over."

She paused for a moment, as though looking for a misplaced thought.

"And I'll be talking about this to your father, too," she said. "I'm not afraid of him. I haven't been afraid of him in a long time."

She made a brisk turn back to the kitchen, leaving him to stand and stare after her.

They spent their evening in the usual way, reading and listening to the record player. Though she owned a TV, Martha kept it in the closet, pulling it out only when there was a something important on: like moon launches, elections, and tornadoes. After supper, she put on an album of folk stories, then sent Henry and his sisters out to the screened-in porch to listen.

Lucy and Betsy sat together in the same chair. When they were older, he thought, maybe they would be different enough for him to think of as two people. Now, he took them as a brace. They had done this folk story listening so often that their eyes even fastened onto the floor at the same spot.

Every once in a while, Henry listened, but for the most part he stared into the screens, watching bugs beat against the mesh.

No matter what Cox said, Martha always made sense. Maybe he was as smart as she thought; and maybe what he was supposed to do—his reason—depended on his mind, after all. She made it sound like he was going to be a king, and he couldn't help but like that. Besides, school was one thing he could trust her about. He read all he could from *The World Book* she had ordered for him. He was allowed to take one volume home whenever he left her house.

The "S" was his favorite. He had spilt orange juice on it a year ago, so the pages had a crumpled, dirty look along the outside edge. Still, it was his favorite. There were colored pages of all the snakes of the world, with a plastic overlay that showed what a snake looked like from muscles to skeleton to skin. He had learned the truth about Santa Claus from the S. At present, it was teaching him about Spain: El Cid, the Alcazar in Segovia.

In fact, though he never told her, he thought he might like going to the school in Memphis, if it wasn't for the sleeping part.

He dragged his attention back to the record. The narrator was trying to sound serious, but his voice was boring. It would have sounded good if Martha had read it. Her voice was somehow just right: low, but sweet, like the moist smell around hot bread. It would be nice if Martha read aloud from the S to him, too, he thought. It would be pretty.

He looked through the door at her, where she sat tearing strips out of the newspaper and putting them in folders. Something for school. He turned away and stared at the bugs hitting the screen.

If he didn't watch out—if he didn't watch out. . . .

The next afternoon he climbed into his father's truck to go home. In his pocket were two aspirin bottles full of pink sand Martha and the girls had dug out of a drainage ditch.

Looking up to the house, he saw that Cox hadn't followed him. He was standing with Martha, just outside the front door. Her hands were crossed on her chest; she was talking fast, and every once in a while, she snatched her head to the side. Cox, with Henry's suitcase in one hand, stood with his head tilted, as though he couldn't hear her. Then Martha nodded at the car.

Henry's stomach turned over. His mother eased into the house, her last look aimed through the glass at him.

"What did she mean by that?" asked Cox, as he drove towards Wolfy. "She said she knew everything and that it better not happen again. What'd you tell her?"

"I didn't tell her anything!" shouted Henry, louder than he meant. "Except what you know. That I got in a fight. She made it all up herself."

Cox looked him over, wary. For a while he drove, glancing at Henry from time to time. He shook his head. "Hell, she's crazy."

He gave Henry one long sideways look. "*I* don't want it to happen again *either*. And it better not. Hear me?"

Henry nodded. It better not, or Martha would call the law.

When they got to the Wolfy sign, Cox slowed the truck and eased onto the shoulder. The chert and gravel ground beneath the tires. With the engine idling, Henry rolled down the window, snapped the caps off the aspirin bottles, and poured the sand onto the pavement. Then he put the caps back on and shoved the bottles deep into his coat pocket.

Chapter 4

Cox couldn't sleep. He always ate too much when he was mad. He had followed his supper—chili and grilled-cheese sandwiches—with half a box of Eskimo Pies and two bottles of Coke. The food fizzed and boiled inside his belly. He rolled around on his water bed for an hour, then got up, poured a bottle of Pepto Bismol into the milk carton, and drank down the whole thing.

It was after midnight when he plugged in the projector and threaded a new mail-order film through the reel. The customer who had first told him how to get the films highly recommended this one. It was set in a skyscraper office and had a surprise ending. Cox was ready for a surprise. He had a cigar box full of movies now, and after twenty or thirty showings, they got stale.

His fingers fumbled with the reel, feeding the end of the film through the slot. He flipped a switch and the projector started to run, making a loud clacking noise as it gorged itself on the tape. A pulsating square of white light appeared on the wall above the sofa, in a space Cox kept blank. He swiveled his recliner around and settled down.

Every movie started the same. Tease and bait, tease and bait, using a woman with melon-sized breasts, hoisted up to her throat. She'd lean over, then fall against, a parade of slobbering men—neighbors, field hands, salesmen, or—in this particular movie—her boss. The movies were like silent films, simple enough to follow without words. In fact, that was what bothered him. They didn't need words for what they were doing, so why bother him with a plot? This was a skin-flick, for God's sake, so why not just show it? He wasn't the kind that needed, or wanted, teasing—let alone a story. Just show it.

As he waited for the boss to make his move, he tried to think up what he should have said to Martha that afternoon. Her meaning hadn't fully sunk in until he had gotten into the truck.

He clenched his jaw. She knew him better than that. Never, not once had he done anything to make her ask what she had. Like always, she had made it up and sold it to herself, so that now she was convinced of her own story. And as usual, it was just to get back at him for something. This time, it was because he wouldn't let Henry go to school in Memphis.

But why should he? What good would it do to haul him up there every day? It would iron him out, change his blood to dishwater. Henry didn't need any help being strange; he was practically a weirdo now. He didn't have any friends, he listened—to radios and TVs and old people—more than he played, and he boxed himself inside his head for whole stretches of time.

Cox frowned at the film. The girl in the movie wasn't the usual type. She was skinny, with brown hair piled on her head and a big horn-rimmed pair of glasses. She looked hateful, and too smart for the man playing her boss. He was the same pompadoured guy who had played a race car driver in another film. Despite his business suit and tie, he still looked like a race car driver.

Cox rocked back in his chair. The couple still had a ways to go. He closed his eyes.

Sometimes his heart would stop when he came across Henry staring, with his eyes hammer dead. Cox would stamp his foot, and the boy would surface and blink, like he had just awakened from a nap. Then, the next thing he knew, Henry would be asking questions—*why* this and *what for* that—as though he had been digging around for the answer to something Cox was keeping from him.

Cox opened his eyes. That's what aggravated him the most: being looked at like he was keeping something back; something important, like the right way to breathe, or the real way your heart should beat. As though Cox would keep anything—*anything*—from him that he needed.

For a moment, he dug around in his mind to see if maybe he knew something that he hadn't told. Maybe he was supposed to tell Henry something.

He shook his head. Tollet had never told him anything. He'd just made it through on his own. Of course, what could Tollet tell him? How to lift a bottle? How to lie in a bed? How to piss money?

His eyes felt for the flickering pictures on the wall.

The man was shutting his office door. The woman was lying over the desk, hiking her dress.

There, thought Cox. That there was what you needed to know. He turned sideways a bit, as the man tugged down the woman's panty hose.

That was the one thing Tollet could have helped him, Cox, with. He had never been any good at getting women. They said he was too rough, treated them like they were heifers in heat. In fact, one girl had even told him to go practice on a heifer, then come back.

But Tollet. He had been good with women. Cox knew that now, or at least he would admit it now. When he was a boy, he had lied to himself about his father. His mother—a thin, quiet little lady with iron-gray hair—had always worn a face that seemed freshly hurt, continually tricked in some unforgivable way that she was too brave to cry about. For her, Cox had told himself that he hadn't seen his father in certain places, doing certain things. He would play like he had imagined the looks Tollet gave the girl at the feed store, barely older than Cox himself. But what was it? What was it his father had said, or how was it he had smiled, to make her whisper back?

If Tollet had told him that, then maybe the sight of the old man wouldn't make him sick now. If he had helped him through back then, maybe things would be different. But all he had done was drink and lie, drink and lie, and make up stuff that embarrassed him when he found out it hadn't really happened. Coming after lies like that, ones you had believed, the truth was too hard. When he had learned, Cox had felt shunted and small: a stunned pain, like he had fallen to packed earth from the top of a high tree.

He shuddered his shoulders, focused his eyes. He wouldn't let that happen to Henry. And he wouldn't let him be that kind of little liar either.

The springs of his recliner creaked under his weight. His gaze grew fixed, narrowed.

The woman was naked now. Her breasts were small, but firm. Her arms and legs were hard as cedar posts. She didn't roll around with a dumb look, but kept her face straight. It was a smart face; the boss wasn't fooling her.

Cox rolled his tongue over his bottom lip, then pulled it in and bit down, gently.

Martha had looked like that. Her hands were something like that too, but she used them in a different way. She could put them on the sides of his head, just so, like she was handling glass. And then, by God, all the stuff inside it would settle down, fade off into the soft pull and push of his breath. At times like that, she would keep very quiet, the air clean of words. She would almost smile. As smart as she was, right then, she could almost act like she liked him. And for a time, just that time, all the things he hadn't believed in anymore, all he had come to think were just lies, seemed possible.

The film ended, clattering in a spin at the top of the projector arm.

Cox jumped. He rose, exchanged the reels, and watched the film again. It ran over and over, until morning light poured through the windows, fading the pictures away.

━━━━━━

There had been no sign of the boy at the end of the previous week, but Henry was nervous again on Monday morning. Cox watched him take every bite of Frosted Flakes, so that his appetite left him entirely. He gave up on breakfast, grabbed his books, and set off for school with the money in his billfold. Before he got by the table, Cox leaned out of his chair and stopped him. He ran a hand over his front, frisking for the blackjack. When he felt it inside the coat, he let him pass.

With his gaze glued to his boots, Henry made his way through the dewy pasture. It was a quiet morning. What noises he heard—a dog barking, a tractor—were distant and faint.

After he entered the woods, it took a while to get close to Shreva's trailer. But when he was near, her chickens always pulled at his attention. He glanced to the right, to find the sight that went with such a smell. This time, however, she stood there herself, between the trailer window and the sheet she used for drapes. She was smoking a cigarette and eating a Pop-Tart.

Henry swung his gaze around and tromped past the trailer, stopping at the place where he had first met the boy. The ground was spongy from an early morning rain, and the early heat of the sun brought out the stench of trash, rotting. He scanned the woods, then shouted.

"I got me ten dollars in my billfold right now!"

He moved his head an inch to one side, then an inch to the other. There was no wind. The creek sounded in its regular, slow babble. Some rustling came from the woods, but it was only birds building nests. He sighed. The boy wasn't there. He couldn't feel him this time. The place was empty.

Henry turned towards Shreva, looked straight at her and shouted.

"Said I got me two five dollar bills! Once! Twice! Gone!"

When he looked, Shreva had pulled out from beneath the sheet, letting it fall against the glass. Henry jerked his chin at her and ran on to the bus stop.

The boy wasn't there in the afternoon either, or on either trip the next day, or for two days afterward. Henry grew less and less afraid. On Thursday afternoon, he had stopped directly across from Shreva's window, with her staring tunnels through him, and shouted until his voice cracked.

"Said I got me ten dollars! Asshole. I said 'Asshole!' Here I am! Come get me."

His voice echoed and disappeared. And each time, when it was obvious that the boy wasn't coming, he had raised his chin at Shreva, who moved away from the window, disappointed.

When he got back to the house, he sat on the floor in front of the television, looking at a Godzilla movie and eating Fig Newtons. Shreva was due for a visit, and he was eager to hear her report to Cox. He had to make sure she told the whole truth.

From time to time, he clambered to the back window to look for her. She was late today, for no reason. He took it personally and was about to give up. Then, as soon as supper was on the table, she appeared in the yard, hollering about her eggs. Cox got up to meet her; despite Tollet's smacking and slurping, Henry could hear their conversation through the screen door.

"Hadn't seen nothin'," said Shreva. "Now gimme four dollars."

"Hold on a minute," Cox shot back. "Did you look both days? Yesterday and today?"

"I watched both days and nothing come of it. He passed my house and hollered. That's all."

"No sign of that boy?" asked Cox.

Shreva made a pestered sound. "That's what I said."

Henry looked up at Tollet. He'd stopped eating. His gaze lingered around Henry's head, on the bandage. An expression that was both smirk and smile sat on his lips.

"And you heard him shout?"

"Raised hell," said Shreva. A moment passed, and she spoke again. Her voice was low, as if she knew Henry was listening. He strained to hear.

"But that don't prove nothin'. If he's sorry, that don't prove he's not. Only been a week."

Henry glanced at Tollet, who chuckled as he tore at his bread.

"Take this money and get your ass gone," Cox said. "Come back here Tuesday and let me know what you see." He changed his voice to a smug warning. "And by the way. I'm asking Henry to tell whether *you're* watching too, so don't think you can fool me."

Henry blinked. Tollet coughed.

"What you gonna pay Henry?" asked the old man, as Cox stared at the two of them. Henry cut his eyes at his grandfather.

"Never mind," said Cox, waving a hand. He walked over to the table, yanked the chair back and sat down with a rush of air. He was about to pick up his spoon when he stopped and leveled his gaze at the boy.

"Did you see Shreva looking out the window? Both times, both days? Tell me. I'll know if you're lying."

Henry nodded. With an angry, disappointed look, like he had been disgraced, Cox lifted one hip from the chair and pulled fifty cents out of his pocket. He shoved it across the table, picked up his spoon, and began to ladle stew into his mouth.

Henry watched him for the rest of the meal, wondering why Cox didn't like Shreva's news. If the boy was gone, and nothing happened again, it would get Cox off the hook with Martha. Things would settle down. There would be nothing to misunderstand anymore. But it didn't seem to matter.

Cox's left forearm rested against the edge of his table as he ate. His chapped hand was clenched in a fist, and it tightened and relaxed as he leaned over and slurped his soup.

Henry frowned. Cox wouldn't be satisfied unless there was a fight. He wouldn't be happy unless Henry split the boy's head open. Because Cox thought he was sorry, just like Shreva said.

At length, he dropped his spoon and went to his room, where he fell onto his bed. He rested his chin in his fist. For a long time, he'd known he didn't exactly suit his father. But then, nothing suited his father exactly, so it hadn't bothered him too much. Now, however, the thought stoked a fresh anger, banking ashes in his chest.

Then, happily, he spent a long time imagining Cox in jail. A deep satisfaction spread through his body, warm like syrup. He pictured Martha reporting him, calling the law out; Cox, pushed around, his hands behind his back, shoved into a car, laughed at. His body went tense thinking it; he felt better.

As the night wore on, he heard things begin to settle. Tollet was next door, flopping around in his chair. Later still, the old man burst out with parts of half-asleep sentences, bits of song, as he drank. Mi-Fa-Sol-La.

"It's not what you think!" he screamed. Then quieter, "Yes, it is. Yes, it is."

Henry turned over to search for a cool spot on the pillow. The silhouettes of the old furniture—black chifforobe, chest, chair and table—loomed about his room, in the same places where they had stood since it was Cox who slept in this bed, since it was Cox who was a boy here.

What difference did it make to Cox? If he got around the boy in his own way, what did he care? But no, it had to be Cox's way. Nothing else mattered. The boy in the woods might be gone, but if it wasn't Henry that ran him off, it was just another thing to be frustrated about.

Henry tightened the muscles in his chest and pushed all the air out of his lungs, squeezing until he shook. His mind grabbed at ways that would make his father sorry.

Let him come back. Let him beat me blind, like Tollet and them did to that boy. Then she'll see. And tell. They'll take him away then. Good. And maybe while he's in there. . . .

His lips curled over his teeth. The thought rolled in and out of his brain until he grew drowsy. Odd voices called in his sleep, people he knew—his teacher, his mother, his sisters—lulling and pulling him down into the dark. Words mostly. Senseless words.

But then, somebody was singing. Tollet? Old songs. Old, sad songs—threaded and laced with unanswered callings—notes without words. Sol—Fa—La . . . what Tollet sang, but with Cox's voice. Couldn't be. Couldn't be. Then again, it sounded like Cox.

For a long while, he swam in and out, out and in, plunging and rising.

His left arm and knee spasmed; he jolted awake. His eyes shot open, darting along the lines of the room.

Was it day yet? He looked at the glow-in-the-dark alarm clock beside his bed. Only an hour had passed, but it felt like morning was just outside the window, over the hill. He picked up the clock to see if it had stopped, but it ticked in its dull, metallic rhythm. A heavy feeling grew over him, menaced him as though something were out of sequence—a confused wandering—a normal thing, outside its natural place.

He lifted his hand to graze his brow. It ached beneath the bandages, the wounds burning with a bright fever. The revenge that had burned in his chest had given place to queasiness now. Tollet's snore was sawing through the wall, as always, but right then, he wanted to hear Cox; there was no reason he should, at that time, that hour, but still he wanted to, and listened for him.

He sat up and stared at the clock.

The boy would come back. He knew it, as surely as he knew it was night. And on top of what he was sure of, he knew one thing more: whatever Cox deserved, he didn't want him to get it.

After a while, he turned on the light to think by. In time, it came to him. He left his bed and padded around the dark house. He dug loose change from beneath sofa cushions and took scattered dollar bills from the kitchen drawers. He emptied it all into the jelly glass full of money he kept under his bed, stuck the jar in his bag, then crawled beneath the covers.

The next morning, he grabbed a biscuit from the skillet and ate it standing up. Tollet, in a red flannel robe and leather house shoes, leaned against the sink, smoking a cigarette.

"Oh, no you don't," said Cox. He sat on the sofa, pulling on his boots. "Not so early."

Henry started before he could finish. "I thought I'd go early this morning. Catch him."

Bent over his feet, Cox narrowed his eyes. With his hands holding his laces in mid-knot, he hesitated, then pulled the strings together.

"No. Sit down. Leave when it's the right time."

Henry sat at the table and ate. The dough hung in his chest, trying to maneuver its way through his tight throat. Presently, Cox joined him.

"Go on then," he said, after five minutes. "But take your coat."

Henry grabbed his bag, careful not to let the jar shake, then his jacket. Out of sight, he tied his coat around his waist, the pipe making a strange angle in the cloth.

The field grass was coming back, a tender yellow-green rising out of the brown patches from last year's dead. The ground was still soft under his step, despite the fact it hadn't rained in days. The sky was a sanded, cloudless blue. A slight breeze moved the branches of the fence-row sumacs and black gums. The sun was strong and fresh, cracking the last scum of winter varnish off the ground. Henry's feet alternated under him, taking him towards the hill and the woods at their base. For the first time that spring, he noticed a soft haze of green resting over the forest, a tender, juicy color brushed about the limbs. The color disappeared the closer he got to the trees themselves.

Even before he entered the forest's lip, he felt the boy. Flares went off in his blood—on his face, on his back, in the bowl of his stomach. He tried to swallow.

The day was all quiet with morning sleep. He shuddered, but moved in deeper, wandering off the path, then back again. The trees seemed to step back from him as he walked.

As Henry passed the bend that gave out onto Shreva's, he saw him standing further on, in plain view. This time, the boy didn't step out from any place, or come up from behind. There was no surprise to him. Still, Henry stumbled backwards at the sight. His knees buckled, stooping him so that his torso turned to one side, his body preparing to bolt him away.

With a soft grunt, he forced himself on. His head throbbed in a rhythm that matched the pulsing along his back—each pain falling into slots left by the other—a music that hurt like torches being laid, then lifted from his skin. His heart rose into his throat, the thrusts of his blood killing him as he came to stop in front of the boy.

The long, threaded hair, the tattered pants, the triangle of red cloth he wore as a coat. He stood on a small incline in the path. He loomed over Henry, so that the stove wood he held in his hand already had a power to it, a hard promise made from the height at which it would swing. Henry's eyes watered, his wounds sweating.

He forced his gaze to the boy's face, to where his eyes smoked, a furnace smoldering in the lids. He was both old and young, his skin lined with trenches, but ruddy and flush. And he looked at Henry with a face so serious, so free of lies, or anything near lies, that standing there might have been all he was ever meant to do. And under the stare, Henry's skin wept—with sweat or blood, he could not tell—so that he felt a trickle course across his head and back.

But before the blows came, he had to say his piece. Before the blows came, he had to talk.

He snatched his head to the side, yanking his lips apart.

"No," he said—a whisper. He struggled his voice clear of the rock in his throat.

"Listen," he began again. "I got ten dollars. More than ten. It's yours. All of it. I'll give it to you, then I'll get you some more."

The stick rose at an angle, creating a wind.

"I'm not through," he rushed on, amazed his voice could come. "I'll give it all to you, and then, if you still gotta hit me, then hit me where it won't show—where it won't cause my Daddy trouble. All right? Hit me," he stopped to tug his shirttail up, holding it across his chest. "Here."

His own gaze fell to where a breeze grazed his skin: his dark nipples, his bruised ribs. His voice came out mannered, desperate.

"You can still do it. I'm not saying you can't. But just don't let it show. Hurt me where it don't show. So it's just me. See? So it's just me you're hitting."

The boy held the stick in a way that it seemed a part of his body, another arm, something to which he had grown fixed. Henry's gaze traveled up his shoulder, fumbling for his face.

From his chapped red mouth came a sound, whispered—taps, like two drops of water—a word Henry recognized at once, in form and shape, but at once forgot. For the boy's eyes bore down with a dreadful heat, burning up his thoughts. The light they carried reared, then lunged. Henry stumbled backward, his head falling to the side, dangling from his neck like a boulder. He clamped his eyes shut. A storm of heat rushed from an open oven door, scorching him. It cooked through his flesh, seeping into his bones, dividing and entering, dividing and entering—towards the place where he knelt, cowering within himself, curling into the smallest thing he could manage—the tightest cradle. The flame towered, then surged through his chest in a hot, furious plunder.

———

The first thing he heard was the creek, then the chickens, then the smaller sounds of branches moving in the woods. His eyes were open, not closed. He stared into a mesh of limbs and a small span of blue sky. When he could bring his head forward again, he was surprised to find himself erect, in the same place as before. Searching for the boy, he found the last of him in the distance, his head and shoulders still visible as he walked down the far side of a rise. The back of his head bobbed below the top of the ridge, and he was gone.

Henry looked at his fingers. He moved his right hand back to his pocket, felt for his billfold, and pulled it out.

The money was still there. He raised a cautious hand to his face, passed his palm over its glazed surface, then drew it away to look. Except from the glisten of sweat, his hand was clean. His head and back no longer throbbed. Cautious, he sawed a gust of air into his lungs. His ribs warmed in mute pain.

There were bubbles in his blood now, shimmering, exploding. He picked up the books that lay about his feet. Then he set trembling legs off towards the road. When he saw the yellow bus waiting for him, he thought to glance at his watch. Only ten minutes had passed, but the morning was already ancient.

———

Cox had to edge through the woods to keep from running into a tree in the dark. A rind-colored light had lingered about the top of the hill as he had come across the pasture, but it was black night in the woods, and he had forgotten to bring a light. He couldn't see Shreva's trailer yet, but he smelled chickens and garbage. He opened his teeth and breathed through his mouth, then continued around the bend, shoving his chilled, stinging hands into his jacket pockets.

A yellow light glowed from every window in the trailer. It fell heavily from the glass and laid a dirty luster along the leaves outside. Cox stomped up the concrete blocks that served as steps and pounded three times on the metal door.

"Open up. It's me. Cox Tollet."

"Who's that?" came her voice. "Who's that out there?"

"I said it's Cox. Open the door."

"I'm in my night gown."

A wave of nausea passed over him. As she shuffled towards the door, he backed away, nearly falling off the steps. The door came open, but Cox was out in the yard by then. He swung his head towards the woods.

"I just wanted to know what happened today," he said. He felt a terrible pull at the back of his head, like something was trying to force him to see a horrible sight. "Henry left acting weird at breakfast," he said. "Came home even weirder this evening. Won't say a thing."

"Where's my four dollar bills?" interrupted Shreva.

Cox pulled out his wallet. He edged over to the steps with his head still turned, then shook the paper at her. She snatched it away, and he backed off to a safe distance again.

"Well? What happened? Did he whip him?" Cox stiffened his back, his gaze darting about the black trees. The cold lay a coat over his skin, driving his neck down to his shoulders. Air whistled in and out of Shreva's nose.

"Your boy come to stand in fronta the other," she said. "Stood there and commenced to talk. Pointed to his back pocket. I edged up to the glass to hear him, but—" Her voice turned strange.

"But he was talkin' so soft I couldn't make it out."

Cox shifted sideways a bit, so that he could see her out of the corner of his eye.

"Go on," he said. "Tell it or you won't get another dime."

"Then that other 'un lifted the stick," continued Shreva, "but your boy yanked his shirt up and showed 'im his belly. Then his eyes glassed up and his head dropped back like he wasn't gonna look."

Cox's mouth fell open. Shreva paused; he had to prompt her.

"Well?" Instead of going on, she shut her mouth with a clack of teeth.

"That's it," she said, disappointed.

"That's it? Nothin' happened?"

"Other fella eased off the path and headed over the rise."

"That's it? He just left?" Cox moved his head a bit further, so that he could see her better. She was nodding.

He squared his shoulders as a rush of pride swelled over him.

Henry had dared the boy. Taunted him. Turned his head. But the bastard had run off.

He smiled a broad smile. He knew it. He knew it!

"That don't prove nothin'," said Shreva, her voice black. Cox nearly looked at her, the way she sounded. "Besides, your boy's turned idiot. He started laughin' like a fool."

Henry had run the other boy off.

He turned to face her full on. It wasn't so bad. She had on a man's plaid robe and a pair of men's house shoes, like Tollet wore.

The worst of it was her head, which looked all the more like a skeleton's for the hair she'd pinned up in back.

He swung around to leave, then threw over his shoulder, "I won't be needing your detective work anymore. I'm closed for business."

Before he could get out of earshot, she shouted back. "Lyin' bastard! You promised me two weeks! Said 'guarantee'! That shows what you are, right there!"

Cox was already well into the woods. He laughed in a long, loud mock, strong enough for her to hear him through the slammed door. He strode home through the deepening dark, forgetting how cold he had been. When he got home, he'd let Henry keep the marked money. He'd earned it.

Chapter 5

Several days passed. Henry showed no fresh bruises or welts, so Cox felt certain the whole thing was over. The boy had proved that he wasn't a coward, and in a bigger, braver way than Cox could have hoped. What's more, Henry didn't brag, either. Though Cox gave him plenty of chances, he never discussed what happened.

"Saw him again, I hear," offered Cox, the morning after he'd met with Shreva. He was casual, so as not to seem too interested. Henry looked up, like someone had poked him with a pencil. He nodded, then found an excuse to leave the room. Cox had tried him again in the evening.

"What about this I hear with the boy? Shreva told me you ran him off."

Henry's head wobbled about in a gesture that wasn't quite a nod and wasn't quite a shake.

"Something like that," he said. His tone was reserved. It made Cox suspicious.

"You haven't seen him again, have you? He hasn't come back?" Henry's expression was loose and wild, like he'd fly apart at another question.

"No," he answered. "I haven't seen him. He's gone."

Cox backed up a bit, nodding that he believed. Had he not already gotten the whole story from Shreva, he might have pressed Henry for details. But the boy's reluctance filled Cox with new admiration. He himself would have bragged.

After supper, Cox studied his son, who was bent over a comic book, his bandaged head resting on one hand.

Maybe Henry was better than he was. Maybe, despite Martha's best efforts, he was a boy who would kick your ass and leave everybody else to do the talking. Those were the kind Cox had wanted to be like. For some reason, he had always had to fan the flames of anything he did. Whatever he beat or kicked or fucked had to be talked about, often, loudly—to get anyone to take notice. And even then it died away.

But others, rare ones, could do their work, sit back, and leave it alone. They made wakes and left things in them. Maybe Henry would be one of those. At any rate, here was the first indication he might be, if given the chance. Cox decided not to rush him, but just prepare the ground, as he had by making Henry face the boy from Camille. There were other, subtler ways to help, too. Cox would try to work that way, though admittedly it wasn't a style he had used in a long time.

During the week that followed, the weather got warmer. After supper, Tollet had started using the longer days to set off for Felix's house, to drink. Sometimes, he'd pass out there and wait until the next morning to come staggering back up the road. With him out of the way so early, not stumbling around under foot to disturb things, Cox decided to start bringing out his projector sooner than usual. When Henry settled onto the cleared table to do his homework, Cox got out the card table and began to reel a movie onto the projector.

They were easy little movies at first, plots that allowed for a bedroom scene every ten minutes or so. They stopped short of sex, but Cox decided you didn't have to be as smart as Henry to make the connections. All he wanted was to whet the boy's appetite. Henry was the wary type, like Martha had been. But then, Cox had found a way around her, too. And that kind, once you got them started, were something else again.

Back in school, she had wondered why he was paying so much attention. Though everyone knew her, mostly because she couldn't keep her mouth shut, she did nothing with her looks: straight hair, plain clothes, big glasses. But she had a firm body that the boys talked about, and imagined differently. One night, some friends had dared him. So he had edged up on her, careful not to talk, careful to go soft.

He hadn't known himself that he could go soft, if that's what it took. She hadn't known it either; and neither did Henry, now.

Following a week of easy movies, Cox decided to move on to lay-out films, the whole point of which was to look at women naked. But though they were naked, they were shot in beautiful places, so that the whole thing had a classy feel. They even superimposed the girls' first names on the bottom of the screen: "Elsa"—"Marie."

One evening, when Cox was part way into a movie, he froze the film. Though he had just eaten supper, he had grown hungry again, and decided to root around in the refrigerator. As he rose from his chair, he noticed that the frame was stopped on a black-haired, beach-scampering girl named Oona. Her head was cut off, but her breasts and stomach were in full view. After getting the leftover cold cuts and cheese out of the refrigerator, he turned back to his chair. But out of the corner of his eye he saw Henry hovering over his math book, head bent, eyes on the girl. Cox looked away quickly, trying not to smile. He settled down again, tore the Saran Wrap off the bologna, and ate.

Not only would Henry grow up into a bad-ass, mused Cox, he would be good with women. Bad-asses didn't have to buy whores. Whores, even like Lois, laughed while they counted your money. Women would come to Henry instead of the other way around.

When the weekend came, Cox had to run his usual Sunday errands alone. He wasn't due to pick the boy up until late afternoon since Martha was taking them all to see her mother, who lived at the nursing home. So he had all day, and planned to pop in on Lois around eleven thirty, to make up with her. All these tame movies had begun to aggravate him, fading away as they did, just as the girl was starting to fondle herself. It had put him in a bad mood, which boiled over into his last time. He had gotten too rough, and she had smacked him when he bit her on the shoulder. He decided to take her a sack of groceries to the house. Sunday was the only day he was allowed to come there instead of to the gas station.

He filled up two sacks with things she liked—mostly chocolate candy and deviled ham—but before he got out of the parking lot, he remembered he needed salve for Henry's head and back. For some reason, the wounds were slow to heal and the scabs wouldn't fall off. He made a U-turn, then drove to the far corner of the shopping center where a drugstore had opened only a month before. He'd never traded there, but it was the closest one.

Heading for the pharmacy in the back, he walked down a row of snacks and snatched a bag of miniature candy bars off the hanger. He ripped open the bag and tore into the chocolate as he came close to the raised ledge. Before he could say anything, the pharmacist called from inside the rows of shelves behind the counter.

"I'll be there in juuuust a second."

"Mmmmmm. Take your time," said Cox, his voice caught with chocolate.

As he worked his jaws, he looked around the store. A long row of greeting cards lined the wall to his left, and a swivel stand full of sunglasses stood to the side. He stepped over and tried on a pair of glasses with heavy black rims, then stooped to examine himself in the tiny mirror. He decided to buy them, but when he took the glasses off to see the price, couldn't find a tag. He checked his looks again, then stepped up to the counter to ask. He leaned over and glanced about.

Henry might not have caught his attention if he hadn't been frozen so still. But out of the corner of his right eye, Cox noticed something trying to melt into the scenery.

Cox swallowed his chocolate with a hard gulp. Henry was dressed in khaki shorts and a white T-shirt. The bandage was gone from his head, leaving the jagged red-black scab rising from his face. An open book with pictures of snakes inside rested on his knees. He was as still as the chair he sat on.

"What're you doing?" asked Cox, stunned. "You're supposed to be at the nursing home."

Henry's mouth opened, and he drew a long breath. Then his eyes shifted to look at the pharmacist, who had come around the corner of the shelf. Cox looked too, eyeing a slump-shouldered, balding, dumpy man in a short-sleeve white coat. His skin had a boiled look to it, and his wire-framed glasses dug into the bridge of his nose.

"I'm sorry," the man said. "Did you say something?"

"I said something to *him*." Cox's gaze moved back to Henry. He lifted his arm over the counter and laid it down slowly, pointing a finger at the boy. "What're you doing?"

He realized he still had the sunglasses on and ripped them off his head. The pharmacist made a coughing sound; Cox cut his eyes at the man.

"That's my boy. What's he doing sitting inside this drug store?" He flushed a hard red. "What's he doing back in there—with you?"

The pharmacist took a wheezing breath and stepped forward. He started to offer his hand but hesitated and dropped his arm to his side.

"Hoyt Barnes," he said, a jittery smile on his lips. His eyebrows rose clear to his hairline.

Cox's face twisted into a snarl. He was as disgusted as if a pig had gotten up on its hind legs and tried to introduce itself. He glanced back to Henry, whose face had drained.

"Let me explain," said Barnes, a shaky laugh in his voice. "Henry's just staying with me while his mother and sisters are at the dime store. They'll be back soon."

"How come she left him with *you?*" blared Cox.

The red in his face washed around beneath the skin. "Martha and I are—friends. Sometimes she leaves him with me. I'm the one that's teaching him the piano, you know. And, man, he's a real fast learner—"

"I sure as hell did *not* know it!" Cox slapped the sunglasses down on the counter and motioned for the boy. "You come out of there. I might as well take you home right now. No need to drive back to town this afternoon when here you are."

Barnes stepped forward, but Henry sprang out of the chair and scrambled under the open space below the hinged counter-top.

"Shouldn't we let her know?" asked Barnes. "She's right down there at the—"

"You tell her then, since you're 'friends' with her. You tell her I picked him up."

He waved his hand to send Henry marching towards the door, then swung back on Barnes. The man sucked in a loud mouthful of air.

"Oh yeah," said Cox. "Gimme some salve. Where is it? Cortisone salve."

Barnes nodded at a shelf directly in front of the counter. Cox snatched up the biggest jar he could find. The price tag read "$3.99." He dug a dollar out of his billfold.

"Keep the change," he said. He whipped around and followed Henry.

When he got outside, Henry was making towards the truck, his arms swinging, his legs at one speed below a run.

"Hold it. Right there," called Cox. The boy turned and came back as swiftly as if he were a toy whose feet were on tracks. For a moment, Cox rummaged for something to blame him with.

"What in the hell're you doing?"

Henry folded his top lip beneath his bottom. He ran the flat of his hand up and down his thigh.

"She changed her mind about going to see Big Mama. It's Sunday, and she doesn't like having to go to the church service out there." His words came out carefully, like he was trying to repeat only the things that Barnes had said.

"He comes by sometimes while I'm at her house. And we all go out together. Sometimes." The tone of his voice changed. "He doesn't bother anybody."

The thought was sickening, but Cox let himself think it. "You mean she's taken up with *that?*" He jerked his thumb at the drugstore.

"He doesn't do anything," said Henry, "except come by and eat with us and go to the picture show. You hardly know he's there."

Cox rested his hands on his hips and stared at the sidewalk. Before he'd even gotten a look at the man, he knew it—by the sound of his voice, he knew it— an ironed, pressed sound. And he looked worst than he sounded. Martha had picked him on purpose.

Cox ground his teeth and aimed his stare at Henry.

"You never told me one word about this."

Henry dropped his gaze to Cox's belt buckle. "I know it."

The boy looked to have moved inside his head and closed the shutters on his eyes. Cox hated it when he did that.

"Taking piano," said Cox, sneering. "Look at me. Look at me right *now.*"

The boy raised his eyes, but the shutters stayed closed.

"Have you done this before? Come stay out here with him?"

Henry's shoulders rose and fell. He lifted his hands and rolled one fist into the cup of the other. He nodded. "When she's busy."

Cox gritted his teeth. "Day in and day out, she's all the time nagging me about you—what all I'm letting happen to you. What all I'm not doing for you. What all she's gonna do to me if I keep it up. And now here she is dropping you off with her boyfriend while she runs around. And keeps it hid to boot. Boy, she's gonna find out different now."

"But she's just over there at the *dime store*," Henry said, pointing. "And I don't do a thing except sit there with him and—"

"—and read," finished Cox. His voice rose to a pitch that stopped Henry's fidgeting. "And take piano lessons, and God knows what else. Looked like you were enjoying yourself to me. Is that what you wanta do now? Be fat, and shove little-bitty pills into bottles? Sell lipstick and cold cream?"

Henry's eyes cleared; he came out from behind them, staring Cox full in the face.

"All I do is sit there. He doesn't bother me, and he doesn't *wanta* bother me."

Cox sniffed, folding his arms across his chest. "You don't know shit from short cake."

He rolled his shoulders, throwing his clothes back.

"Got you skipping grades—taking piano—growing up to—"

Henry lifted his head, his eyes flashing. "She's not any worse than you."

"Shut up," said Cox. Henry lifted his shoulders, rose to his full height. Cox loomed up and over him. "Get in the truck."

The boy closed his mouth, but he kept his angry look. Cox watched him, pleased. Henry didn't just get in the truck—he yanked the door open and clambered in, then slammed himself inside with a sound that scared a dog lying against the drugstore wall. Cox gave him half a sneer and half a smile.

Before they left, Cox salved and bandaged Henry's head again. The places needed covering, but it was just like Martha to take his work off, whether it hurt Henry or not. He glanced at the boy's angry face as he doctored him.

He might be right about Henry. Look at him now—the kind to clean your plow and leave it clean. If Martha didn't screw him up.

When they pulled out of the parking lot, he saw Martha and the girls headed for their car. Cox pounded on the horn hard and made Henry wave out the window. Then he tore out to Lois's house. He sawed the car under the canopy at the gas station next door, killed the engine, and gathered the grocery bags in one arm.

"Wait here," he said to Henry, kicking the door shut with his foot. "I got business in this house over here. I won't be long."

He was furious. It would be good and hard. He'd think of Martha.

Chapter 6

Henry lifted his books off the truck floor and got out his homework for Monday. It was hot in the truck, so he rolled down the window and tried to concentrate. But the spring heat had settled in, making the air too damp and close for work. He gave up and watched traffic pass by the station.

Cox knew about Barnes now. It was a shame, too, because Henry liked Barnes. They got along, though they didn't have a lot to say to each other. Barnes wasn't the kind to smother you. Even when he started teaching Henry piano, he hadn't forced it down his throat. First, he had lifted the lid to show how the hammers hit the strings. While Barnes played, Henry stared at the felt mallets, the lengths of tight wire: that all of them together could make a song. One thing led to another, so that he hadn't thought of himself so much as learning piano as making a song. Barnes had taken the time to show him the strings, the reason for the sound.

But as much as he liked the man, Henry couldn't see why he let people walk all over him. A few times, he'd even seen Martha do what Cox had just done. Whenever Barnes came to the house, she all but tied an apron around him or stuck a shovel in his hand.

If he were grown—he stopped to think, then nodded to himself—if he were grown, he wouldn't stand still for that.

A car drove up to the full-service pumps, rolled over the cable and set off a bell. A sluggish, fat man with short arms, dressed in a football jersey, came out to pump gas.

Mrs. Carberry ran this place, he knew. He went to school with her boy and girl. Mona Lisa was in his science class, and people said she had already been married once. Her little brother, Curtis, was bigger than Henry, and liked to make the point. Because Henry couldn't climb the rope up to the third marker, he had to leave junior high every day and take gym next door at the elementary building. It would've been fun, being back with people he knew for a little while. But Curtis spiked volleyballs into his face, and slung him to the ground by his shirttail when they played football. Once, he had singled Henry out in the shower, just to piss down the side of his leg.

He ground his teeth at the memory. Times might be changing.

Lately, he had decided that maybe there was some kind of toughness in him he hadn't known about before. Maybe Cox was right after all, forcing him to take the boy on. Now he knew he could stand up for himself if he needed to. In fact, in a way, he had stood up to Cox, just now.

He closed his eyes and pictured himself slamming Curtis's head into the asphalt and saying—"Times've changed"—into his face. A stir passed through his muscles, pump and pulse. Stretching his arms over his head, he yawned. His hands clutched and his fingernails dug into his palms.

The passing traffic made gentle sounds outside the window, like cars riding through water. From inside the store came the scratchy noise of a transistor radio. Occasionally, he heard the clank and echo of a tool being dropped in the garage. The still, muggy air lulled him to drowsiness. He slid around the edges of sleep.

He imagined himself beating Curtis in front of the whole sixth grade, and Cox, and Tollet, and even the boy from Camille. And then, for some reason, the girls in Cox's movies were there, too—the ones from the beach. The girls were all watching the fight. The wind blew their hair all over their heads, along their collarbones, and lower. . . .

He bolted awake. His gaze shot about, and he was scared of the wild sounds in his heart. With a loud sucking noise, he slurped up the drool that dangled from his bottom lip. Glancing down at his watch, he saw that twenty minutes had passed. He snorted and sniffed, then looked around.

No one was outside the store. No cars passed on the road. The music was the only thing that was the same, straining out static. The floor of his stomach tingled.

Maybe Cox had put the bandages on too tight. That could make him feel queasy sometimes. So he worked at the adhesive to loosen the wrapping. The hot weather had weakened the glue, and the gauze peeled away easier than he expected. Little by little, the bandage came unstuck. With one side free, the air rushed underneath to cool his skin. The places were healing, and he fingered the bumps and ridges of the scales. He had half a mind to pick at them, just around the edges. But before he could start the job, Cox rounded the corner, tucking his shirttail into the back of his pants. He had made it all the way to the truck, when a voice stopped him.

"I said, '*hey*'—you didn't sign this."

She was leaning against the corner of the building, with one hand shielding her eyes from the sun, the other holding a piece of paper out at Cox. She wore a tight yellow shirt, green shorts, and white sandals. Her frosted hair had fallen down on one side, so that it lay across her shoulder. Her chest and hips were big—soft and round, but not fat. The skin on her raised arms was a flushed pink. For some reason, Henry knew just how hot it would feel if he lay his cheek against her arm— then his mouth. In a slow, lazy movement, she let all her weight roll onto one hip. The rumble in his stomach rose, spread.

Cox pulled a pen from his shirt pocket, walked over and reached for the check she was holding. But the woman snatched it away as soon as his fingers grazed the paper. She laughed a quiet laugh to herself, then let him have it, offering her shoulder as a desk. Cox blushed, coughed. He laid the paper down on the flat space along her collarbone and softly scribbled his name. Then the woman swung around. She snatched both the pen and paper from his hand. Laughing, she strode away and rounded the corner.

Cox cleared his throat. He kept his gaze at his feet until he was in the truck.

Henry felt like he had stood too close to a fire—scorched, unstrung. The oddness in his stomach—lower than his stomach—was a sweet sickness he had known before, but never so long, never so much. He turned halfway around in his seat to stare at the gas station as they drove off.

Though he tried not to, he couldn't help stealing looks at his father. Cox looked happy, but hot and winded. He looked that way whenever he came home from a trip to town.

Henry felt the same way now—like he had found what he wanted, but couldn't get enough of it. One glass of water after a trip through the desert. He stared at Cox as long as he dared. They had never looked so much alike.

———

The woman in his dream started to move. Up until then, she had stayed at his bedroom door, leaning so that only her head and the cross of her shoulders touched the frame. The rest of her slanted out at a diagonal, all the way down to her calf-high boots on the hardwood floor. She had bleached hair, teased high on her head, with a curl plastered at the corner of each cheek. Long eyelashes. Green eye shadow. Red-black lipstick. She wore a green bra and green, high-waisted panties. Her right leg was moving at the knee, twisting in and out, like a gate on its hinges.

All at once, she pulled her shoulders off the frame and took a long, lazy step towards his bed, slinging her leg from the hip. Henry lay paralyzed. Come closer, something said. Closer, Closer, Clos—

His stomach was pressing at the covers when he awoke. His underwear had somehow made its way down around the ankle of his right foot. Suddenly, his eyes shot open; his gaze raked the ceiling. He swallowed, gently.

If he didn't hold perfectly still, something—an attack, a seizure—would happen. The air was all sparks. He pulled breath in and out through his teeth, over and over, until he calmed the feeling, like a ship settling to a sea floor. Slowly he eased out of bed, pulled his underwear up, and padded to the bathroom in the dark.

Turning the faucet on, he stuck his mouth underneath and gulped mouthfuls of cold water.

When she had first come into his dreams, the woman was from a beach party movie he had seen one hot afternoon last fall. It puzzled him that she was so different from the girls in Cox's movies. They were prettier than she was. But though she might have come from the beach movie at first, she had changed now. She had the same kind of look, but she had turned into Mrs. Carberry.

After he had his fill of water, he slipped back into his bedroom. He curled onto his side and clutched the covers tightly against his head. He didn't know what time it was, but he wouldn't be able to sleep. Heat lurked about his groin.

In the window of time after he had last seen the boy from Camille, he had believed he was getting somewhere—that his troubles were, if not going away, at least changing. He had stopped the boy and was confident that he would never see him again. There would be no more beatings to explain and have misunderstood. He was glad, for Cox. And the rest—his reaction to the boy, the swelter he had felt that had lifted him clear of his body. *That.* That he wouldn't let himself think about. That he imagined as a pawed, reamed-out place—a scoured hole floating around in his chest and throat. He didn't understand it. And he had expected it to linger, well past the healing of the tender, scabbed-over spots on his back, head, and ribs. He had made another discovery, he thought—one that wouldn't pass. He could do things himself, in his own way. He had hoped that soon he'd be at his starting point, at the beginning of what he was supposed to do.

But now something had made him forget. It had stolen up from behind and caught him like a hard clap of water, slamming into his back. The start of it was his dreams, but then Mrs. Carberry had come and deepened it. It had taken him with a pull he didn't have the strength to overcome. And it wasn't just Mrs. Carberry—not exactly—but it started with her. It needed her until he was lost in what felt like a sea, rolling gently through his crotch, growing more and more stormy, more and more fierce—until—what?

The time since he had first seen her seemed like one long day, a day that held darkness inside it like an eclipse. He hadn't been able to sleep much. When sleep did come—she was there. When he was awake—trying to study, eat, bathe, or just be—she was still there. Nothing he did held his attention. Any book he started, he stopped within the first three sentences as she came into his head. Even the S was no match for her.

His favorite cartoons faded as his gaze moved to the wall, lost focus, fixed. He ate all day long, but he didn't have a real appetite, not even for pizza. She came for him in cycles, and before he knew it, he had been staring so long that black and blue spots fused into his eyes. There she stood in the door—there she lay on the table—leaning, reclining, her mouth on the brink of laughter.

Had this been part of the world all along, and he hadn't known it until now? How could it not be everybody's life, all the time, the way it felt? How could anybody live and work and carry on outside their heads, when this was possible, *inside* their heads? It felt so good that hours could pass while he stared and thought. And it wasn't like he was unconscious. He was wide awake. He heard sounds in the background: Tollet talking—the cows being fed—cabinets slamming. But he was just below the surface, a layer of glass between him and all that. He lived underneath, in his head, with her.

· "What's her first name?" he had asked, just that morning. He felt he ought to know. Standing at the feed lot fence, he had called up to Cox, who was working in the barn loft. Every few seconds, a hank of hay sailed out of the loft door in a rain of sticks and yellow powder, then hit the ground in a shatter. Henry, cross from lack of sleep, called again when his father didn't answer.

"I asked you what her name was."

"Who?" barked Cox, coming to the door. "Who're you talking 'bout?"

"Mrs. Carberry."

Cox scraped his boot across the floor and sent the last of the bale over the edge. The steers and heifers ambled up, nudging each other aside for the food.

"What you wanta know for?"

He wants to keep her name to himself, thought Henry. Suddenly, he was fearless.

"Tell me. You tell me!"

Cox put his hands on his hips. But instead of anger or aggravation, he smiled an oily smile. He swiped his boot across the floor one
more time.

"Lois." He sang the last syllable to him, in a taunt: "*Looiissss.*"

Henry had taken the name back to the house with him, to sit
and think with it.

He breathed deeply, his eyes on the darkened light fixture. Sleep
was impossible. It was as though he was mostly dead, and now only
lived in her going and coming. She had always just left, and she was
always just now coming again. And she seemed to promise something. It had almost happened a while ago, but he had awakened in
time to stop it.

What if she was going to leave? It had felt like that. What if her
promise was the first and last one she would make?

He had to keep her. If the best she gave—and that was what it
had felt like—meant that this had to end, he didn't want it. He
would live with just this much. It was enough.

He turned over, his face damp. Finally, a strange, buzzing half-
sleep caught him, moving him along a twilight crest.

She was there again, against the door frame. He was only half
asleep, and this time he partly put her there himself. He didn't care
that she came to the same place, did the same things. He liked it,
since he knew what to expect. He shifted, turning so that he lay face
down. In a rich, round moment, he felt his stomach loading with
feathers. He had to touch it, feel himself swell into it.

She moved from the wall and came to him, standing at the foot
of his bed, a full smile on her face. His feet twisted beneath the warm,
clammy sheets.

For the first time, she eased her hands behind her back. Her top
fell off, her breasts bouncing gently, like the girls in Cox's movies had
done. A tremor passed through his crotch. He pushed against it, and
struggled over a slight gag in his throat.

Suddenly, he was afraid she was going to speak. He clamped his
eyes shut, squeezing his cheeks towards his brow to hold her in, to
keep her from saying anything. It didn't work.

She was going to give it all to him—anyway—no matter what he did.

Then, all at once, it had nothing to do with talking—nothing to do with words. He pitched onto his back, pushed his underwear down to his feet.

She was on the bed now, just above him, straddling. With a thrust, he pushed towards her. He wanted her heaviness on top of him, to feel her weight settle onto his hips, crush him with her round cheeks. He pushed again, up and against where she should be. He met only air—air, where he wanted weight, where he wanted her weight.

His face twisted. For some reason, she wouldn't meet him. She wouldn't sit down. He gagged again, his throat snaking inside his neck as he rose to her.

"Sit down. Sit down, damn you!" His voice grew in the dark, whispered like a man's, hoarse with fury. Everything in the room was something else, separate and apart from what used to be whole—his voice, the dark, her weight, his heat and swelling.

With a furious pitch he rolled onto his stomach again. His eyes opened, kneading the dark where, now, she lay beneath him. His stomach and hips pounded into the mattress—at the pillow—grinding in brutal twists. The bandages on his head loosened. Sweat stung the wounds beneath.

Now she was the bed—nothing but the bed. Then she was nothing at all—just a gathering tremor—an unfolding black he was about to feel.

Ropes, cords, knots—filling—rushing—foam, salt, flowers. A secret—nearing. Too late to stop and too late to want it to stop. He rode the thrust, entered a dark shaft, flared into a black maw. A shudder broke against his belly: flurries, shimmers on a knife blade. He groaned and bled with pleasure. On and on and out. His hips rocked into the wound between his legs—pause and bleed, pause and bleed—larger—better—a skinning that traveled down to his toes, laid on the underside of his arms, in the palms of his hands—an unlit sun—consuming itself, melting even the black pitch where it lay.

Finally, breath came again, rising steadily with his heartbeat. It flogged at his chest bone.

Time crept back. His eyes shot open, fixing on the outlines of his dresser and chair.

He sent a shaking hand down to feel the blood. It was thick, like oil. It stuck and dripped from the balls of his fingers.

This would be how you bled when you died—thick and weighty—like this. A strangled quiet clutched at his chest. He was too frightened to cry out. He yanked the covers back, slipped from the bed, and ran to the bathroom.

The fluorescent light strobed on and off, but when it stopped, he saw that his stomach was covered with some terrible, clear blood— not red at all. His gaze went black for a moment at the sight. Something that should have stayed in, he had forced out with all of his pounding.

I've killed myself, he thought, staring at the strange blood on his stomach. She's killed me.

Quickly, hands shaking, he cleaned himself with wads of wet, soapy toilet paper. He didn't want Cox to find a bath rag and wonder why. Then he crept back to his room and turned on the lights. It took more toilet paper to mop and scrub the sheets, the paper wilting and crumbling against the cloth. He rushed back and flushed the remnants down the commode.

The bed was too damp to lie in, so he sat down in the corner of his room, his eyes growing used to the dark. His stomach spasmed, cramped. He was going to die.

━━━━━━

"You don't know a damn thing," Cox said.

He sat at the table, dressed in his work coveralls, digging his hand into a Frosted Flakes box for the prize. Tollet stood at the stove, turning pancakes as he smoked a cigarette. He wore his flannel robe and corduroy house shoes. Varicose veins spidered through the back of his white legs.

"I know what I remember," answered Tollet, taking the cigarette from his mouth. Cox watched him lay it in the porcelain spoon-rest that had belonged to his mother. Her name—Meriam—was embossed on the side.

"Unh-hunh," started Cox. His voice was choked dry. He took a swallow of coffee so he could talk. "All right, then. Who was it that led the singing out there at Camille, then? Remember?"

Tollet shook his head and smiled, as though to ignore that it was an argument they were having. He turned a pancake over and picked up his cigarette. Sometimes he dropped ashes into the batter, which Cox had to be careful of.

"I can see him, right now," said Tollet, eyes squinting. "Had his hair oiled back and parted down the middle. Had a hair lip and some teeth out." He turned, and pulled his lip up to show the dogtooth and the two beside it. He dropped his hands. "Made his face sink on one side."

Cox rolled his eyes. "That's a man on TV. That's the man on the magazine cover."

Tollet turned around to the stove again and quietly lifted some pancakes onto a plate. Cox gave a triumphant laugh and rammed his hand back into the box.

He had caught Tollet singing the sacred harp when he'd come into the kitchen. But instead of walking out, he had decided to take up the old fight again. He was fierce whenever he dug at the old man's lie, giving him nowhere to hide, like a dog digging for a rabbit.

"Can't call his name, can you?" badgered Cox, leaning back in his chair.

Tollet dropped a spoonful of batter onto the skillet, making it hiss and spit.

"Can't drive me up to his house, can you?"

With his back still turned, Tollet began to hum. Then the hums rose, became notes, a gentle chant. No words, just music, each note making a step in the air, falling and rising in scale, giving birth to the note that followed.

"Sol—Sol—Sol—La, Sol—Sol—Sol—Fa. . . ."

Cox leaned forward. His mouth eased open, as though he would join him.

Alas and did my Savior Bleed—Cox thought to himself, before he could speak.

No. It was *Jesus, Lover of my soul.*

". . . la—la-la—la, mi—mi."

"Stop it," he said. "Stop."

Tollet took a long drag on his cigarette and blew the smoke against the windowpane. It curled back at him and lay smog along the counter. When he spoke, he spoke to the glass panes.

"There's folks around back in there that'd tell you the same thing as me."

"Bullshit," Cox said. The speed of his words trampled all over Tollet's. "There's nothing back there."

"*Now*, maybe" said Tollet, allowing the point. He turned and brought the pancakes to the table, setting them next to the plastic syrup bottle. "But didn't used to be. Used to be real people back in there. Ones that sung sacred harp." He bowed his head a bit, looking from beneath his brow as though he knew he'd regret what he was going to say.

"You went oncet. You and your Mama went to hear it, right 'fore they stopped havin' church back there. You used to talk—"

"Hush," Cox said. His face was stormy with red and white patches. "You make me so goddamn mad sometimes I don't know what I'm gonna do."

Tollet moved to look out the window at the sink. His cigarette smoldered in the spoon rest.

"I know what I'm gonna do," he said, his voice testy. "I'm going down to Felix's. I might talk bid'ness with him."

Cox narrowed his eyes. He started to speak, but stopped himself when Henry came in the door. The boy crossed to the table, very slowly, and took his chair. He had a spooked look to him, drained, edgy. Cox pulled the prize out of the cereal box—a sticker of a souped-up race car with an American flag on top—and handed it to Henry. The boy had been moping around for days, staring into corners.

"What's the matter with you?" he asked. "You look sick."

Henry shrugged, his gaze on the plate rim. He lowered his chin further.

Cox tightened his mouth.

"Make us some more pancakes, Daddy," he said. He glanced at Tollet, who was staring towards the road, and added "please."

Tollet waited a moment, then dumped a load of mix into a bowl sticky with wet batter.

The phone rang just as Cox was about to take a bite. He looked to see if Tollet was going to answer, but the old man stayed put, stirring the batter, making lush, hollow noises. Cox sighed, got up, took the receiver and walked back to the table.

"Who's that? Cox?"

Cox's face dropped loose again. His voice softened. He blushed at himself, the way he acted such a fool for his boss.

"Yes, sir," said Cox. He plucked at the phone cord. "Mr. Porter."

"Mornin'. Mornin'. How'z your girls doin'?"

"They're fine. Just fine. I took 'em to piano the other day."

"Good. Good. How'z your boy doin'?"

He shook his head and glanced at Henry, who was picking ashes out of his pancakes.

"He's fine. Just fine."

The man finally got around to what he wanted. His car wouldn't start. He needed a ride.

"Pick you up in about ten minutes," said Cox. He shook his head, insistent. "No, sir. It's no trouble. Cars break down. Glad to help."

After a few more smiles and nods, Cox said goodbye. As he sat the receiver back in its cradle, the phone rang again, beneath his hand. He cursed, then jerked it up. His eyes narrowed at the sound of Martha's voice.

"Have you been running your truck up behind Barnes's car and blowing your horn? All the way to my house?"

Cox smiled. Yes he had. He had been doing exactly that whenever he saw that pig around town. He had made a point to find out what car he drove. Of course, it was a ten-year-old Bonneville.

"Maybe I have, and maybe I haven't." It was the kind of answer she hated. "I wasn't anywhere near your house yesterday," his eyes darted about. "Except—maybe—once. If I honked, I mighta been scaring squirrels outa the road."

"*You're ridiculous,*" said Martha. Her voice quivered, about to lose control. "*I've never seen anything like you—*"

"Listen. I gotta go. Besides, I don't like you leaving Henry with a perfect stranger. You don't see me leaving Betsy and Lucy with—" he stopped short. "I don't do that to the girls, so—"

"*Don't you dare tell me,*" sputtered Martha. "*How dare you tell me what to do with my son. I'll do what I want, when I want.*"

Cox glanced at Tollet and back again. The old man was pretending not to listen, but he stirred the batter slowly and kept his head cocked at an interested angle. Cox spat the words.

"Go ahead, then. Do it and see. Just leave him there one more time and see."

He slammed the receiver into the cradle then lifted it off and slammed it again, cracking the plastic down the side. Henry clutched the table's edge as Cox leaned towards him, palms down on the table. His weight made the wood pop.

"You tell me if she leaves you at that drugstore again. Hear? Tell me the very next time. I'm gonna check for myself anyway, but I want *you* to tell me."

Henry wouldn't look him in the eye, but he answered sooner than Cox expected.

"I will," he rushed to say. He reached for his ice water. "I'll tell you everything."

Chapter 7

Walking to the bus, Henry felt the sun work its way underneath his bandages. He was already hot by the time he crossed the woods. The trees were flocked with new leaves now—a fragile, yellow-green, not yet so full that the black and gray trunks were hidden. Over the last few weeks, while he was living in his head with Lois, he hadn't paid them any attention. The days spent beneath them—the boy and the beatings—seemed years ago. The thought of last night lay over him like a wool blanket. A sob caught in his throat.

He would have been glad to see the boy last week, glad to have been beaten senseless by him—anything that would have changed the course he had been on. He stopped and blew his nose on his sleeve, then wiped the mucous on his pants leg.

It had all been a mistake. He could see it clearly, now that he was dying. The boy had left him alone because he had gotten tired of the game—or because he thought Henry was crazy—the way he had offered to be hit that day. That was why the beatings had ended. He had been a fool to think that he was the cause.

Downcast, he pushed on to the bus stop, where the rest of the children waited. They were passing time by throwing rocks at a skinny gray mutt in the road. Despite the rain of pellets all around, the dog would not quit its task, pulling at the furry, mashed remains of some animal plastered to the pavement. Henry turned away, looked up the road as the bus rumbled towards him.

The worst trick of all—the worst lie—was the clean, hollow peace he had felt when the boy had left him, after he had tried to save Cox. Now, that was just something he had made up. Maybe he hadn't saved Cox at all. Everything was the same, or worse.

He climbed the creaking bus steps carefully, afraid he might rupture inside again at any moment. He didn't want to die on the bus.

The rest of the day was misery after misery. With his head clear of Lois, he could listen to his teachers and even hear what they said. When people talked to him, he could answer. He could taste his lunch now. But braided through all was the sting of regret, since his life would be over soon. It was only a matter of time until whatever organ had burst would bend him in half with pain. True, it hadn't hurt yet—had never really hurt—which confused him. But it would. And because no one knew but him, he was all the more miserable.

Eventually, he stopped hiding his face. He grew too tired to care. As the day wore on, a strange, cried-out resignation replaced his despair. He had a peculiar calmness about him by the time Martha took him home.

"You seem worn out," she said. "Last week you were cross, and now you're exhausted."

Henry sat on a kitchen stool, watching her cook. Barnes was coming for supper, and she made everything from scratch for him.

He gave her a wizened smile and shrugged. He didn't have the heart to answer. Without protest, he had allowed the girls to show him their new turtle aquarium. He had even helped them pick out some rocks to paint on later. He went about with a detached benevolence—a dying man's grace—as if, at long last, he had learned the slight significance of minor things.

During supper, he moved his noodles around on his plate as Martha rambled on about a science fair she was planning. Mostly, she addressed Barnes, who did little more than smile and nod at her. He acted the same way—smile and nod, smile and nod—whenever Martha asked him to rub her feet, or put flea powder on the cat.

"Barnes," said Martha, pointing to an empty plate, "go out to the kitchen and get us some more egg rolls." Barnes, still chewing, lifted the plate off the table and excused himself.

Henry scowled. It was the kind of thing he had seen at home with Cox and Tollet—one making a fool, the other playing the fool. He glanced at Barnes through the kitchen door.

He might act like he didn't mind, but Henry knew better. Like Tollet, Barnes had to care. He was just afraid to say so. It would show in his face somewhere, if not now, later: a tight jaw, down-turned eyes, sulky answers. It would creep out some way. It had to.

When Barnes came back to the table, Martha looked him in the eye, smiled and thanked him. The man blushed a ripe, reddish-pink. Then she slipped her hand over to pat his.

Like a dog, Henry thought.

He dragged his gaze to her face, to confirm that was the way she had meant it. But when he found her eyes, he saw a slight shadow lingering behind the glass, a warmth that made it seem as though, right then, she wanted to say something nice. Barnes, blushing still further, made a pleased sound, then stuffed a whole egg roll into his mouth.

Henry sat back. He checked their faces again, which held expressions just below smiles. He glanced at the girls, to see if they had seen it too, but they were talking about where they could find more ants. He picked up his fork and reshaped his pile of noodles.

He hadn't suspected this. It wasn't at all what he'd had with Lois. It certainly wasn't whatever Cox had with Lois. It couldn't be what Cox had with Martha. But there it was.

As the night wore on, Martha was as bossy as ever. She sent Henry onto the porch, to paint the rocks they'd collected; made him eat Jello; and forced him to listen to a record of *Peter and the Wolf*. But he didn't mind as much as usual, since he was dying. He listened with a renewed interest, and from time to time stole glances inside at Martha and Barnes.

They sat in the living room, reading and talking quietly. It was the calmest he had ever seen Martha be—like a calm she had worked over the past few months, and finally decided to show. And instead of the whipped dog he had thought Barnes was, the man not only did whatever Martha asked, but also offered to do more. He was anxious all right, but anxious to please her.

The next morning, again surprised not to have died in his sleep, he set out with the others on a trip to the lake. Instead of fishing, which was the only thing Henry had ever done there, Martha led them on a nature walk. Bored with the talk, Henry decided to hang back with Barnes, who was struggling under the weight of a loaded tackle box. It was full of the weeds and sticks that the girls ran back to drop inside from time to time. The load had gotten heavy ever since they had come upon some stones with shell fossils. Barnes strained along, one arm cantilevered out for balance. His face had turned a sweaty red since he had given Lucy his hat. His breathing was loud, like a croupy horse.

"You want me to carry that thing?" asked Henry, squinting into Barnes' face. It seemed right to at least offer.

Barnes looked at him, a ball of sweat dangling from the tip of his nose. Water glistened on his eyelashes. All at once, he stopped, nodding at Henry as he passed him the load. The boy, surprised, took it. Then he set off up the path, the box bouncing against his leg. He was glad it was heavy.

"I'll spell you after a while," wheezed Barnes. "After I get my wind back."

"All right," answered Henry. "We'll take shifts."

The sticky smell of pine gum set the day's heat close to his skin. The brown water lapped against the shore, just above the sound of their shoes scuffing on the gravel path. For a time, Henry walked alongside Barnes at a slow, halting pace. He searched for Martha and the girls, and found them well ahead, far out of earshot. Before he had the sense to stop himself, he asked a question.

"How long—do folks that get that VD stuff—how long do they live?"

Barnes, lagging along the path, looked sideways at him. He shrugged and sighed. "It won't kill you. I heard tell of a boy that went blind once, though. What you wanta know for?"

"I saw it on TV," Henry said. It was true, in a way. He had seen a commercial once on the subject. It was the only problem he knew of that had something to do with your pecker.

"Just wondered." A blush of sweat glazed his ribs. "I might do a report on it at school."

Barnes turned his head and looked him up and down as he walked. "They have ways of helping people out nowadays though. There's drugs that clean it up."

Henry swung his head around so fast he nearly threw himself off balance.

"Do you have 'em? Those drugs, I mean?"

Barnes shook his head, lifting his arm to wipe his brow against his upper sleeve. "Yeah. Penicillin, at least. You can find out about all that. Look it up."

"Under what?" asked Henry.

Barnes shook his head. "Under 'Venereal Disease,' I guess. Or—" he stopped and lowered his voice, "—or 'Sex,' maybe." He bit his bottom lip. "I'm surprised they'd be having you write a report on that. Even at Martha's school."

Henry paled and shook his head. "They don't know I'm gonna do it. It's for extra credit."

Again Barnes looked askance at him, nodding. He stopped at a level place in the path and wiped his hands on his pants. "All right, let me spell you for a while." He held his hand out for the box and Henry passed it back.

The next morning, he excused himself from the breakfast table under the pretense of having to go to the bathroom. Then he went to the bookcase full of *World Books*. Pulling the *U–V* volume from the set, he scanned the article on "Venereal Disease," where he found out you mostly got it from having sex with somebody who already had it, or by getting bit by a monkey. He hadn't done either thing, as far as he knew. Then again, he wasn't sure he knew all the ways you could do things. He slipped the *U–V* volume back into the set and pulled the *S* out.

Thumbing through the volume to find the place, he didn't know why he hadn't thought to look the word up before. But then, it was only last fall that he had learned it meant more than whether you were a boy or a girl. After his promotion to junior high, he had shamed himself during lunch one day. Two boys were telling jokes about sticking "Dick" into "Jane." When he had asked how you could stick Dick into Jane, they had laughed their heads off. That was when he'd checked out the old health book and learned that it had to do with how a baby came into the world. But he supposed the health book was too old to tell the whole truth. It didn't have to do with *just* that—at least the boys at lunch weren't talking about it that way. It had something to do with Cox's movies, and probably was the reason he had killed himself over Lois. But what he didn't know, and had to find out, was why it had caused an organ to burst. He also wanted to know exactly which organ it was that oozed clear blood. He couldn't get fixed if he didn't know what was broken.

"Come back, Henry," called Martha, "I need to ask you something."

Her voice was loud enough to call through a closed bathroom door, so she must have thought he was still in there. He closed the volume and stuffed it into his satchel. After a few composing breaths, he went back to the kitchen. Hope shimmered in his chest.

"I talked to Barnes this morning," said Martha, handing him a plate of sliced cantaloupe. She had pulled her hair into a ponytail, and she didn't have her glasses on. Her eyes were narrow and set.

"I've got some errands to run, so I'm going to drop you off at the drugstore—with him."

The bite of fruit in his mouth nearly slid down his windpipe. He coughed it into his hand and placed it on the side of his plate. Martha frowned.

"I'll go with you," Henry said, strangling on his spit. "I don't mind."

Her eyes narrowed further. "Why? You *like* to go to the drugstore. Barnes lets you have those old comic books. He'll be disappointed."

"No. I don't want to. I wanta go with you today. Daddy'll—" He checked himself, but saw it was too late. Martha's smile grew rigid, then fell. "I oughta be with you," he finished.

She edged the tip of her tongue into the corner of her mouth and drew it back inside. "Well, you can't," she said. "You're my son, too, and when you're with me, you'll go where I say. Besides, I have a meeting this morning."

"Then I'll just stay with Lucy and Betsy."

"No," she answered, shooting her gaze at the girls. "The meeting's with—their tap dance teacher. They're trying out for a role in the recital."

The girls stared at her like a set of owls. Martha glowered back, sealing their mouths once and for all. Her face brightened as she glanced at Henry. "Of course, if you really want to come, you could try out for a role yourself. But you can't come unless you do."

"I don't know how to dance," said Henry, offended.

"Oh, I'm sure we could sign you up for lessons if you're interested. She's always looking for boys to play the—"

Henry could only hope Cox wouldn't come by the drugstore to check. Besides, the most important thing right then was what the S had to say. If he couldn't find anything out, he would be dead soon, so one more lie to Cox wouldn't matter.

As they stood before the pharmacy counter, Martha told Barnes she'd be home by two o'clock. Henry could hear the man's voice catch as he agreed. He looked worried, like he had just been told the roof might fall in at any given time.

"Why don't you come back over here and read," he offered, pulling up the countertop gate. "Get you some candy and a Co-Cola. There's some old *Supermans* in the back room, too. In that big cardboard box."

Henry passed through and nodded his thanks. "Maybe later. I got some work to do."

Barnes's Adam's apple bobbed up and down as he swallowed. "Well, I'll just get on about my business then. Holler if you want something."

Henry settled into the plastic bucket chair against the wall. It was just after dinnertime, so no customers were in the store yet. All he heard was Barnes—knocking glass bottles together, pouring and swiping pills. The bank of fluorescent lights buzzing overhead, and the odor of cherry cough syrup, helped him settle down. Opening the S, he set the book on his knees, leaned over, and read.

"*Sex* is what makes males and females different from each other." He stopped and skipped down the page. He needed to know how you could kill yourself with it, and what to do if you had.

". . . Because sex usually involves much deeper personal feelings and desires than other areas of life, it is not discussed so openly as are other areas. As a result, many people are confused and bothered by their sexual feelings. Some view sex as something to laugh or joke about. But throughout history. . . ."

He backed away from the book, groaning. This sounded like something they taught at school. He wanted to know what to do! A hot, flushing anger spread to the tips of his ears. But as he was about to slam the book shut, he saw the word "puberty," which he'd seen before, in an article on "Adolescence." He skipped down to read about a girl's maturity—"her breasts become larger and round out, her hips become wider. . . ."

Lois must've been in puberty—in his dreams—since her breasts were huge. The thought of her made his stomach flutter. He tensed his muscles, his eyes shifting back and forth. He felt the stir in his groin again.

He had thought she was gone for good, but she was still lingering about. He shook her out of his head, afraid he would rupture again.

"The widened hips make it possible for her to give birth. The enlarged breasts will allow her to feed her babies milk from her own body."

He gritted his teeth. That was the reason. It was as though he were being reminded of what he had known, but lost sight of. Her breasts and hips weren't just to make his pecker swell. They could do that, too, but they had another purpose. It wasn't just to make him bust an organ and bleed.

". . . feed her babies milk . . ."—he thought of Curtis and Mona Lisa, Lois' children. Martha must've fed him milk too, though he couldn't imagine it. She had probably given him a bottle. He read on.

"Menstruation, a monthly discharge of blood and tissue from the vagina, is a normal part of a woman's life."

The words stopped him cold. A freezing fear raked his skin and nearly forced him to cry out. He had bled *himself*—after a fashion— just the other night. He read it again—"a monthly discharge of blood and tissue from the vagina."

His hands shook. But that was what a *woman* did. It was normal for a *woman*—not a man. His gaze jittered about the page, trying to find his place. He read the sentence again, to see if it really said that. He was confirmed.

"Most girls start to menstruate when they are about twelve years old. . . ."

I'm twelve! he almost screamed. A blanching horror drained all the blood from his head. He leaned back against the wall to gain his breath. The book slid down his knees.

They'd stick him in the circus, at the fair. He had heard about half men–half women in sideshows. This is what he was meant for? He lay against the wall, as miserable in his agony as a lame, beaten dog. Driven, he read on.

"As a boy goes through puberty, he becomes taller and heavier. His shoulders broaden, he gets stronger, and his voice becomes deeper. Hair grows on his face, under his arms, around his genitals, and on other parts of his body. Most boys consider the appearance of hair on the face one of the most important steps to manhood."

Worse and worse and worse. He didn't have hair in any of those places—he was the littlest one in his class; even with a father the size of Cox, he was still the littlest. And his voice was high as a kite. What would be next? Something like ". . . if by the age of thirteen a boy hasn't shown some of these changes, something is seriously wrong and he should see a doctor as fast as all get out."

For an instant, he thought of leaving, not saying a word to Barnes. He would just keep walking until he was in the woods, where nobody would ever see him again. But he decided to read the rest, just in case there was something else he didn't know. He was sick with surprises.

"When a boy nears sexual maturity, his sex organs become larger, and he may experience nocturnal emissions, also called "wet dreams."

He flushed; his eyes teared.

"Nocturnal emissions occur when a whitish fluid called semen is released through the penis while a boy or a man is sleeping. They are a natural way of releasing semen."

The trembling started in his elbows, then worked down to his hands and up to his shoulders. A matched feeling radiated from his knees to his hips and feet. He swallowed and read it again.

". . . a natural way of releasing semen."

The waves of blood met in a vast, illuminating joy, spreading throughout his chest. Breaths shuddered from his lungs, again and again, like the last throes of a long fever. He had to re-read it.

"a natural way"—

"natural"—

"natural."

He hadn't been bleeding from a vagina! He didn't have VD and it wasn't a busted organ! It wasn't blood he'd had on him! It was natural—expected. He wasn't going to die! His mouth spread open and he closed his eyes.

In fact, he was becoming a man. He was even going to grow. It said so, right there! In the *World Book!* And get hair where he was supposed to, even on his face. Everything was all right! Everything was all right!

He was excited enough to call out to Barnes, but stopped himself, since he didn't want anybody to know how crazy he had been.

Ignorant. He was ignorant. That was why he had been so scared. Damn Cox. Why hadn't he told him? Why hadn't he?

But though he was annoyed, his relief overwhelmed his annoyance. He began to laugh quietly, and clutched the book against his chest. He should have known the S wouldn't let him down. He set it on his knees again to read on, ravenous for news.

". . . sexual tensions," it went on to say, "are relieved by masturbating (rubbing or handling the genitals). In the past, many people believed that masturbation caused various mental and physical problems, including insanity and pimples." Henry's breath caught. *That's* what he'd been doing with Lois—and it *did* cause him to go crazy—those people were *right*. He swept his hand over his face to see if he had acne.

"These ideas have been proven false. But many people believe that masturbation can be morally wrong because it is a misuse of sexual powers. Masturbation can become an emotional problem if it causes people to feel anxious, guilty, or ashamed."

He gave the sentence a sharp nod. He had felt all that. It was true. But even *that* was better than being dead. He could fix feeling "anxious, guilty, or ashamed."

A shudder of joy passed through him, and he stretched his legs and arms. He smiled at the fluorescent lights. In time, he grew aware of an odd, luxurious peace sitting inside him somewhere, resting in a place he couldn't identify. It was the peace and pleasure he'd seen the cat feel when it woke from a long nap in the sun, stretching and arching its back and limbs, like it was giving thanks. It came from the same place, was in the same place, he had felt when the boy left him—the shadowed hollow. It made him feel— he grappled for the word:

Thankful. Whispering, he said it aloud, from the scoured-out place in his chest and throat; so it was there after all. He closed his eyes, breathed into the hole, and let it come again.

"Gimme some Rolaids," came Cox's voice.

Henry's eyes shot open so fast a firecracker might have gone off beside his head. He looked, and found Cox's gaze burrowing into Barnes, who had come out from behind the shelves. He was as white as his coat.

"I said I need Rolaids," repeated Cox. His voice was too loud for the place, bouncing off the walls. "And some Q-Tips, and some Alka-Seltzer, and some more tape and gauze for *his* head."

He flicked a hand at Henry, "aaaand two bags of Red Hots. And a bag of peanut M&M's."

Barnes tried to smile, but the gesture slid off his face as his color rose.

"Ubb—well—we've got all those things, Mr. Tollet. But I've got some prescriptions to fill. You're welcome to help—"

"What kinda place is this?" boomed Cox, his jaw falling slack. Henry closed his eyes.

"I thought the customer was 'number 1?' So that's justa load of bullshit, huh?"

Barnes stepped to the counter and leaned towards Cox. His eyes bolted about as he checked the other people in the store—a woman with a baby, and an old lady with a walker.

"Mr. Tollet, please don't yell. If you'll just wait a second, I'll help—"

"Wait? I hadn't got time to wait! I'm a busy man. I sell tractors, not face powder." He crossed his arms on his chest, grabbing his elbows. Henry saw a gleam in his eye that matched any small sliver of pleasure he had ever seen Cox show.

"Now, I'll tell you what. I'm gonna stand here for five minutes— give you a chance to help me," he stopped to lower his voice, "—then, if you don't, there's gonna be some excitement in here."

Barnes shook his head and backed up, his face frozen into a stiff grimace. At length he moved, his steps cautious, as though his momentum might fail. He lifted the hinged counter and came out into the store. Henry grabbed his books and followed.

Stop, Barnes—thought Henry. Don't do it. Let him kill you first.

Watching him move among the aisles, Henry was amazed to find that he wasn't red with shame, that he walked at a smooth gait. Barnes's face was firm, like he was trying to die quietly, without bothering anybody. Item by item, he collected the things into the crook of his arm.

Henry silently moved from Cox's side, aiming for the candy row and a bag of peanut M&M's. But before he could get away, Cox's arm slid out in front of him, the fingers spread stiff as sticks.

"Don't you even think about it," said Cox. Henry's foot dangled in the air, then set down again. He stepped back.

"That comes to $8.14," said Barnes, a touch of salesman's cheer still in his voice. He rang up the items, then shook out a plastic bag and stuck everything inside. Cox, who had been fumbling in his bill-fold, took the bag and handed him even money.

"Here's five dollars. That's all I got on me." He rolled his shoulders. "Things are too damn high in here anyway."

Henry lowered his gaze to his belt. He moved further from Cox, then turned to face the door. Barnes would have to say something now, he was sure. But it never came, not even when Cox started away.

"Come on," said Cox, throwing the words over his shoulder. "I'm taking you with me."

He followed as fast he could, anxious to get out before Barnes went and did something, like tell him "Goodbye." He would yell out, right there, if Barnes went and told him "goodbye."

"I'll be by to get his suitcase this afternoon," called Cox, turning to walk backwards. "Tell her. I'll be there after a while."

When they were outside, Cox all but skipped to the truck. He flooded the engine, backed the truck around with a screech, then stamped the accelerator to the floor. He forced the clutch and gears so hard that Henry nearly hit the dash with each shift. He sent an arm out to guard himself.

"I guess you were gonna tell me about that?" Cox asked, his head cocked so that he led with his chin. "Her leaving you there—after I told her not to."

Henry nodded. "I was."

Cox let out a bitter laugh, his fingers drumming the steering wheel. He sped them on through town, towards Wolfy, but at the last turn whipped the truck into a parking lot and turned around. Henry's stomach leapt as the truck roared on. From the starved look on Cox's face, he knew they were going to the gas station. They were going to her.

Even though he had been wrong—even though she hadn't killed him—he was afraid of Lois. The thing that she caused had a hold of him, just like it had a hold of Cox. It was the same thing the girls on the beach caused, the girls in Cox's movies. And with a sharp, unpleasant jolt, he understood that, for Cox, Martha caused it most of all, and she didn't even want him. Cox was crazy, and he was headed that way himself.

The sickness splashed about as though a stone had been dropped into the well of his belly. The truck sawed into the gas station and braked to a jarring stop, throwing him against the seat.

"I got some more business in here," said Cox, already out of the car. "I won't be long." He fished around in his jeans pocket, then pulled out some money and handed it to Henry.

"Here. Go inside and get you something to eat. Get you another funny book."

Henry took the bills. They were wilted and damp, moist with sweat from Cox's thigh. The man snatched his checkbook off the dash and went up to the house. He entered without knocking and slammed the door shut.

It was still and clammy inside the truck. The truck oil ticked and clocked underneath the hood. The view outside—store and house and road—was frozen, no cars or people to make it real.

Henry rolled his gaze about. He had been left with a lion outside the door. He looked down at the bills in his hand, pulled out his wallet, and lay them next to the two bills with Cox's signature.

Cox is in there, he thought. Then, though he hadn't intended it, his thoughts went on.

With her. In there with her.

Before he could raise his hip off the seat and replace the wallet, she came into his head, exploding onto the landscape of his brain, full-formed, like thick paint dashed onto course canvas. Thighs, breasts, arms—everything about her rushed at him—busting seals, busting strings. She was big and hot, rocking against his bedroom door with a raving power.

He swallowed as she came towards him, mortified. He hadn't started it, but it was here now, again. The crown of his head fell back against the rear window. His hips eased forward as his eyes shut tight. His neck tilted to the side, as if lifting towards a knife blade.

The nauseous wash in his stomach was rising steadily, on a track of acid. He felt it climb towards the middle of his chest. But it was as though it were all happening beneath a screen, kept from his sight. Lois was in his sight, above the screen, and while he pushed himself towards her, the misery crept on, up, to where the hole lay exposed and waiting. For one clear instant he knew that it was as real as when he had first known it—while standing beneath the shadow of the boy's arm. As real as when he had just felt it—with the news of nature, and what it was doing to him. And for an instant more, like the faintest smell of the oldest scent, he remembered peace, and thanks, and what it was like to be free.

He gripped the seat, pressing his legs into the floorboard, lifting from the cushion as though he'd found himself in rising water, a flood lapping at his chest. Lois danced in his head, over him, astraddle and ready to sit.

And this time she *would* sit, and the sap in him would spill like a vein ripped jagged. It would never stop coming and, like Cox, he would never stop giving himself to it. Crazy like him; eaten alive— every day, eaten alive. He shuddered to stop it, but it kept rising, matched by the acid that traveled towards the hole.

The stick flashed through his mind, the promise of its pain, the roll of its wind on his cheek. The clarity it brought. Come down, he whispered. Come down.

He shifted in his seat—strengthened, vested, and lifted his arm, so that it was square with the bandages. With a blunt, mean thrust that took his wind, he drove the heel of his hand against his brow. He gasped, his breath thinned to shrieks, and did it over and over, until he felt the wounds pound back, like another hand inside his skull, meeting his own. He smeared the bandages, with a brutal back and forth, dug his nails underneath the edge, and ripped the gauze away.

"*I'll tell you!*" he said, a scream without voice. "*You don't tell me when! I'll tell you!*"

The pain made bruises in front of his eyes, blue and orange spots— suns, shattering and reforming. His blood welled, then spilled from his head, like milk brimming over a glass. It fell along his temple, into the bristles of his eyebrow. His heart beat in a savage hammer, but the sharp dance of pain was stronger still. A globe of blood sagged from the ledge of his brow. He shut his eyes, and felt it ooze down the closed lid.

Lying back against the seat, he broke the jars of stale air in his lungs, let the volume pour from his mouth in rows and flutters. Nothing was left. His stomach was cool and calm. Not even the scream remained, the one he had heard. It might have been his own scream, but he could not tell. All he knew was the pain, and the clean, sweet peace that waxed and waned with each pull of breath. The hole had grown over him, melted through him, spread so that layer on layer, gristle and cord and pulp, was all one thing, all one space. His head rocked to the side. He fell into a deep, wrapped sleep.

Cox stood beside the bed, hitching his pants up around his hips. The breeze from the air conditioner blew against his bare back, cooling the sweat. He had managed to pull his shirt over his head before he fell on top of her, but he hadn't been able to unlace his boots and take his trousers completely off. It had taken an embarrassingly short time—not more than five minutes—and he wasn't sure that Lois had ever stopped watching the TV over his shoulder. She was crazy for Bugs Bunny cartoons, and every once in a while, between his thrusts, he thought he heard her giggle.

That was where she was now, brushing her hair out to the ends as she sat cross-legged on the mattress' edge. Within a minute after Cox had rolled off, she had pulled on a red terry-cloth robe, fixed her face, and sat herself in front of the TV again, in the same spot where she had been when he stormed in. It frustrated him how quickly she could get herself back on track, as undisturbed as if she had only just taken a shot, or swallowed her daily medicine. She didn't ever tell him to get up and go, but it was hard to lie there when she was up and going.

Cox wiped himself with some Kleenex and zipped his pants. He saw in the dresser mirror that pink blanket fuzz was matted into his whiskers. He drew close, inspected his cheek and jaw, then scrubbed them off. Staring at her reflection, he watched Lois rock forward, silently laughing at the screen. A tree had smashed a dog's head, so that he walked away playing accordion music. Cox pulled his gaze from it. He was all at once cold and reached for his shirt.

She wasn't like Martha. Oh, she was in a *way*; she liked sex. But she didn't hold you like Martha did. Martha held you even after it was done. In fact, that was what Cox remembered most, the way she would run her hands up and down his back—just the very tips of her fingers—always cool, like she was swabbing him with alcohol. And she would lie there, still as night, holding him as though she were trying to keep him just that way, as though in that way he pleased her. It made him afraid to move because he did not know what it was about him right then that she should want to keep.

a house all stilled

There was one such time, right after Henry was born, and her stomach flesh was still loose, when Cox came close to saying something beyond anything he had ever spoken. It came on him with a rush, a swell, right when her cool fingers found the cross of his shoulders. It was a power forceful enough to scare him, make him start. He had pulled himself back and fought to force it down, so that when he did speak, he said something else entirely, something that surprised neither of them, and made them both cringe: "Not bad."

He blinked at the memory, and reached for his cap.

A sharp, barking laugh came from Lois. "Where do they get all that dynamite?" she asked, and Cox could tell by her voice that she truly wondered where.

"I wish I could get me some dynamite," she added, wistfully. "That'd sell, sure enough."

He reached for his checkbook and began to write in her usual fee. But this time he wrote slowly, each number and letter, a chore. He lost his place once, and became tired enough to sit down when he came to the signature line.

Now what? he asked himself. It was what he always asked when it was over. An overwhelming, despairing sense of boredom set in, as though he were frozen, as though he had stuffed and filled and stroked everything until his nerves were numb.

Was it better to be hungry all the time? No. That was painful. He had to let it out, had to have somewhere to put it. Otherwise it would strangle him. But then, whenever he was fed, glutted, he was as depressed as a dying man staring at a cemetery plot. Only the in-between would do—the brief time lost in the climax, where he could forget himself, where he could lose his body and his sight and become one single, solitary thing—the forward push and drift, push and drift. But that didn't last. He couldn't make it last. And whenever it left, he felt abandoned altogether, mean and hopeless and at a point which always seemed lower than the time before, at some place further down a slope filled with sand.

"Ohhh, you better watch out," Lois warned the coyote, who was sticking his head into a canon.

Why wouldn't it go off when the bird ran by? Why did it go off at the wrong time, never the right? Cox stood to watch the coyote's head get blown back into his shoulders, then pop out again—his head sooty, black, bewildered.

He handed the check to Lois, who stuck it under her thigh without shifting her gaze, then turned to leave.

The outside air made him notice that his chest was wet. When he looked down, he saw that he had snapped his cowboy shirt up wrong. He pulled it open again, then stutter-stepped his way to the truck as he refastened the snaps.

He finished the last one as he got to the truck door. When he saw Henry, an odd, strangled cry tore from his throat.

The boy sat slumped in the seat, his head resting against the rear glass. Courses of cherry-red blood had run down his brow, across his eye and cheek, into the top of his shirt, painting his face in a crow's foot. Pieces of dry scab hung from his forehead, and the twisted bandage gauze lay in his open hand. Henry's head bobbed up at the sound of door hinges. His gaze found, lost, and found Cox again.

"What happened?" Cox asked, his voice cracking. His head jerked about, looking to see if anyone was there. A hot breeze blew against his left side.

"What happened?" he repeated. The back of his tongue hung to the top of his mouth. "What'd you—what'd you do?"

Henry's head lolled about, as though his mind was too jumbled to make sense of the question. He stirred himself up hazily and shook his head.

"I got—" he said. He was strangled sounding. "I don't—"

Cox looked about again. No one was there. No one could've been there.

"Did you—did you get out and fall down?" he offered. "Did you hit your head?"

The boy stared at him blankly, like he was a stranger. Cox didn't know whether to get in the truck, rush around to the other side, or stay where he was.

"Did you pass out?"

"I don't remember," Henry answered.

Cox thought of his handkerchief. He whipped it out of his pocket and shook it at the boy.

"Here. Here. It looks like it's—it clotted up—but here." His nose crinkled as he stared. "Maybe I better take you to the hospital."

Henry shook his head. "No, I don't want that," he said, stronger voiced. His face seemed to clear as he took a few breaths and coughed.

"I just knocked the scabs off, that's all. I remember. I—tripped and hit on the side of my head. I'm all right now, though. Just dizzy."

Cox wasn't sure. He shifted his weight back and forth. His hands brushed his hips, then fell to his sides.

"I wonder if I better not take—"

Henry shook his head, himself once again. To Cox's surprise, he even sounded agitated.

"I said I didn't *want* that," he snapped, then added, "Did you sign your check?"

Cox shut his mouth. The gravel crunched loudly under his feet as he moved an inch. He climbed in, cranked the ignition, then turned it off again. Shifting sideways, he took the gauze and tape out of the drugstore bag.

"Well, let's at least clean you up some. We can't let anybody see you like this. Come on in here to the bathroom."

For light, Cox left the door open to the station's gritty, closet-sized toilet. As he dabbed his handkerchief underneath the faucet, Henry stared up at the condom machine. Cox daubed the warm, wet rag against his face, the sting driving the boy's eyes shut. Cox sucked in loud breaths, tried to hold the cloth more lightly, tried to graze it over his son's flesh, the way Martha would have. Cox swiped the blood off places he was surprised to find it had drizzled—across the back of the boy's neck, down inside his collar, and across the bone. Finally, he finished, and began to re-bandage Henry's head. The clean, antiseptic smell of glue and cotton overcame the stench of dirty toilet paper floating in the commode.

"All right," said Cox, relieved. "Now people can look at you. Let's go get your suitcase."

"No," said Henry, swagging his head back and forth. "Let's go on home. I'll get her to bring 'em to school tomorrow. She's at the dance teacher's, anyhow."

Cox blinked, cocked his head. "What?"

"She had a meeting at the tap dance teacher's house. That's why she left me with Barnes."

Cox's jaw worked against his teeth. He might have just been slapped himself.

"Well," he said, "I know for a fact the dance teacher's on vacation. She told me so last week." He scrambled his gaze about, as though to find a place for a firm footing.

"You gotta have your toothbrush," he allowed. "So let's go."

The lie stoked him as he drove, feeding his anger, turning it to rage. She had left him with Barnes just because he had said not to. She had done it and laughed all the way. Cox felt his muscles gorge with blood. He had to shift in his seat. She wasn't done with him. She wouldn't play these games if she were.

By the time he got to Martha's street, he was so wild he could hardly see. He honked the horn before they had gotten within four houses, which sent Martha storming out to meet him. Cox ran his tongue over his teeth at the sight.

She stopped at a mid-point in the sidewalk, standing at a slant with all of her weight on her front foot. He jumped out of the truck, his shoulders rising and falling. Henry climbed out too, following in his wake, but Cox didn't have the mind to shout him back.

Martha's face boiled—a mean, fiery sneer. Barnes was at the front door, at the foot of the stairs, with Henry's suitcase beside him. The man's face was Martha's opposite—a sucked-clean white.

"Just what do you think you're doing?" she let out, in a low, hard voice. "Tell me just exactly what you think you're doing?"

Cox sniffed, coughed up a wad of phlegm and spat it onto the sidewalk. She was close enough to grab.

"I told you not to leave him with that guy. I told you—"

"There's something you don't understand," she broke in, raising her voice. Her eyes flashed. "You don't tell *me* a blessed *thing*. Especially not about my own son!"

Cox's voice rumbled from his throat, building into a full-fledged shout with each word.

"He lives with *me!*" He pointed over her shoulder at Barnes. "And I told you not to leave him with *that!*"

Martha shook her head so fast her hair rustled. She balled one hand into a fist and pointed the fingers of the other in Cox's face.

"Listen—I'll say this as slow as I can—I let Henry live with you out of the goodness of my heart, but if you think for one second—one *instant*—you're going tell me what I can and can't do, I'll get full custody so fast the hair on your tongue will stand up!" She stepped forward and screamed louder still. "Understand? You don't treat me like this. Not *me*, or anybody around me!"

Cox took what was left of the concrete, the part that Martha hadn't claimed, and practically touched noses with her. She was nearly breathing into his mouth. He was nearly breathing into hers. As close as they were, standing like that, Cox thought anything could happen. He could almost say something right then; almost. But before it rose to his lips, he looked over her shoulder at Barnes, who had stepped back inside the front hall. His arms dangled uselessly, and his jaw worked his mouth down and up, like it was priming a pump. Cox flushed. He jerked his thumb at Barnes.

"Does he know you like it when I'm dirty?" said Cox, in a whisper. "Hunh? Does he know you like to crawl all over my back when I come in from the field? Does he know you nearly break my ribs?"

Martha blinked, whitened. He thought he heard a cry come from her throat. Then he heard it again, and knew it had come from Barnes instead. The sound brought Martha to her senses. She looked over her shoulder.

"Don't just stand there!" she yelled to Barnes. "Go call the police." She shuddered as though ice had slipped down her back. When she swung around, her eyes blazed at Henry. The expression on her face made Cox lose his words.

"Go back to the truck, Henry!" she yelled. "Go back—No! Go in the house!"

For a moment, Cox noticed something, as if the ground had moved beneath his feet, or a small shadow had passed by the corner of his eye. It was clear enough to startle him, and he wanted to stop. He knew he should stop. But in another moment, his fury returned full force.

"The hell he will!" He rared his head and smiled broad enough to let all his teeth show. He swung on Barnes and stomped his foot at him, like he was spooking a cat. Barnes flinched.

"What about it, Martha?" said Cox, grinning. "You meet him naked at the door, like you used to do me? You claw his clothes off when he comes in from the drugstore? Pull him down on top of you where he stands? What about it? Has he got any steel under that little outfit he wears?"

Martha groaned. She hopped back, as if she'd found herself standing next to a corpse. Her face was patchy with rage.

"Liar! God, kill him!" she yelled, and whipped around. Cox laughed as she marched up the steps, shoving past Barnes. Then she dashed down the hall to the kitchen.

"She's gonna get a knife, Barnes," said Cox in a loud voice that beat the other man lower. "She used to get knives all the time. Likes that. Likes to play like she's gonna kill me, then have me force it out of her hand." He smiled and flashed his eyes. "Wanta watch? Wanta see how I do it?"

"Liar!" screamed Martha, rambling through the kitchen drawers. "God kill him! God kill him, or I will!"

"Ooooh, listen to how smart she sounds *now*! She doesn't like me saying this—she's got too much framed paper on the wall for that to be the truth—she's not supposed to like it hard that way. But you hold on and you'll see. Give her five minutes, and she won't give a shit about that paper anymore."

Barnes turned his head to his shoulder, like a bird hiding under his wing. A drawer slammed shut; then came the sound of the phone being snatched off its hook with a small ring of protest.

"Calling the law on me, now," said Cox. At the sound of his voice, Barnes turned further towards the wall, so that he all but faced it. He looked to have been pinned there.

"Answer!" Martha screamed, her voice shattering. "Pick up the phone!"

"Better go," said Cox, his hand on the doorknob. "You take care of things for me, Barnes. Don't let anything happen. You protect her. Like a big boy."

He traced the broken line of the man's back, the way he slumped heavily into the entry wall. Somebody would have to talk him away, he thought—the way they talk people off ledges. And even if they got him away, he would never come back here. Not with Cox Tollet in the world.

He scuffled up the porch steps and lifted the suitcase off the landing. Back on the sidewalk, he took Henry by the shoulder and turned him in the direction of the truck.

Chapter 8

When Henry went home with Martha the next week, he found that Barnes hadn't been by. If he had, there would have been new notepads littering the girls' room—in the shapes of capsules, feet, and doctor's bags, gifts from drug company salesmen. Lucy and Betsy doodled on them. There would also be out-of-date comic books with the front covers torn off. Barnes brought two or three each visit.

As usual, Martha carried them to the lake again on Saturday. Before they left, she pulled her hair into a tight ponytail, did the same with the girls', then stuck caps on all their heads. And as usual, she read aloud from a dingy pamphlet put out by the park service: "A Nature Guide to Verona Lake," nodding at the brown water as she talked. Henry fanned himself with his cap and rubbed a foot along his shin to shoo flies. But things were different, and for the worse.

"Let's go get us something cold to drink," he said. His head was scabbing over again, and the hot sun was filling his fresh cotton bandages with sweat. They grew heavy, made his head feel plugged. The wounds were angrier than before, itched and burned at a higher pitch. He had kept their freshness from his mother, to keep her from getting ideas again. If she asked, he would tell her what he had told Cox, or say that the scabs had come off with the dressing the last time they were changed.

Martha looked up from her book, her mouth open in surprise.

"I'm not finished yet."

"Well—let's go anyway. I'm not feeling good. I need me something to drink."

She gave him a dense look. She closed the pamphlet, then nodded towards the car.

Henry sat alone in the back, his cheek against the cool glass. Turned sideways, with his gaze at a slant, he watched the others. All three heads were balanced like spelled boulders. It had probably been this way all week.

He had been moving slower lately himself. All the trouble last week, the highs and the lows, had worn him down. He had avoided Cox as best he could, wary of him in a new way after what he had done to Martha and Barnes. The only time he sought him out was when his bandages needed changing. Tollet had been on a week-long drunk, so Cox had taken over all the nursing duties.

"They're gonna heal up soon if you don't go falling down again," Cox had said, cuffing Henry on the shoulder. "They got a good thick layer to 'em. They'll be hard as washed concrete soon."

Henry nodded. The scabs itched more than they had, and they throbbed whenever he got up from tying his tennis shoes. He started away, but Cox caught his sleeve.

"You hadn't seen that pig from the drugstore have you?" Light blazed in his eyes.

"Not since you have."

Cox held him a moment longer, then let loose of his sleeve. He nodded and cuffed him on the shoulder again, two light, playful pats. Henry looked down at his arm.

"Well. I've got an errand to run before work. I'll be there to get you next Sunday." His breath smelled of grape jelly and biscuits. "You tell me if he comes by," he added. "Hear?"

He had left through the back door, shoving a jar of Vaseline in his coverall pockets.

Henry rolled his head off the window and sat up straight. They were only a few blocks from the shopping center. He shuffled to the edge of the seat, so that he was behind Martha's right ear.

"Why don't you turn in up there. We can get a cold drink at the grocery store—then drop in and get us some comic books." He sniffed, adding in an afterthought way—"at the drugstore."

a house all stilled

She stared at him from the rear view mirror, driving well past the shopping center. They turned in at a car dealership and bought drinks from a machine.

The night followed the same routine, but without the usual trouble he was accustomed to from Martha. Instead of making supper herself, she had bought frozen dinners. The food hadn't cooked evenly, and Henry had to leave a couple of ice-laden forkfuls in the tin. Martha didn't eat at all, but sat in one of the sling-chairs, writing. She hunched over her work, straining to concentrate. Henry walked up to the side of her seat. He cocked his head and studied her.

"What're you doing?"

She didn't look up. "Grading papers."

He glanced at the blue pamphlets stacked beside her, then at the adult handwriting on the open one in her lap.

"Whose?"

With a red marker, she wrote—*"illegible"* in the margin of the booklet, next to the words *"doesn't make sense."*

"I decided to help out at the community college, teaching a night class."

Henry stared at the paper, which she'd covered in red circles and lines. She had curled sideways in the chair, feet beneath her. The papers were too close to her face.

"Do you care if we don't listen to records?" he asked, his jaw shifting his bottom teeth below his upper. "I wanta—I wanta watch TV."

The girls' chairs shuffled back. They stared at him, breathless. Martha glanced up for a second, but her gaze failed to catch hold.

"Okay."

Henry sniffed, looked aside. "I wanta watch—cartoons. Stupid ones."

She shuffled about and dipped her head further, blocking him out of her vision. "All right."

Lucy and Betsy raced to the hall closet and began yanking the TV set out from beneath the coats and umbrellas. The two of them hauled it into the kitchen, away from Martha's view.

Without a decent antenna, all the channels were snowy. The sound was filled with static. Eventually, they got an old western to come in fairly well. The girls sat before the shimmering screen, soaking in the blue light like prisoners released into sunshine. They were amazed, but Henry lost interest. He went over to the piano to practice a song Barnes had taught him. It was the first one that had any black keys in it, so he must have been getting better. He was only through the first line when Martha stopped him.

"That's too much noise," she said, holding her pen out like a pointer. "Read or watch TV, one or the other."

He hadn't even gotten to the part with the black keys yet. Scooting the bench back, he hit them anyway—making a sharp, metal-on-metal noise—then went to his room. He returned with his book bag, replaced the S volume into the set, then pulled out his second favorite—the two-volume C. He sat on the floor, his back against the sofa, and began at the front of the first book. Turning the pages one at a time, he scanned the columns.

Ever since he'd read about "puberty" and "sex," he had wanted to know how it was supposed to work. One day last week, when Cox was gone and Tollet was passed out, he had mustered enough courage to go into Cox's room.

The shades were pulled down beyond the sill. He was afraid to turn the lamps on, so he felt about using only the light from the hall. Clothes were piled over the chairs and dresser, and the bed covers were heaped about on the floor. But underneath the bed frame, he spotted the box of movies. He pulled them out, only to find another box with magazines inside.

Thumbing past pictures of naked women riding an escalator, he found pictures of a man and a woman together. The man was shoving his hips inside the woman, his face squirming in pain as she wrapped her legs around the small of his back, in a scissors hold. She was clutching at the bed board.

That was the right way. He couldn't have said it before, but it was exactly what he'd wanted in his dreams: for her to sit down on his hips and press.

Everything fell into place—Tollet and the girl from Maben, the one that had held onto the back porch eaves—the boys on the bus, Dick into Jane. His stomach began to flutter, then he felt himself stir.

His skin tightened, as if he smelled something.

It was all still possible. It would always be possible. Always. He closed the magazine.

Martha let out a heavy sigh, which made him look up. Her face didn't show anything new. He went back to the book, unsure of what he was looking for. His mind wandered as he scanned "California." "Calpurnia."

The people in the magazine were doing it right. If Cox had just told him, then he wouldn't have had to go through all that. From the hungry, anxious feeling came the need to rub and press yourself into a woman, and from doing that came relief from *wanting* to do that— at least for a while. But he remembered, too, what the S had said about babies, and added that to the rest.

From relief came a baby.

He nodded at his conclusion. It seemed right, explained a lot. That was the purpose of wanting the relief then: to get a baby. Babies grew up into people, and people made farms and cities and schools and books and encyclopedias. It all made sense, spreading out in a huge fan that he couldn't see to the end of. That's how it all started, and it came from being hungry in your crotch. Women probably got hungry, too. And what were they hungry for, really? For something to come of it all. He thought for a moment, then felt embarrassed, as if he had been surprised by a compliment. He, and to a lesser extent, Lucy and Betsy, had been hungered for.

But then, he thought on, was that why Cox went to Lois Carberry? The thought of it made him sick. And had he himself wanted a baby with Mrs. Carberry? No, but then he hadn't known yet that that was the reason for it. But Cox had known. And Cox couldn't want that. So Cox must do it for meanness, like everything else. Because something had rubbed him the wrong way.

He glanced up at Martha. She was bearing down on her work, digging pencil into paper with furious scribbling noises. Occasionally, she would make a violent stroke, then circle it, which Henry assumed to be a bad grade. The more time passed, the more violent the strokes. Eventually, she began making disgusted sounds when she marked. It distracted him so much that he couldn't concentrate on

"Caligula," which he had found very interesting. He gave up when she began calling the papers names—"idiots" and "fools."

He expected her to throw the papers onto the floor and get up for some coffee. He had seen her do that plenty of times. But now she hunkered down over the sheets, coiling over the work. The sight made him take a breath, stretch his legs. When she closed the book-let and picked up yet another, he rose and walked over to her chair.

"Why don't you quit for a minute?" he asked.

"Fool," she said, snatching at the corner of one page. It took a few moments before she surfaced and faced him. "What'd you say?"

He furrowed his eyebrows. "I said 'quit.'"

She blinked back. "I've got at least fifteen more essays to grade. I can't quit."

"Yes, you can," he said. "You're all worn out. You're gonna start messing up."

Except for canned laughter from the TV, the house was quiet. Her gaze dropped an inch, lingering around his mouth, then his chin. A strand of hair came loose from behind her ear and fell into her face. She looked younger than he ever remembered, and more lonely.

"There's no reason to," she said.

Henry looked at her hands, at her fingertips stained with red ink. Her voice was as soft as her hands, smooth and round and sad.

She had cooled the stripes on his back with her hands. She had hungered to have him.

He nodded, slowly at first, then built it into a gesture.

"Daddy buys Mrs. Carberry, three to four times a week." His voice was sharp, vibrating through his neck.

"What did you say?" Her eyes broadened, caught light.

"At her house. And at the gas station." His buttocks tightened as he watched Martha rise from the back of her chair. She leaned towards him, away from the dim floor lamp over her shoulder.

"What do you mean 'buys' her?"

He thought of the movies and the magazines. "You know. Writes her a check, so—" He blushed, lifting his shoulders. "So he can rub around inside her. Sex."

Martha flinched. "How do you know—"

"I wait in the truck."

She edged further out, the booklets slipping from her lap one at a time, softly rustling against the hardwood floor. Henry backed up a step, swallowed, and shook his head.

"How do you know about all—*that?*" she asked.

"I just do. People at school. And health class."

She flinched again. "That's not how you know. Is it? *Is it?*"

Henry's gaze slid onto the floor. He was messing up. It was going in a way he hadn't meant. He tried to steer it back.

"See? Now you've got as much as he does," he said. "Tell him you know. He'll have to let you alone if you do."

"What?"

He backed his head into his neck, surprised she hadn't put it together. "He'll be scared you'll tell Mr. Porter on him."

She eased back into the chair so gradually he barely noticed it. She sat there, in the seat's swallow. Her face churned with what he'd told her. Henry nodded to put an end to the silence.

"Barnes'll come back, once Daddy lets you alone."

A glimmer lit her cheeks. He was glad for a moment. Things had been taken as he meant. But then her face clouded, and her lips came clear of her teeth. Henry blanched as their eyes met.

"He's taking you to a whore," she said to herself. Then she pulled the hungry expression back beneath the skin of her face. "How many times have you gone?"

Henry shook his head. "Just two or three times. But that's not—"

"Is it *Lois* Carberry? The one that runs the gas station near the river?"

He blinked a yes.

Martha smiled so that all her teeth showed. "Filthiest thing he could find." She sat up. "How much does he pay her? Do you know?"

"No," muttered Henry, scared again. "Leave that part alone. All you have to do is tell him you know about it, so he'll stop bothering you." He nodded. "That's all you want."

Martha rolled her chin from one shoulder, across her breastbone to the other, as though she needed a new place to stare. She breathed sharp, fast breaths.

"I can't believe him," she mumbled.

"What?"

She looked up suddenly, her eyes losing their cast. Henry shifted from foot to foot, watching her think about what to do with what he had told her. Then she placed the back of her fingers against his cheek, brushing it softly. He thought she said "my poor baby" underneath her breath.

"Thank you, Henry."

He smiled a silly smile, in spite of himself.

"I'll take care of it," she said. Her tone was faint and liquid. She scooted closer to him. "Don't you ever, ever go with him again. Not if you can help it. Understand?"

Her fingers ran down to his chin. His smile fell.

"That's all you want, isn't it?" he asked. "Barnes?"

Martha frowned, turning red.

"It's not like that Henry. It doesn't have to be the way—what your father does—it doesn't have to be like that. That's *his* way. But it's not mine, and it won't be yours either. Understand?"

Henry frowned. That's not what he'd meant. He watched her face gain color, like morning sun hitting a white wall. She looked over his head into the kitchen where the girls sat in front of the screen.

"Cut the TV off," she called, full-throated. "That's enough of that."

━━━━━━

Cox signed the box marked "X" and gave the green slip back to the mail carrier. The man winked at him before he left, like he already knew what the letter said.

Cox glanced behind him at the shelves full of tractor parts, then looked out over the counter to scan the display floor. They had just opened up, so no customers were lolling about the new weed eaters and lawn mowers. He figured the two sorry boys that "helped" him were still in the back room, eating doughnut holes and drinking coffee. He decided to let them alone until he had had time to read the certified letter.

He wiped his hands on his coverall pockets a couple of times, eyeing the return address. It was from Martha's brother, the lawyer. Two weeks had passed since the scene at her house. Cox had been wondering why the police had never called, but now. . . . After a shaky breath he ripped the end open.

Under the word "Petition" he found "Mary Martha Macby Tollet—Petitioner."

He scanned down the white space below Martha's name and found his own.

"Henry Cox Tollet, Sr.—Respondent."

He shut his eyes. What now? He was doing everything he was supposed to do. He eased his lids open and scanned for the gist of it— past all the "Whereas" paragraphs that explained things he already knew: that he was a resident of Taxamingo county, that Martha was too, that they were divorced, the names of the children and the custody arrangement. His gaze hung on the allegations.

"And Whereas Petitioner claims that Respondent has, without thought for the welfare or proper guidance in the upbringing and nurturing of the minor child, Henry Cox Tollet, Jr., repeatedly and on dates certain, exposed said minor child to environments unfit for. . . ."

His eyes fluttered. A cold snake crawled up his spine, fanning into his shoulder blades.

". . . namely, conduct involving extramarital sexual relations between the respondent and parties certain, the identity of whom will remain undisclosed until such time as the court. . . ."

He gripped the paper with both hands and pulled it closer.

"Now therefore, Petitioner does hereby petition the court, in the county and state above-mentioned, to terminate, rescind, and otherwise revoke, *in toto*, Respondent's award of partial custody to said minor child, Henry Cox Tollet, Jr., and all rights consisting thereof, and to award full custodial rights to said minor child, Henry Cox Tollet, Jr., to Petitioner, and in addition, to terminate Respondent's rights of visitation to said minor child, Henry Cox Tollet, Jr., and to said minor child, Mary Lucy Tollet, and to said minor child, Elizabeth Macby Tollet, indefinitely. . . ."

Further down he read: "Petitioner also requests that the court, by exercising its jurisdictional authority in domestic matters, place Respondent under a bond of peace, leaving Petitioner's person, household, and place of business in quiet enjoyment, within a distance of one thousand feet of said Petitioner's person, household, and place of business, at the penalty of one thousand dollars ($1,000.00) per violation of said bond of peace."

Cox lay the papers on the counter without finishing. His gaze shot around the store again, worried that by some stroke of bad luck, Mr. Porter might decide to visit. He put the papers inside a notebook that he could easily slam shut. Then he saw a small envelope underneath all the rest. His name was written on the front, in Martha's handwriting. He ripped the letter open so hard he tore the paper in half. Placing the pieces side by side, he leaned over and sped his gaze down the lines, like a dog lapping at water.

"Here are the documents Clark drew up for me. He doesn't know it, but I stole an envelope from him and sent you my copy. He'll file them as soon as I say."

Cox shuddered. The papers weren't signed or stamped yet. He dragged in a few steadying breaths, then read on.

"You can contest this if you want. ('Contest' means disagree. 'Disagree' means you don't think something is true.) But I've got proof. Your whore cashes her checks, so we'll get copies. And no matter what you say, your truck doesn't need, or hold, as much gas as all that. . . ."

She went on to warn him away from her and Barnes, then said that unless he kept Henry from Lois's, and let him go to school in Memphis—without a fight—the petition would be filed. She wouldn't even have to win, she said. Everybody would know, and Mr. Porter would fire Cox before sundown.

Cox clinched his teeth. He tore the paper sideways, in quarters, and eighths before piling the scraps in a glass ashtray and torching them with a solder gun. His chest heaved up and down, so loud he was afraid the boys in the back would hear him wheezing, come out to see what was wrong.

She was lying. Of course she was. *What* proof? The paper shriveled into black crisps.

But how did she know about the checks?

The truth came to him all at once, but he dismissed it as impossible. Henry couldn't have.

A finger of white and black smoke curled towards the rafters. His top lip grew moist. But how else could she know?

He held himself still, his eyes darting about as though something were sneaking up from behind. Stifled laughter came from the back room—the boys winding up their break.

After a few more minutes, Cox was surprised to find he wasn't particularly mad. Numb, yes, but not mad. A small, nagging fear twitched about the base of his skull, above his neck, the snake flitting its tongue.

It wasn't a lie Henry had told. It was the truth. Finally. But of all the true things he could have said, why this one? One that thrust Cox under the Adam's apple, dug its nails into his throat?

He had the taste of dirt in his mouth, and his tongue was too dry to wet his teeth. The smell of smoke made it worse. But the drinks were in the back where the boys were, and he couldn't see anybody right then. He couldn't be seen. The smoke faded to white strings.

He didn't understand anything about Henry, not one blessed thing. The past few weeks—the fight, the movies, his ideas of molding the boy into what he needed to be—even his budding pride—they were all a mistake. They dropped away, whole and complete, like clothes falling to the floor. The memory of them went too. They hadn't really happened—or might as well not have—so what was to remember? Why keep it around in his head? He bit the inside of his mouth, chewing the soft flesh.

And now, from the looks of things, Henry himself would be gone. Soon. Either Henry, or Cox's way to provide for Henry and everybody else, one or the other.

He stared at the ashtray, then stepped sideways, as though someone wanted past him. He found himself trying to avoid a false memory that floated into his mind from time to time. No matter. It came anyway.

Someone approached where he was playing on a dusty, scarred oak floor in an old house; someone singing. All he could see was a grown man's feet, a grown man's shoes. And he had watched, amazed, as his—what? Soldier? Car? Drum? Whatever it was, it was his—and it was being lifted away—carefully, kindly—but still away, out of his arms. And he hadn't been finished with it. He hadn't even gotten *started*. . . .

He blushed as the boys came from the back room. Waving his hand to clear the smoke, he shut the notebook on his papers.

That was one of Tollet's stories, too. None of it had happened; none of it, except, maybe, the dust and the floor.

Cox stumbled through the day, sustained by a smoldering anger at Martha. She thought it was taken care of, but he wasn't through yet. He had tricks of his own.

When he got home, he rooted around in the refrigerator for a beer. Behind him, Tollet moved slowly around the kitchen. He had drunk enough the day before to turn his blood to lava.

Apparently, he had given up on cooking some red, burnt thing that was stuck to the sides of a pot. On the counter were white bread, bologna, cheese slices, and Fritos.

"Whatza matter th'you?" wheezed Tollet. When Cox looked, he saw the effort the words had taken. The old man stood achily on one leg, leaning against the counter. His arms and hands fussed for a place to rest—on his hips, at his sides—like flies trying to light. Cox struggled his gaze away from him, turning back to the staggered rows of half-full jars in the icebox.

"Martha's blackmailing me," he said, deciding in an instant to give him the whole story. He might as well know. It would give him a reason to be drunk, at least.

"Whaaa?" asked Tollet.

Cox wouldn't let himself look. The old man's eyes would be fighting to come up through the murk, lose, and fall back again. Bleary pools, the glaze on lily pads.

"Says I'm taking Henry to see my whore." He sucked at his teeth, disgusted. "Like I don't buy gas and bread and charcoal from her, too."

"Whooo?"

Cox fixed his stare on the bottom drawers, pulled one open, and found a beer under a head of soggy, brown lettuce. He wiped the can against his pants leg.

"Lois Carberry, that's who. Says if I don't leave her and her steer alone, and send Henry to school in Memphis, she'll sue me for custody."

Tollet stumbled back a step, like he'd been shoved. Despite himself, Cox looked over at him. A pale sheen lay on the old man's face. One good thing about Tollet, he was never too drunk to understand the situation.

Cox went out onto the back porch to wait for Henry. He would cross the field from the woods any time now. Popping the beer top, he leaned his left shoulder into a porch post, crossed his legs at the ankle, and held the can alongside his right hip.

The sun had started lingering in the sky lately, so there was plenty of light to watch the boy come. He looked at the border of the yard where the field met the lawn. There wasn't much distinction between the two anymore. When his mother was alive, a calf-high lattice fence separated what was to be lived on and what was to be lived off of. A clutch of irises guarded against hay and corn and Johnson grass. But each side ate into the other now, creating rough, ragged borders, like a fight between river and shore.

It wasn't long until Cox spotted him. Henry's silhouette looked like a scorched place bobbing about on the field of green alfalfa. Even at that distance, Cox could tell he was thinking. His head and shoulders were slumped down, and he was walking too slowly.

Always, thought Cox. Always mulling over things; never just walking. Never like he should be. Cox lifted his shoulder and lay his back against the post, so that only his head faced the field.

It wouldn't matter if Henry just thought about school things—things that didn't interest Cox. That would've been all right, in the end. The encyclopedia—even the piano—would have been all right.

Things that just occur to you, and you pick them up, then set them down again. That was fine. Everybody did that. But it wasn't just that.

He lifted the can to his mouth and took a swallow, washing the beer from side to side. Henry drew closer, the black spot growing on the green. Then, suddenly, the boy stopped. He froze stock-still, staring at the grass as it rippled in the wind.

Cox stiffened to see it. He stood on his toes, hoping to spot what the boy was studying. But just as sharply as he had stopped, Henry started again, like someone had prodded him from behind.

Cox jerked his head back, then spat into the grown-over calla lilies at the porch's edge.

There! That was it, right there—what he detested—what was ruining the boy. He worried. He stewed. He brooded like an old woman over things that weren't there—things normal people went right over the top of and didn't feel the bump.

Why are you doing this, Daddy? What's the use of that? Who says so? How come? Questions like that were underneath all his sulking and moping, though Cox had barked at him enough to stop his speaking of them. Henry never put *anything* down—all of it mixed up and twisted together—trying to see how it all worked. Normal people got on with it, let that stuff alone and just lived. But not Henry. When he came up on something, he had to dig around at the beginning of it— or dig around at the end—to know where it was going. He wouldn't just *be*. And no matter what answers you gave him, he wasn't satisfied: you were lying or ignorant, one. His face would squirm up like you were keeping some disaster from him, like it was really a tornado outside, not a train. Then he would take his questions and fold inside himself—become one of those people Cox couldn't abide—one that sinks to the bottom with whatever he's brooding on, scumming around like a catfish, doing God knows what. And everybody else was up top, living and breathing on dry land.

Henry crossed into the yard, his gait steadier as he left the high grass and came onto the lawn. When he noticed Cox, he stopped at the clothesline. Its length was hung with dingy white bed sheets Tollet had put out that afternoon. The amber sunlight made them glow.

"What's the matter?" asked Henry.

Cox took a sip, then bared his teeth before speaking. A quiet stir of pride rumbled through his chest. See? he thought, I'm not mad at all.

"I was just about to ask you the same question."

The boy backed up, as though he needed a running start, then came on. He moved to a point directly in front of Cox. His jaw was tight and his eyes were lit up—sparky.

Cox gathered a scowl. He swallowed, rummaging around for the time when he had last seen Henry this way. It was when—it was when—

His jaw tightened. His lungs grew hard as concrete sleeves.

"Come here. Come close."

Henry walked to a spot just below the porch. He was wobbly on his feet, and all at once Cox could hear flames—pops and hisses. The bandages were still on his head, wrapped tight. They weren't torn off like before. Spotted with old, rust-colored blood—whispers here and dime spots there—all of it was dried, old. Nothing new.

Still, Cox thought, turning cold. Still.

"Pull up your shirt!" His voice shook free of control. He winced at the loss.

Henry dropped his bag, yanked at his clothes. His shirttail rose to his chin, then he locked gazes with Cox. The glass of the boy's eyes was both steady and wild. Cox gritted his teeth.

He won't say a word, he thought. He knows what I think, but he won't say a word.

What was left of his composure shuddered off like dried skin. Groaning, he felt himself fall into his old grooves, saw Henry do the same: puppets under strings.

I can't help it, he thought, his gaze raking over the boy's body. I can't.

He stepped off the porch, turning an ankle in his haste. He drew near, stooping down so that his head was level with the boy's body. Henry quivered breaths under the search.

Nothing new—bruises from the stomping, turned yellow now— old scratches—old moles—and *still*. Cox's fingers trembled out— grazed the flesh. The boy shrank back, came forward again.

"Turn around," said Cox. "Turn around," louder, insistent.

Henry wobbled about, working the shirt over his shoulder blades. Trickles of sweat branched and rushed down into the gully of his back. Cox watched his own huge hand move out to the young skin, to the hills of baked, dried blood on its surface. He ran the balls of his fingers over the scars, knowing, *knowing* that anything new in the blood, his son's blood—his boy—he would see, he would feel. It wouldn't fool him. It couldn't, could it?

Hot, baked ridges—crust—spaces, white as flour dust—new flesh where scabs had sloughed and fallen. On and on he traced them—through the ditch in the boy's back, white sweat mingling with red blood—each scab so easily torn with a nail, so easily lifted away, too soon, before it was finished, just as it had gotten started. The thought made him press the scabs harder, push them down until the boy winced and gasped.

Cox came to himself, drew back. He stared at the pattern—scuppernong branches, ivy vines. It looked the same, and yet, by God, it had to be different, didn't it? It was!

"Turn around again."

The boy dropped his shirt and swung to meet him, his face flush with something Cox had never seen. The man's throat closed. Henry was on the bottom, beneath the murk, drowning.

"You're getting beat," he said. His voice came out like scattered marbles, flying everywhere, into the grass, into the weeds. "Tell me—tell me the truth—he beat you—just now, coming through the woods. He beat you." And Cox wanted to add, but was unable to add—"I'll kill him—for you, if you can't, if you need me to!"

"No," said Henry. "He didn't."

"He did! He did!" cried Cox. "Tell me! I'm right! I know I am! Tell me!' He tilted his crown back, closed his eyes for a moment. "I won't—make you this time. I promise I won't. But tell me!"

Henry shook his head, shoulder to shoulder in a swag. "He never touched me."

Cox trembled with fever, his concrete lungs calling for breath.

"Where is it?" he demanded, his eyes flying all over the boy. "Take off your britches."

"He didn't."

"Take 'em off!"

"He didn't!"

Cox raised his hands—to crush, to pull—he dropped them again.

"You saw him though? You saw him, didn't you?"

This time the boy's face calmed, slid into some old, schooled pattern Cox had seen before—known by its name. Whatever he said, however he put it, what came next would be a lie.

"No."

"I know you did," Cox muttered. "I know you did—you did."

The boy's face fell deeper beneath the water, so low Cox could barely make it out. And Cox drew back, jumped clear, as though he had been studying something that proved to be something else—a coil of rope that was a snake, a nail that was a spider.

"What's the matter with you?" he said, a horrible whisper, rolling like fog through a trench.

Henry's eyes gave him pity, the last, best light before a shadow falls. But nothing came from the boy's open mouth—round and silent—filling and filling with water.

And now Cox knew this was something he could not fix. It was all getting loose from him, tearing itself free. And all he knew to do, all he had ever known to do, was to chase it off in return—to run it away as hard as he could—as though he had never wanted it in the first place.

"All right then" His voice shook in catches. "If that's the way it is, here's the rest of it. You've fixed it *all*, now."

He said it in as mean a tone as he could manage, raking it over his teeth to cut the words.

"You told her—about Lois. Called her a whore. I know you did, so don't let's fool with that part. She told me to stay away from her and that pig. Either I stay away, or she'll sue me for custody."

Henry stood for him, just like he always had and always would. Cox saved the best for last, brandishing it like a whip over his head as he chased. Go on then! he thought. I never wanted you anyway!

"And she says you'll have to go to Memphis to school because of what you told her. From now on, I hadn't got any say." He backed off another step, then another. The boy's face drank it in like dry ground under rain.

"And I'll tell you another thing. I'm gonna let you. I'm gonna let you! Hear? By God, I am! No more of this. No more from me! Lying when you want to, the way you want to." He smirked, nodding. "There's shut-mouth lies too. That's your kind now. Staying down inside, when everybody else is up here. So by God, go ahead! Ruin it—drag it all down there. Go on—you l'il—"

He backed off, still jabbing a finger at Henry, where the boy stood staring a hole through the world. Cox turned, stumbled up the steps, snatched the screen open and slammed it so hard that the crack made his eyes water. He was exhausted from running him, and he couldn't watch him disappear.

Chapter 9

Henry stood in the back yard and listened to his father roar through the house like it was on fire—snatching things off counters, off tabletops—finally, a rattle of keys. Then he heard him barrel out the front door and climb into his truck with a squeal of hinges. The engine fired, the tires tore at the grass, and the truck raced down the chert road. The sound gradually lessened, like sand being poured over tin. Henry looked over the roof and saw the peach-colored dust billow into the sky, sift, taper. The truck wound through the hills, gears following each other to a high ledge, then leaping off into the soft night air.

Something in his leaving brought Henry back to himself. Before, standing with his shirt around his shoulders, he had been there and not there, like he was jumping loose from his own body, sailing upward at one moment, yanked down by his heels the next. He had seen it as though by the flashes of a camera—shutter and light—long blinks. What had been far away was suddenly too close, on top of him. It wasn't until Cox had spoken that Henry had found his tongue, and what he had said was more of a reflex—like a gasp in cold water—than anything else. But he had meant it all, reflex or not. All but the last part had been true.

He had seen the boy. He hadn't been touched, but he had seen and been seen.

This time, he was just off the bus and headed towards the first little ridge. Even under the trees, it was the kind of hot that made the clay ground seem closer, right under his nose—grainy rocks, patches of damp soil that gaped like cuts. For a while, he wandered about, not wanting to go straight home. His uncle's visit the Sunday before had troubled him, and he had wanted to think about it. He hadn't even seen the man more than ten times in his life: three with black hair and a beard that reached down to his paunch, and the rest with gray hair and no beard.

When he topped the crest, he skipped down the other side of the ridge, through the clutter and crunch of oak leaves. The creek was up ahead, drier now from lack of rain: a series of black, oily puddles, oozing and trickling into each other.

His uncle's paunch was big so that his belt and pants barely had hold of his shirttail. His voice had been firm, but not scary.

"You haven't had sex education in school, have you Henry?" Not exactly.

"You know what 'sex' is though, don't you?" Yes.

"From school or at home?" Both.

"Talks?" No, not talks.

"How else, then?" Well. There's other ways. Books. Magazines.

"School or home?" Mostly—home.

He should have kept his mouth shut and played dumb. But he had thought Clark was there to educate him. From time to time, Martha invited him to school, to talk on courtrooms, laws, and about staying out of strange cars. He'd come to the house years ago, to tell Henry and his sisters what it would be like when they didn't live with both parents. So when Clark had started off with questions, Henry assumed the man was just figuring out where he should start teaching. Then he slipped into another gear:

"And you've been with your father when he goes to see women?" Henry was nodding before he knew it. Only one woman, he corrected. He shot a look at Martha.

"But several times?"

Martha nodded. Henry answered "several times."

"And you said he pays her—with checks?" He had said that, yes.

There had been a second when he almost lied. But Martha was there, and he never lied when somebody was around to catch him.

He had walked over a rise in the path, coming to the edge of the black creek. Clark was going to do something to Cox with his answers. Barnes might come back, and Martha would be all right, but now Cox was in trouble again. He shook his head. His breath skipped.

Things see-sawed back and forth like that, out of his control, no matter what he had meant to do. Tell this one thing, and look what happens. Tell that, and see what you've done. Things flew out of his grasp, wrenched free and swung back on the other one, mowing it down. He couldn't get it right. He didn't have the skill to keep it in the middle. He shouldn't have tried.

All at once, his breath was labored. He stopped to lean over his knees, his rump against a tree.

The boy was hurrying across the path, fifty yards ahead. All Henry caught of him was a glimpse, but the sight trussed him like a new rope—a rough, seizing catch above the ribs.

The boy's hair trailed behind him. He held his arms out from his sides, fists clinched. It seemed he was headed somewhere—headed *back* somewhere—like he had come for only one thing—something he had left, but needed. But before he made it inside the cover of trees, he swept a look Henry's way, chin to shoulder, then back. Short, but purposeful; he hadn't forgotten; he knew, very well. But he could pass Henry now. He didn't have to beat him anymore. He had somewhere else to be, someone else to see.

Henry's shirt was drenched and stuck to his back. His fingers stung at the tips. The ground's smell forced itself inside his head, seeping into his mouth with the light breeze. It lay a raw taste across his teeth. With a push of breath, he trudged on, each step a high stair.

And now he was here, in the yard, where his steps had brought him. His thigh and right hip tingled with sleep, tired of standing so long. A metal chair sat in the middle of the yard, surrounded with shattered walnut shells from part of Tollet's afternoons. Henry dropped down onto the seat. It was still too warm from the day's heat to lean back against.

He didn't know why he hadn't told Cox. Because he would go back there, if he knew? Because, this time, it had looked like Cox would try to do it for him?

Cox's face had been scared to his skin's edge, bristly as a spooked horse. He hadn't known, hadn't even suspected, that some of what Cox wanted was really for him, Henry. Wrong or right, it was for him. Even before, when he had sent him off with a wooden club—wrong or right—some of it, more than he had known, was for him.

Still, he couldn't say anything just now. Hadn't he just learned what words, his words at least, could do? Not saying had run Cox off, but what good would telling have done? Even if he had found the boy and pounded his head into the dirt, what good? And no matter how it had started, or what any of them thought—even the boy—it was something different now. It was Henry's, now.

He had understood that coming across the alfalfa field, headed towards the house. This whole thing was his. It didn't have a floor, or a wall, or a roof—not to speak off, anyhow. He couldn't back off, get a good look, and then name it. He couldn't tell when it was coming, how it was coming, or the way it would play out. But it was his, and it was making him. At the end, maybe he would know.

Cox had to keep his hands off that. Cox and Martha and Tollet, too. This was his.

He walked into the house, dropped his bag, and looked around for something to do. He wasn't through thinking yet, so he turned on the television and sat down. The screen brightened, focused, and brought a picture to meet the newswoman's voice. He didn't bother to change the channel. Her drone wouldn't interfere with his thinking, like cartoons could. In time, a mat of muscles tightened across his stomach as he remembered what Cox had said.

The school in Memphis. That was what Clark had done with his answers. The thought of the place ran off every other thought he had: the boy, the alfalfa field, the way Cox had looked. Henry stared at a hole in the floor boards as he rolled the school around his brain.

He had been scared of the place as long as he had known about it, and for no good reason. They had science labs there, Martha told him, and they even expected you to read the encyclopedia. The brochure showed pictures of the rooms; your own desk and chair. It showed two boys sitting on their beds, looking over books at each other, smiling like they couldn't get enough of it. His gaze rose from the carpet to the opposite wall, stopping on a sunburst clock—black face, gold hands to match the rays shooting from the circle.

If he didn't have friends there, all right. He didn't have any now. If the teachers were mean, all right. He was good at school, and they were mostly mean to the ones who weren't. If he had to take gym class, all right to that, too—he could play sick and need to go to the bathroom a lot. He could take everything but the sleeping part— having to sleep in a strange bed, with somebody he didn't know lying five feet away, breathing at him, watching him in the dark.

Acid washed through his stomach. He stood up.

He would take what he knew over what he didn't. Even this mess here, he would take.

He stopped to look at Tollet's closed door. What he knew, he could handle. It couldn't sneak up on him because he knew how it would come, and what it could do. But what he didn't know—like the boy in the other bed—a boy cut loose from a house and a family and a room that hadn't been a stranger's. Who knows what he would do? It wouldn't just be pissing on him in the shower, or throwing his clothes out the window. Cut loose like that, drifting in outer space, what would stop a boy like that from doing whatever he wanted? Who would care? While he slept, he might sneak up and—the idea crawled up his skin like a stump full of spiders, legs faster than touch.

Tollet was right. The things that had been were better than the things that might be.

He cut the television off, listened for the old man, then crept to his door. He pushed down on the knob as he turned it, to keep the hinges from squeaking.

The night-light cast a woolly, yellow ring beneath Tollet's chair. His knees were spread wide. His arms had fallen off the rests and hung loosely. As Henry crawled towards him, he saw that Tollet's head rested in the corner, propped in the angle. He looked like he'd been knocked back into the chair by a punch in the face. His sour breath hung about like a molded sheet, so Henry reversed his crawl until the scent faded. He stretched out on his stomach and waited, coughing loudly to bring Tollet up.

The eyes fluttered, sank, rose again. It took a few moments for them to move. At length, they slid down at an angle, as though adding Henry into what they saw.

Tollet's head wobbled free of the wall, turned a fraction to face him.

"Henry?"

Henry braced himself. It had always started with a song or a story—never with him first—never with him at all, except to say that he had missed out on what was to come, had been born too late to see.

"You're not gonna stay—" he began, lifting a shadow hand, "—here?" His voice was full of water, trembling through pipes. He nodded with great effort, then swallowed. "You're gonna go."

Henry's back stiffened. Suddenly, he felt disrespectful, lying across the floor as he was. But moving now wouldn't do.

"You'll—be sorry," said Tollet. His mouth lifted a mournful smile. A vague dew puddled in the corners of his eyes. Henry blushed, his throat straining to hold his head up. Was he not drunk?

"You. You don't know—a thing—'bout that," he said. The old man's eyes cut to the shaded window where the light dug its nails around the border.

"Think it's better? What you got comin'? Think it's better just 'cause it's all white and lit and numb feeling? Think it's better 'cause you can paint anything you want on it?" He swelled up an inch, his eyebrows lifting him. "Think you can hold it still when you got it like you like it?"

He tried to laugh but coughed instead. His face twisted towards the center as he belched spit, the color of his tears. When he had gotten the better of it, his head went back, eyes shut tight.

"It won't hold still. Won't be like the picture you've made." A slight laugh, all he dared, came through. "It don't want your plans. Got its own. Be givin' 'em to *you*, for *you* to work off of."

Henry's spine was a wrung dish towel. His neck and jaws burned. He couldn't swallow over the ropes in his throat.

"You'll see. That's the same as this—'cept worse, 'cause you don't know it. When this stinks and rots—you know it, know where it is—can get around it." He shook his head, flicking a hand at the window. "But not that. You're as liable to think it's pretty as not—walk right in—deep—all the way up to your mouth."

Tollet sighed. His high, sour breath ran up Henry's nose. In a joined movement, Henry rose to his knees, then swung around to sit where his elbows had rested. His heart pounded in relief—sent blood into all the robbed, starving places in his trunk. But the motion startled Tollet so much that his face stormed with color. His nostrils flared, his stare grabbing Henry by the shoulders. Right then, Henry remembered what he always forgot: Tollet was Cox's father.

"You think there ain't whores anyplace else?" he jeered. Henry shrank down.

"You think this is the only place? Hunh! Won't you be surprised? When they're there to meet you! They're here, there, and everywhere—some hide and some don't—and the ones that don't, at least you know 'em—they give off a smell so you can decide 'Yes, I will' or 'No, I won't.' But the ones that don't—they hide and—and—" He swelled with a laugh that choked him worse than before. Hacking, he clutched at his chest. But when his face cleared this time, his eyes weren't done laughing.

"Won't you be surprised?" Tollet leaned forward, to give him something, or to take something away. Henry edged back, ready to rise and run.

"Your own *mama's* a whore. That's where *you* come from! And her so *smart!* Wasn't smart 'nough to keep her legs together! Wasn't even smart enough to charge for it! Not then—but *now—now* she comes collectin'—got a bill for your Daddy to pay!" His face ground into a mean point.

Henry shivered. Tollet could beat a boy's eye clean out of his head. Tollet could pull a dead man from his box.

"See? It's all over you. Running hard the other way, but still headed right for it. You're just something for one to snatch up and beat the other one with—"

Henry spun around and crabbed towards the door, scratching his way through its opening before he was on his feet. He ran through the kitchen, out the screen, across the yard and lot to the barn. Then he scrambled up the ladder to the loft, a place too high and rickety for Tollet to follow. He ran to the wall beside the open loft door, shoulders rising as he heaved for breath. After a moment, he leaned around to peek out at the house.

The old man finally tottered into the kitchen. He stood peering through the screen. Tollet rubbing his elbow, then his shoulder, places he had probably struck against the wall or door on the way. A hand pressed against the screen, making the mesh dimple and shimmer in the heavy afternoon light. The springs sang as the door inched open a bit, hesitated, then slid back with a pop. Tollet stumbled off into the dark house.

Henry sat on a low stack of hay, its straw sticking him beneath the knees. The loft was as still as asphalt. The air might never have been moved here, never been disturbed by Cox busting and scattering bales.

Before too long, he was soaking wet. His insides began to churn under the heat, rolling over and flopping back. He sat as still as he could manage.

In time, he heard a scratching noise from across the way, near another, taller stack of bales. The cat's head peeked out, green eyes staring. Slowly, she eased from her hiding place and padded towards him, her steps all in whispers. She stopped, looked up.

As hot as it was, as hot as it would be to hold her, he lifted the cat from the floor and held her deep against his chest, until his heart slowed to the rumble of her purrs.

He waited until first dark—until purple-blue water stood between him and the trees, and grass, and house—until lightening bugs rose and fell like tossed candles. Then he moved down the ladder as quietly as he could manage, wincing at every cracking sound the wood made. He lowered himself to the sawdust ground.

The house was dark and silent—a tight, black box. Cox hadn't come back. Tollet hadn't stirred. The old man was probably still in his room, too drunk to eat, feeding himself stories—breathing them out on sour breath, sucking them back in before they drifted too far.

Henry eased through the screen door and turned on a single floor lamp, the light stinging his eyes. He pulled bread and candy from the drawers, a plug of cheese and a can of Sprite from the ice-box. When he turned to go outside again, his eyes weren't used to the dark anymore. He made his way back to his room, careful to tiptoe past Tollet's door. He stole through the dark, sat in the corner behind his bed, and ate.

If it hadn't been for hunger, he wouldn't have left the loft. After a while, when the sun had gone down and the hot air had risen to the tin roof, the loft had become the perfect place for him to be, with hot, thick smells: molded hay, pigeon droppings, ground dust, and most of all—beneath his feet, coming through the cracks in the planks—the rising smell of the pony, the aged saddle mare with cataracts, and directly beneath him, the two steer calves with pink eye.

He had looked down through the cracks and watched them stamp their feet from time to time—hidden from light and flies by the white patches covering their eyelids. He had helped Cox when they had put the patches on. They had caught the calves in the head-catch, doctored the swollen eyes with ointment guns, then glued the cups to their heads. Released, the terrified calves had stumbled, risen, gathered speed until they crashed into the cedar posts, then the barn wall—heads cracking against boards. Henry had cringed at the impact. They staggered about, dazed, witless.

Cox cursed them because he hadn't wanted them in the first place and had had to buy them when his bull bred the neighbor's milk cows. Then they went and got pink eye. But with their steering, he had gotten his revenge, Cox said, for having cost him so much. Finally, they had managed to herd the calves into a stall together, to isolate them, so they would heal. In time, the dark, quiet place had calmed them, so that they were peaceful now, all silent and stilled. Even when Cox came in to feed, they would only turn their blind faces toward him, to sniff at the oats and molasses. They had to rock themselves to move.

Would they be calm, Henry wondered, when Cox took them to the scales? to the truck? to the slaughterhouse?

His chewing sounded loud—grind and mill and a hard swallow. After a sip of his drink, with all its gurgle and fizz, he grew tired. He sat the food aside, half-eaten.

His head bandage had slipped down from the sweat and grit. It sagged along one eyebrow. Heat rushed about the scabs and sores, from one side to the other, like a string pulled on a feed sack. With his fingers wet from the Sprite can, he ran the water underneath the gauze to cool his brow.

He thought of the calves—each calm, even with the blast of a gun firing into the brains of the one before it—even with the wind of a sledgehammer rushing down at their skulls. They didn't care, or know to care, of anything but food and sleep—and, had they not been steered, an itch in the crotch.

He sat up, to think of all the calves they had ever raised, each of them planned on the clipboard Cox kept hanging on a nail inside the door:

"Number 251—hot—put in pasture with Colossus bull #5—8/15." He understood what those words meant now—since he had seen the man and woman twisted together in Cox's magazine—since the movies—since Lois.

And later—*"#251 calved 4/21"*

After that, a separate line for the calf, to chart its shots for lepto and blackleg, the dates it was wormed—the dates it got tattooed inside the ear, tagged outside. A number that meant all of the things on the clipboard, to show all the thinking that had gone into it.

Henry put the whole can of Sprite to his head, rolling the cold over his soaking brow.

But not the two steers with pinkeye. They were mistakes. No plans, no clipboards—nothing but surprise and disappointment. The Angus bull had gotten over the fence to the neighbor's milk cows. Henry hadn't understood why at the time, but what followed was a problem.

"A mistake," he'd heard Cox plead to his neighbor.

"A ruin!" Mr. Dindy roared back.

Cox had paid the vet to give the milk cows shots—shots that made them piss thick, lumpy blood. His father was too mad to be asked questions, but Henry found out that some of the cows hadn't bled. They had had their calves anyway—half Angus, half Holstein—and Cox had been forced to buy those mistakes.

That's what they had stayed, too. Mistakes. Coming hadn't changed that. The others had moved aside—shifted over—grumbling as they made room. Of all the calves they owned, Henry knew these two and for that very reason. They were the first steered because they had cost so much.

The cold from the can gave him a headache.

It could be a lie. Tollet had been mad and drunk. It could be a lie. It didn't help to think that, as far as he knew, Tollet had never told him a lie, least of all when he was drunk. He shook the thought out of his head.

Lifting the bedcovers, he slid underneath, fully dressed. He held his feet out over the side and kicked his tennis shoes off.

Tomorrow was Friday. He could ask Martha when he went to her house for the weekend. He closed his eyes, unable to sleep for his listening, ears keen for the sound of his father's engine.

When he came onto the back porch, Martha and the girls were laughing. He had been in the bathroom, changing out of his school clothes—checking face, underarms, and crotch for signs of new hair—when he heard them start to giggle. The laughter built on his way down the hall, and now they were all three red-faced and speechless.

"What is it?" he asked, looking around the group. Martha sat in a wicker chair with her hands over her face. Lucy was sitting on a stool in front of her, swatting at her hair. Betsy rolled around on the floor.

"What? What?"

When they couldn't answer, he got aggravated. It was hard not to look like a fool with everybody all around you laughing.

"What!"

"She—she—she—" wheezed Betsy. They fell into another gale. Henry could only roll his eyes and wait. Since Betsy was the closest to finishing, he looked to her for the explanation.

She was tan all over, and prettier than Lucy, who was getting kind of stubby-looking—more like Henry and Cox. Lucy even acted stubby: quick to slap and shove. She had raised a bruise on his arm last week when he hadn't carried on over her new guinea pig.

"She—she was driiiinking Cooooke," Betsy managed over another round of giggles, "and—and—she took too big a swaaalllaaah. . . ."

Henry looked at Martha, guessing she was the one Betsy was talking about. His mother was wiping her nose on her hand. She took a napkin off the table beside her and blew it hard.

So Coke came out her nose, Henry explained to himself. He tried to laugh and think it was as funny as they had, but since he hadn't seen it, he couldn't muster much enthusiasm. He smiled and shook his head, the way he had seen old people do when witnessing something foolish, then left them for the kitchen. He got himself a Coke of his own, but set it back for something dry—crackers—instead.

"Come out here with us," Martha called from the porch. Henry took the square, wax paper sleeve with him and went out to sit on the swing, stuffing his mouth with two crackers at a time. He wasn't in much of a mood to laugh. He looked down at the package of crackers, and all at once determined to eat every one of them, without out a drop of water to help him.

"You should take those bandages off your head now, Henry," Martha said. "Let some air get to them. They'll heal better."

Henry nodded, unable to talk. He swallowed a few times, painfully.

"Some of the bandage's dried to the scab. I'm gonna wait 'til it pulls away, so the scab won't come off too." He loaded his mouth again—three at a time.

Martha raised her eyebrows and nodded back. She reached beneath her thigh and pulled out a strand of ribbon. After tying it at the bottom of Lucy's braid, she patted her shoulders.

"Turn around," she said, her eyes happy. Lucy looked over her shoulder.

"Good. Good." She glanced up to Betsy and waved her over. "Your turn."

The girls switched places. Henry studied his mother's face as she set to her work on Betsy's longer, shinier hair. Martha looked young.

She had more energy. At school, she showed up everywhere—visiting classrooms, announcing events every thirty minutes, calling assemblies. She had taken over his Mississippi History class when it came time to discuss the Chickasaws, Choctaws, and Natchez. It was his favorite subject, and she had done it the way he liked—color slides and stories of sun worship and sacrifice by strangulation. On the way home, she had mentioned a program she had heard about, one that let the students write and illustrate comic books.

"What kind of comic books?" he had asked, sitting up.

"They take ones that you like, and let you use the characters to start one of your own. You change the costume and their powers and everything. You want to try it?"

When they'd gotten to the house, he had gone into the girls' room and found a whole box full of new comic books, their covers torn off. A new Rex-all calendar was on the wall.

"I couldn't find a new *Superman*," strained Henry, his throat tight with dried crackers. "That's my favorite one—but they," he nodded at the girls, "only had *Archie* and *Richie Rich*."

Martha rolled her gaze up to him, blinking to make sense of what he said.

"Oh. Well, that's okay. We'll go by the drugstore and get you some."

Henry lifted his chin, looking down his nose at her. "When?"

Martha shrugged, her hands busy folding hair. "Anytime. Tomorrow maybe. Barnes's car is in the shop, so I'm going to pick him up at the store and bring him over for lunch tomorrow. We can get a *Superman* then."

It wasn't until after supper that he spotted his chance. When Martha told the girls it was time to go take a bath, he lied and told her he had taken one earlier. He meandered about the kitchen, helping her put things in the cabinets and pantry.

Did you mean to have me? He had decided to say, straight out. But that didn't sound right when he imagined it, and before he could think of something else, the girls were padding around the kitchen in their nightgowns. After a while, Martha sent them all to the back to sleep. He pulled his clothes off and lay under the cold sheets, waiting for Martha to tell him goodnight. He had noticed her long sighs in the kitchen, seen her hand placed at the small of her back. She wasn't one to linger when she was tired. When she came to the door, she called goodnight and flicked the lights off.

"Wait." He wished she hadn't heard him. This wasn't the time or place, with her tired and headed for bed. She wouldn't take the time.

Martha swung back around the door frame, flicking the lights on again.

"Hmmmm?"

"Come here." He felt like a fool, lying flat as he was. He struggled up to a sitting position.

"What?" she asked, walking to the bed. A worried look faded in and out on her face.

She must think I'm gonna ask her about Memphis now, Henry thought.

"I gotta ask you something."

"All right. What?"

He opened and shut his mouth several times. Martha frowned.

"Go ahead," she said, bumping the mattress with her knee. "What?"

"Don't get mad."

She rolled her eyes. "Ask me, then! What? What?"

"Sit down?" he asked, glancing at the chair beside his bed.

"I am *not* going to sit down. Not until you tell me what it is."

He thought of asking for some water or crackers—or about the comic book program. But he rattled out what he wanted to know before he lost courage.

"Tollet said you didn't mean to have me—you and Daddy—didn't mean to have me." The words formed in his mouth, a glass stone on his tongue.

"I was a mistake."

He had said too much. Her skin bleached and her eyes shrank back. He shouldn't have said how he knew. The hand on her hip came down. Her arm hung loose and away from her side, like she had broken it.

"Sit down?" he asked.

Instead of the chair, she eased onto the side of the bed, so that he had to scooch his legs over. She stared at her hands, running one over the back of the other, calming it with long strokes.

Why had he asked? He didn't want to hear after all.

"I'm not going to lie to you, since you asked me." The cast of her eyes, and what she was doing with her hands, sent a wave of dread over Henry's chest. His legs shivered, tingled.

Lie! Lie! he wanted to say.

She stayed still as she mustered up the truth.

"You need to know the truth, so you can—see—that it's not so bad."

No, he thought. It is. It will be. Lie.

For a time, she shook her head. Then she brought her voice out in a pace and pitch that matched her movement.

"What he told you isn't true."

His head twitched to the right, an unexpected spasm. Then he relaxed. He was surprised at how tight his shoulders had been. He let old air out of his lungs.

Tollet was crazy, saying such a thing. But then, he was old. He'd been drunk, and mad because Henry was leaving him. So naturally—

"We," started Martha, "—got *married*—because of you. But you—I meant to have you."

His shoulders clamped tight again.

"I don't mean I *planned* to have you—I wasn't trying to trap Cox, like Tollet meant." Her eyes flattened. "But—that doesn't mean I didn't want you. Once you came."

She squinted at him, her teeth gritted as if she were watching something she knew must hurt, a bullet being dug from his chest.

"You—know what I mean? About 'planning' to have you? You underst—" She stopped in mid-question, remembering. "Oh. Of course you do. That's what got all this started, isn't it?"

Not that, he thought. Now that it was out, he wanted to hear it all, even the worst. But he wanted to hear about *him*, not about her and Cox.

"Tell me," he said, pulling her back to what he wanted. Martha lifted her hand from her lap slightly, as if she needed a moment.

"We got married because—we were young—and that's what you did back then. Accidents happen to people when—they're young and they don't have sense, or anybody to help them." Her lips drew tight against her teeth. "I didn't have anybody."

Henry knew better than to ask about Big Mama. Often she said "My mother's job in life was doing without things on your behalf, just so she could turn around and say you didn't appreciate it."

She shook her head fiercely. Her cheeks blushed red.

"Accidents and mistakes are two different things. Understand, Henry? And you weren't a 'mistake.' I made a *'mistake'* when I married your daddy."

She must have felt him stiffen, but it only stoked her.

"It *was* a mistake, Henry," she said, too loud. "I'm sorry, but it was."

Henry stared at her hard. Even in the dark he could tell she was blushing, uncomfortable. When she spoke again, her voice was lower.

"Well, all right. I didn't always think that. There were times— he was always somebody you felt safe with, and everyone admired him for that. There were even times when I thought he—liked me. It seemed that way, at least. But I was stupid, and now I know it was all a waste, because—"

Her gaze wandered as she spoke, as though she were just now putting words to something she had thought for a long time.

"I was going to go away to school," she said, smiling. She switched her hands, so that now her left soothed her right.

"To a college in New Orleans. I'd already had to wait a few years, working to save money. But then one of my old teachers gave me a scholarship application. And I won." Her eyes widened, shrank again.

"That doesn't mean much to you, but see—see—nobody had expected it. Not even *me*. To get to leave here, and go someplace else, where I wasn't—odd." Her eyes found him, smiled a quick fragile smile. "Like you're odd."

Henry swallowed hard.

"It was free, too," said Martha, her eyes narrowed to pinpoints. "It wasn't going to cost my mother one red cent. It wouldn't have cost her one thin dime."

She drew a fast, gasping breath that made Henry flinch. She spoke in quick, choking lurches. "But then, you came along. And—when something happens you don't expect—you have to think fast. It doesn't matter that you're young." Her eyebrows rose, her mouth opened, still amazed at the fact.

"You're so *young*, and you have to make decisions like that—like *that*. But you don't get any excuses. It happens so fast, and then you make a mistake. And the next thing you know," she snapped her fingers, "you're married and have children and you can't leave. Night school's the best you can do."

Henry nodded, blinked.

You made the mistake because of the accident, he thought. Because of me.

"I suppose there were other ways," she continued, low and to herself. "But I was young and—I didn't know then what I know now." She grimaced, as though staring at some thought that had forced its way on her. "But that's not the point," she said, shaking her head. "I *wanted* you."

He didn't feel better. In fact, it made him move away. What if she hadn't wanted him? Would he not be here? All he was depended on what she wanted? He stiffened again, angry.

She ran the flat of her hands up and down her legs, as if warming herself to finish. She took another full breath and shuddered it out. Her voice was solid now.

"The point is, after that mistake—I decided to live the rest of my life thinking things through. See? All the way out. All the way through. Not to do things just because they 'seemed' right. I wanted all my options, from then on out."

Her voice broke, and she looked at him in a way that seized him—like she was snatching him back from a cliff. A knot bound his throat.

"That's what I want for you. You're like me. I didn't know how much until just this past year. But you are. And this place—this isn't—"

She raised her hand and shook it at the whole outdoors, fending it off.

"No mistakes for you. No accidents that *make* you make mistakes. Things can happen here—people come along—I should know. And you can't count on what they'll do. I want you to go where you can be in peace, where you can think. I didn't get a chance to. Because I didn't know."

She put her hands on either side of his face. Her breathing became a muffled, husky wheeze.

"But you will, if you'll let yourself. If you'll let me help you. That's all I'm trying to do."

Her eyes misted. She smiled.

Henry rocked his head up and down in the brace of her hands. Her palms and fingers moved in slight kneading motions, small circles, tenderly moving the flesh of his face.

The smells of the drugstore blew against Henry as soon as he opened the glass door. He had come from the steaming day into the cold, air-conditioned cleanness of the pharmacy. When he got to the back, the air worked beneath his collar and turned his sweaty shirt cold.

"Barnes? You back there?" He tried to peek around the shelves. "Bar—"

"Hey," came a voice. It was followed by footsteps coming up stairs. "Hold on. I'm coming out there."

He must've been down in the storeroom, thought Henry. He heard the door slam in the back corner, behind the shelves. Barnes appeared from between two rows. He was drying his hands on the bottom of his white coat.

"I was washing my shoes off." A smile flitted on and off his lips. "Got 'em muddy at the lake the other day—hadn't had a chance to."

Henry smiled weakly. Barnes kept drying his hands, then swiped his feet back and forth on the carpet for a long time. It was the first Henry had seen him since the day at Martha's.

"How're you doing?" asked Barnes. He kept his face turned down towards his shoes. Lifting one wing-tip up, he rested it on a shelf and retied the knot.

"I'm all right," said Henry. He looked at his own shoes, then at his hands where they clutched the ledge. The last time he had seen Barnes, the man had been slunk against a wall—shamed, trying to make himself smaller.

"How're you?" Henry asked.

Barnes laughed a little, stopped, then laughed a little more. He changed feet and untied the other shoe. His face was beet red. "Oh, I'm all right."

Once he had finished retying the laces, he stared at the ground, as though regretting the lack of another foot and another shoe. His gaze skittered around the floor as he turned towards Henry.

"It's been a while since I seen you. I've been—busy." He smiled with one side of his face, giving Henry a string of rapid nods. "I was busy."

Henry gave the nods back. "I know. I've been busy, too." He lifted a hand from the ledge, then laid it back down, in the same, hot place. "You're gonna come back, now." He stopped himself and bit his lip. "I mean—you're gonna come to lunch today."

Barnes face reddened. His Adam's apple bobbed. Henry rushed out his purpose.

"Mama's down at the store, getting the food. She said she'd be here in a minute. Said I could get a new *Superman*, 'cause they're doing a new thing at school and you can make your own Superman— 'cept you have to change him and all."

He shrugged and lifted his hand once more. "So. You got any new *Supermans*?"

Barnes smiled at him without looking, then jerked his head at the comic book rack. Henry took the first one he could find—one he already had. He glanced at Barnes again.

"I need to get some Merthiolate and Band-Aids and some new salve, too," he lied. "For my head and back and all. They're healing up finally—and—"

Barnes motioned towards the right with his eyes. Henry moved to the aisle and took what he needed. He came back to the ledge and put the things down. From Barnes's face, Henry might have placed a dead body on the ledge, something too strange to touch.

He took some money out. It was his own, since Martha hadn't given him any more than he needed for a comic book. He fingered a bill, wondering if it was enough, then slid it towards Barnes.

"$5.28," said Barnes, taking the money off the counter.

Not enough. Henry reached around for the billfold again.

Barnes was studying the paper, his face tight and red. He stood flat-footed, as though ready to take a blow.

"Why—why does this—have your Daddy's name on it?"

It was a second before he understood. Then Henry took a shallow breath, the air reaching down his throat for what he needed.

"Because he's sorry," he said.

Barnes stared at the bill in his hand.

"What?"

"He says he's sorry. For not paying you enough before." He rolled a shoulder at Barnes, and the money he held. "He signed it so you'd know it was from him. That's what he owes you."

Barnes stared on, his head moving back so his eyes could take another angle. All at once, Henry felt him begin to slip again. He took out the other signed bill and slid it across the counter.

"Here's the rest," he said, watching Cox's name glide across the surface to lie flat beside the register. "He said to keep the change."

Barnes looked down at the paper, read the words, and picked the bill up. With a throaty, gathering cough, he placed the money carefully into the drawer and closed the till. Then he took a breath, nodded, and looked Henry square in the eye.

"Go get you another book," said Barnes, his voice solid and full. "It's on me. You'll need more than one."

Henry stood for a moment, watching Barnes take root again, blossom and bloom. Then he went back and found the book he wanted—one with Superman on the cover, blasting from a tunnel of ocean water.

"So you decided to go up to Memphis to school?" asked Barnes.

Henry wheeled around to face him.

"Sir?"

Barnes' head was cocked to the side. "You said you're gonna do this thing with the comic books. That's up at that school in Memphis, isn't it? At least, she told me so."

Henry looked down at Superman. He had known just what he was going to do with him. He had planned it the night before. Change the blue to red and the red to blue on his outfit. Make his hair longer. Take the cape off and give him the power to turn into a fireball or an iceman, whichever one he needed at the time.

"I just guessed you were going to go up there," said Barnes. "You'd like it, what with all the stuff they got."

Memphis, thought Henry, with a silent shudder. But then, Superman.

"I don't know," he said. "It's come on me too fast. I might do the wrong thing."

Barnes coughed. His tone was high, playful. "Might do the right thing, too."

Henry looked at him.

"Might," Barnes repeated, as though placing the option in the air. "I've had things come on me by accident before, and it was the best thing coulda happened. Lucky strikes. It's why I'm here today."

Henry moved closer, below the ledge.

"You were an accident?"

Barnes frowned. "Uhh. No. But I'm a pharmacist 'cause of one." He moved directly in front of Henry, resting the heels of his hands on the ledge, settling into a posture for telling stories.

"What're you talking about?" he asked. The question pleased Barnes, who smiled a thanks.

"I mean my Daddy wanted me to be a barber, like him, over in Pyland." He nodded to the front of the store, out the glass, his eyes towards Pyland.

"He said I had the fingers for it. And I probably did." Barnes raised his hands, wiggling the thumb and forefinger, showing how they'd have fit the holes. He snipped imaginary scissors.

"So that's where I was headed. But I went next door from the barbershop one day—to get me a cold drink at the drugstore. And while I was fishing a bottle outa that drinkbox, a man come rushing in—never seen him before in my life—but he's all hot and crazy looking and says to me, says—'my wife's come on with the terrible diarrhea and vomiting—she's gonna shrivel out if this keeps up— help me!' And I looked around to see who he was talking to— thought maybe George was behind me—George was the pharmacist. But then I looked and there wadn't no George—musta been out back or something. And it flew into my mind—he's talking to me!"

Henry watched Barnes face change, an amazed look flitting through his eyes.

"I know he saw that white coat I had on, the one Daddy made me wear to sweep the barber shop. And that man decided I was the pharmacist. And—" he stopped to squint at Henry and hold his chin out, "—you know what I did?"

Henry shook his head.

"I said, 'Well, come on back here, right now,'—and I started back to the pharmacy."

He stopped to give Henry a chance to be shocked. Then he laughed, raising a hand and waving it in the air at his foolishness, his bravery. "I don't know what I was thinking—or what I'da done—and here comes George from the back. But I didn't miss a step—not a lick. I said to George, said—'this man's in a hurry—his wife's got the terrible diarrhea and vomiting. No time for questions.' And all the time I'm pointing at George—like I was telling my help what to do."

Barnes eased back and smiled. "George got right to mixing things together, and me all the while looking over his shoulder and nodding, like I was saying—'that's right, that's right—you're doing fine'—so the man wouldn't notice. I walked out with him and said come back whenever he had trouble."

A moment or two passed, then Barnes crossed his arms on his chest. "I don't know what woulda happened if George hadn't come back. But what's worse is—I don't know what woulda happened if that man hadn't thought I was George. Because that's what did it."

He ran his hands along his sides, down his white coat. He slapped the counter twice, as though to show it was really there. His face darkened.

"See? You say he was just worried. He was in a hurry and made a mistake. And maybe you're right." Barnes lifted a finger. "But *maybe* he saw something in me, like the way you see a stick and know it'll make a good staff. Or see a rock and say 'that's gonna hold my door back.'"

Henry nodded—deep, sure nods that Barnes drew out of him with his eyes.

"I took that accident and made something of myself with it. Coulda just walked off—like when somebody bumps into you on the street. Don't change a thing about either one of you. But it did me. And for the good—'cause—here I am."

He slid the comic books into a bag, on top of the other things.

"No, I'll hold those," said Henry.

Barnes slid the books back out and shoved them into his hands.

That afternoon, at Martha's house, Henry sat beside Barnes on the piano bench and worked on a song he had never been able to finish. It had always given him trouble, caused so many mistakes. But he concentrated hard this time, and forced Barnes to play it again and again. He wanted to hear it all the way to the finish—the whole thing—to see how it came out.

Chapter 10

Cox sat in his brown corduroy recliner, his head resting against the pillow. Whenever he dozed off, the sound of Tollet's wheezes and snores coming from the back room nudged him awake. The old man had stumbled home from Felix's an hour before. Now he lay face down across his bed, his soggy house shoes dangling from his toes. He would sleep for hours, then jolt sideways and swing a wide-eyed gaze about the room, calling out like a baby who had been dropped to the floor.

By the time he wakes up, Cox thought, I'll have gone to pick up Henry. I'll be halfway to Martha's.

No one would be there to tell Tollet it was "all right" then. It happened often. He would come home to find the old man in a dark room, clutching his knees to hold his feet off the floor, waiting to remember.

Cox ran his tongue beneath his top lip and row of teeth. He pinched his eyelids shut, squeezing them tight.

He would sneak out when it was time to go, on hands and knees if he had to.

The phone jangled behind him, and he started from his seat, cussing, already mad at the caller. As he swiped the receiver off the hook, he heard the faint sounds of Tollet rustling himself upright.

"What?" Cox grumbled.

For a moment, there was no sound at the other end. Then came a loud, collecting breath.

"It'd serve you right if I was Mr. Porter," said Martha. "It'd serve you right."

Cox blinked, set his jaw.

"*Well?*" Martha raised her voice. "*Are you going to talk?*"

He waited a moment more.

"You called me. And I said 'What?' So—What?"

Once again she gathered a breath. "*Henry's going to stay here tonight. There's no need for you to come over. I'll take him to school with me tomorrow.*"

She raised her voice higher and higher as she spoke, as if trying to race to the top of a scale before he did. Cox gnawed the inside of his cheek with gentle, pulsing bites. His gaze shifted to stare down the dark hall. Tollet was moving about on the covers, wading back into life gently, soothed by hearing Cox's voice.

He lowered his tone and held himself still.

"All right," he nearly whispered.

"*What?*"

Cox shook his head. It was hard to stay quiet when he was mad. "You heard me."

Her silence was so full he could hear the sounds of her kitchen—a cabinet slamming—someone cracking an ice tray—one of the girls asking Henry if he "wanted some too."

"*In fact,*" said Martha, tentative, as if she were feeding a lion, "*I may keep him here for a few weeks. He's going to be in a geography bee. He can practice better here.*"

Cox nodded. "Fine."

"'Zat you?" Tollet squeaked, his voice all pipes and whistles. Cox held his breath.

"Son—'zat you?"

Cox smiled. At the other end, Martha was fumbling with the receiver, confused. She might be fingering a straw in her hand, wondering how much his back could bear.

"*Bring him some clothes,*" she said in a careful voice. "*To school. On your way to work.*"

"I will," he whispered.

The afternoon air was close and heavy inside the house. The windows popped in their casements. Cox heard Tollet gasp.

Now, he thought, listening. There. Tension. Nerves. A soaking, hazy fear that the house had somehow been sewed up while he slept—sealed away—with some horrible thing sliding around the musty, sweltering insides—from room to room to room. That was the old man's fear, or so he said whenever he was still too drunk and frightened to raise his guard: "I coulda sworn somebody was in here—Who locked the doors on me?—Did it on purpose!"

Cox listened at the rustlings from the back room, plucking at the pillows, feet scraping the floor. He let out small groans.

"Who's out there?"

"*Henry,*" said Martha, her voice muffled by a hand over the receiver, "*you and Betsy go out onto the back porch. Go on. This is private.*"

Cox smiled on—one ear to Martha, one to Tollet.

"*All right,*" she said. The screen door slammed in the background. "*What's the matter with you? Are you trying to pull something? 'Cause Clark told me to let you know that—*"

"Be quiet," mumbled Cox. He shoved his face close, so that his lips felt the holes of the mouthpiece. "Told you last week he's yours, to send or to keep. Memphis—Wolfy—Cellarsville—Korea. Aaaaalll yours."

Martha moved about at the other end. Probably pushing her hair behind an ear, he thought.

"*Well, that's exactly what's going to happen,*" she said. "*He told me yesterday why he hadn't wanted to go all this time. It's because he was afraid of sleeping up there. But some families from town hire a shuttle to take their children to school in Memphis, so he can ride up there and come back every night if he wants. So—*"

"Good," whispered Cox.

She stopped, then continued. "*So. Don't think you'll have to pay a dime for it. I'm putting up the whole cost.*"

"Good," he said.

"Cox!" Tollet screamed. The sound could have ripped the old man's throat. "Cox! Son! Help me!"

He turned towards the hall, staring at the place where the scream came from. He took a few heavy steps, ones that made the floor creak. Then he stopped again, waiting until he felt Tollet's next scream. It was just hanging in the back of his old throat, ready to rip the air.

See? Cox thought, biting his cheek harder. When you lock somebody in a car—go in the beer joint and don't even motherfuckin' wake him up first—don't even tell him what *street* he's on, and—"

"What's the matter with you?" asked Martha. *"What's that noise— what—"*

Cox blinked at her, then dropped the phone to hold it against his thigh.

"Hush," he yelled down the hall. He stuck the point of his tongue into his raw cheek, massaging it with small, circular strokes. "Hush. It's me."

The house held still as the old man clutched at the words.

"Cox? Cox?"

"Hush. I'm on the phone." He lifted the receiver to his ear.

"Hello? Hello?" she was asking.

"Be quiet. I had to calm Daddy down." He leaned against the wall, suddenly tired. "He just woke up from a drunk."

All at once he heard Martha make a disgusted noise, followed by the sound of the back door slamming shut. The distant sounds of the children ceased altogether.

"That's the real reason I called. Right there. You know what that fool did, don't you?"

"Who?" asked Cox.

"Tollet! Don't play with me!" She lowered her voice. *"He told Henry that he was an accident. Told him you got me pregnant! Don't tell me you didn't know that."*

Cox shifted his gaze about the room, from one wall to the other: TV, sofa, sunburst clock.

"I didn't know that."

"Where—are you?" Tollet asked, weakly. From the hall came the sound of rising, stumbling and falling back onto bed springs.

"Well he did," snapped Martha. *"He did it in one of his twice-a-day sots. It practically ruined Henry. You're both set on ruining him. But I won't stand for it. I don't expect you—"*

"What do you want me to do about it?" The edge in her voice sparked one in his own. He rose from the wall and stood square-footed. "He sneaks in there and listens to all that drunk-talk while I'm gone. I can't stop—"

"Yes, you can. Yes, you can—"

Cox nearly bit the phone.

"How? He lives here! I can't chain him down! He even owns the goddamn place!" He started to shout the rest, but caught himself. He narrowed his gaze, drew in a gust of air through his nostrils. He worked to keep his voice cold.

"You're so smart, why don't you keep Henry with you all the time? You're threatening for custody. Go ahead and take it. Take it!"

There, he thought. She didn't expect that. She was struggling for an answer, probably grazing her hand along the curve of her jaw.

Once more, he heard Tollet try to rise, fail, sink back onto the bed.

"Because," said Martha. *"Because he doesn't want that. Not right now, at least. Don't think I didn't ask him. But I tell you one thing—if he has to live there with Tollet—I'll sue for custody no matter what he wants. It's not good for him—"*

"And you got it all figured out what's good for him, don't you?" said Cox, shoving the words at her. "You got it all figured out."

She collected herself for a moment. Then he took her quiet, thoughtful response, like he was being held and hit.

"If you don't get Henry away from Tollet, I'll sue you before God gets the news."

Cox lifted his chin. "Go to hell."

She shifted from side to side. Her voice came back broken and low, not what he had expected.

"Listen to me. Listen. What if—what if the next time he gets drunk—and tells him. . . ." She took a faltering breath and started over. *"What if the next thing he tells is—what we thought about doing?"*

Cox flushed. His tongue caught against his palate.

In the balls of his fingers, he could feel the money—three, one hundred dollar bills—crisp, ironed, new—money Tollet had given him. Martha had sat in the passenger's seat of his Chevrolet. They had stared at the paper, more blue than green under the mercury lamplight. For some reason—and why?—they had not driven to Memphis, to an address a nurse had given them on the sly. Instead, they had driven home. They had gotten married. They had had a—

"That isn't true," he said, his head shuddering.

"Oh, Cox—"

"He's here, isn't he? He's here."

"Cox. Cox."

He heard her move back from the phone, as if to distance herself, the way she would if they had been talking face to face.

"Lie if you want. But that'll be the next thing Tollet tells. And then it'll get you no matter where you try to look!"

A moment passed when Cox guessed she was looking out the window at Henry, trying to see if he had heard any part of what she had said. When she came back, she had control.

"And that boy can't take it. Now that's the truth, Cox. He'll shut down. He'll take that thought and fold up with it for years and years—"

Cox remembered Henry in the alfalfa field—standing—staring as he thought—and thought. He remembered how he had wanted him to move, and how he had been afraid that he would never move again.

"Put him in a nursing home," she said, *"where they can take care of him. It's only a matter of time before he hurts himself. My mother—"*

Cox sniffed, pinched his fingers at the top of his nose. "You hate your mother."

He wiped his wet upper lip against the cuff of his sleeve.

"I do not! I do not hate my mother! How dare you say that? That I hate my mother!"

He shrugged. "Besides. This is *my* farm. I've saved it all by myself. But *he's* got the deed. And he's always throwing it around that he can leave it to Felix to build a bar on if he wants to." He sniffed again. "This is *my* farm."

"Commit him then."

Cox's head bobbed back.

"If he's declared incompetent, he can't change his will on you. Clark told me that when we were dealing with Mama. He just wanted me to know the law."

Cox passed his gaze about the floor. Martha jumped into the silence.

"There's nobody more incompetent than Tollet. Nobody. He's a drunk and he's dangerous. He could hurt himself. Clark can do it." She sounded almost helpful.

"Anyway, you won't have that threat hanging over your head anymore. You said yourself, you've done all the work to save that place. It's your farm. It's only fair."

Cox nodded. He moved a step to the side, so that he could see out the kitchen window: the fence he had built, the cows he had bought, the road he had cut through weeds, with nothing but a grass blade. All by himself.

"Fa—la—sol—sol—la. . . . La—mi—fa—sol. . . ."

The voice, wet with new liquor, strained to sing the harp. And beneath it, like another instrument, keeping time—glass knocking against the bedpost.

"Well. Maybe," Cox said. It was as quiet as he could manage.

He hung up the phone, swallowed hard, and walked towards the room where his father lay.

Tollet could pass through all the stages quickly: dead sleep, wide awake, terror, calm, back to thirst. Now it was full cycle. Cox had shouted his singing to a stop, to which threat Tollet had merely fluttered his eyelids. He was out again by the time Cox reached the bed.

After he dropped the old man's house shoes to the floor—onto the clumps of clay mud he had trailed in—Cox swung his legs back onto the sagging four-poster. He pulled the bottle from where it was wedged upright between the mattress and headboard, then started out the door. Before he shut the light off, he stopped and thought for a moment. Turning, he walked over to the bedside table and placed the bottle beneath the fringed shade of a tarnished copper lamp. In a glass ashtray lay the moist, brown body of a forgotten banana, its top mashed off by Tollet's toothless gums. With a pass of his hand, Cox shooed away a constellation of gnats. He went back to the den and dropped into his recliner.

The song rang in his head with an aggravating clearness. He wondered if Tollet did it on purpose, pretending to be too drunk to know he was singing. That was the trouble with drunks. They could get away with murder, because you never knew how much they were responsible for.

"Fa—sol—la—Fa—sol—"

Lies, Tollet-style. Not the kind Henry told, which were false from start to finish. Tollet's kind might have a little truth in them, but they pulled it all askew, deformed it until you couldn't recognize what was real anymore. Tollet liquored the truth like dye dropped into rainwater.

He swiveled around in his chair and pulled the shades up until he could see the two steers he had let out into the feed lot. Their pink eye had healed up. But though they were no longer in the dark stall, they still stood together in one corner, their heads at an odd tilt, like they'd gotten in the habit of being blind. Like they were listening to something far off, far away.

If there was really a place that sung sacred harp in Camille, thought Cox, as he eyed the breadth of one steer's stomach, somebody besides Tollet would remember it. But though he thought to ask people from time to time, at the barbershop, or when anyone old came into the tractor store, nobody could recall such a thing. There was a church there at one time, and people knew of harp singing in the area, long ago—but not harp singing at Camille. True, Cox had never asked anybody that lived back in the crevice that used to be Camille. That they still lived in that butt crack showed them to be too crazy to fool with. It had never even been a town; not really. It was just a place people referred to, to get their bearings from. People were headed ten miles past Camille, or three miles to the east, but never, ever, to Camille itself.

Cox moved his gaze from the feed lot to the alfalfa field. It was a deepening green, headed towards violet blooms. Beyond the field stood the hills in the far back. In the late afternoon light, they were flat and distant.

Every once in a great while, when Cox had business behind those hills, he saw people coming out onto the highway from a sunken road that led to Camille. They had a smoked-look to them—short, dirty, yellow—like cigarette butts with arms and legs. They looked worse than Shreva. Probably lived in houses worse than hers. Foggy people that nobody knew. Cowards. The very idea of them made Cox's skin itch.

"Where was it then? The singing?" he would ask Tollet from time to time. "Tell me. Take me there and show me and I'll believe you."

He would get out of his chair, pulling the keys from his pocket.

"Come on! Let's get in the truck right now and you take me there. Why not?"

But Tollet would only sulk and look away. He'd mention Felix.

It was just another thing his pickled brain had invented, and Cox had been fool enough to believe. How many times had he discovered that what he thought was true hadn't happened? At least not all of it. That was what irked him. Vivid memories of a lie. One in particular, one he couldn't forget, made his chest hurt:

Men in white shirts, the sleeves rolled up to the elbow—sunburned necks and white chests—sunburned forearms meeting white upper arms—the hair on their heads rose-oiled, slicked back.

Fa—sol—fa—sol—la—mi. Tenor voices.

The room was brown wood, black pews. The smell of medicine in glass bottles.

Somebody spilled a jug. A big red-faced woman, with a body like a sack of feed, rushed to the back—contained the liquid with a blue dishrag. A young girl with a coarse face—harsh skin—stood over the woman on the floor. The girl held a restless baby against her glistening neck—her eyes jumping, embarrassed. A shuffle of paper, and one man with a white line on his finger—from where a wedding band used to be?—held out sheet-music to sing from. Their faces hidden behind paper—cream-colored pulpwood—tenor voices, so high they might have sat on a shelf, out of the reach of children.

Fa—sol—la—sol—mi.

And somebody—to and from—his mother? had said, explained "the notes are shapes."

And Cox had liked it. He had thought all his life of shapes and notes and harps as one thought, the same breath, coils of a spring that brought the next one out with it. It had to harp, then shape, then note. Fa—so—la—mi.

His breath suddenly jerked in his lungs as though he had been frightened from sleep.

Lies from a bottle.

He yanked himself out of the recliner and stomped over to the kitchen counter. Swiping the keys into his palm, he turned and went out the front door and headed for his truck. In mid-stride, he remembered he didn't need to go get Henry. Henry didn't want to come home.

Cox checked his pace, thought of Lois's breasts for a moment, then stuffed the keys back into his pocket and veered from the truck. He walked around the house to the backyard, picking up speed as he continued through the field.

By the time he got into the woods, he had half of it planned. He had to make sure the house was stocked with the kind of liquor Tollet always squandered his share of the farm money on. Cox himself drank beer, since Tollet wouldn't. That way, he didn't have to worry about whether the old man had drunk straight from the bottle, as he was prone to do.

To have Tollet put away, he would have to start buying fine whiskey—Kentucky bourbon. Any kind of cheese worked on a mousetrap. And anybody—lawyer, social worker, judge—whoever it was that committed people—would have to see there was a problem.

Cloverdale Nursing Home. It was all right, he had heard. They didn't steal everything. They had a big TV and decent food. Tollet would have to dry out, but it was high time.

Still, he would need more than whiskey.

He turned along a line of sumacs to take a shortcut to Shreva's trailer. A buzz-saw droned out from somewhere back in the hills, somebody still too poor to cook with electricity. Cox sneered. Whoever it was sawing, he would bet the wood they burned would be better than the wood their house was made out of. Of course, some of them lived in smashed tin boxes, like Shreva's. He didn't know which was worse.

He half-skipped, half-loped down a little hill, careful of the mud underneath the leaves. The route he had picked took him up to the

back of the trailer, beside the rows of tacked-together chicken coops.
As he passed, hens stuck their heads out of the squared-off houses.
They pecked along the ground and fluttered against the sides of the
cages. The smell of stale, shitty water lay beneath the rankness of
birds being kept too close together. After he saw a drowned chick
floating in a dishpan, the fluff plastered against its bluing skin, Cox
glued his gaze to the ground.

Just as he lifted his hand to knock on the back door, he heard
Shreva talking to some boy at the front, something he "should've
done, but didn't do." The voices were mumbled and hard to make
out, but Shreva's had been a nuisance too long for him not to recognize it at once. Cox knocked and called at the same time.

"Hey, Shreva! You want me to come 'round?"

"Shiiiit!" she screamed, the shout curling out of her mouth in a
sing-song. It flipped backwards over the trailer to Cox. He had scared
her. Good.

His gaze fixed on the doorknob as Shreva sent whoever it was
away, one of her boys, probably. The footsteps faded beneath the
sounds of cap pistols blasting from one end of the trailer. Cox noticed
three of them up on the hill, playing around the Buick with cellophane windows.

"Hang on!" she called, slamming the front door. "Don't move.
I'm comin'."

The back door swept open and busted Cox in the shoulder. He
stumbled back, rubbing the socket.

"Damn! What's the matter with you?"

"Stand out from the door," she snapped. She wore blue jeans and
a black and white tank top. "What do you 'spect? Standin' up on the
door thataway?"

Cox lifted his arm and rolled his shoulder in a circle. He gave
her a mean stare, but was careful not to cuss her. He thought a
moment, then started with his biggest carrot.

"How'd you like to make a hundred dollars?"

Shreva pulled back and leaned against the door frame, smirking.

"I thought you'd done *fired* me! I thought I was a *fired* woman.
You stood right out there in that yard and—"

"Never mind that," said Cox. "Now. I need a witness. I need somebody to say they've seen Daddy out of his head—acting dangerous."

Shreva's smile broadened. One of her bare feet started scratching the top of the other. The nails were painted an orange-red. "I toldja he was crazy," she said.

"Shut up. All you gotta do is remember what I tell you, then tell it to whoever it is that gets people put in nursing homes."

She shook her head. "Not me. Not me for a hunnerd dollars."

Cox sighed and put his hands on his hips. "You for a hundred fifty dollars, then."

She kept her head shaking. "Me for seventy-five up front and seventy-five after the job's done." Her flat gaze wandered back to Cox. He took a breath.

"All right. It's a deal."

Shreva didn't nod. She looked bored, as though whatever was worrying her had been fixed. She slapped at a fly buzzing around her head. "Who's gonna believe me?"

Cox already had an answer for that. "You're the only one he ever sees, besides Felix. And Felix is a drunk, too. You're a lot of things, but I hadn't seen you that way."

"You don't know nothin' 'bout me," Shreva said, quieter. The skin beneath her eye twitched. She held out her hand.

Cox sighed, holding up his. She was ridiculous.

"You think I got it now? Hell, woman. What makes you so goddamn mean?"

Shreva lifted her eyebrows, then glowered her contempt from beneath them.

"What makes anybody?" she answered, a low mock. "What makes you?" Her hand slid back to her side. Cox lowered his own. When she spoke again, her voice regained its wire.

"Now. You have that money when I come by with the eggs tomorrow—which you'll start buyin' again—or else, I don't open my mouth. Else, your Daddy walks on water and 'suffers the l'il chillren.'"

"That'll change by tomorrow," nodded Cox. He lifted his own eyebrows. "But it *better,* or you'll be looking for some place to hide what little I hadn't torn up or burned down, one."

He watched the smile slide from her lips. As he walked through the woods, the image of her falling face brought a satisfied grin to his own.

La. Te. Do.

Chapter 11

Before she took the girls outside, Martha gave Henry her tape recorder. She sat it on the living room floor and plugged the hand-held microphone into the side.

"You can read in a question, pause it, then read in an answer. After you're done, rewind the tape. Then quiz yourself by playing the question and stopping it—using this little switch on the microphone, see? You don't have even have to use the stop button on the machine. After you've made your guess, switch the button on again to see if you're right."

It was a good idea. He had studied all week, before and after school. But by the weekend, everybody was sick of quizzing him. Besides, he would need some way to question himself at home, since he couldn't ask Cox or Tollet.

He sat on the floor next to the recorder and leaned against the low-backed sofa. On top of a stack of *World Books* lay his geography text opened to a map of Alabama. He figured the geography bee people might try to trip them up with questions about their back door—"Alabama," "Tennessee," "Louisiana"—ones they'd neglect to study in favor of "Egypt" and "Spain."

He held the little microphone close to his mouth, flicked the switch with his thumb, and spoke.

"What is the capital of Alabama?" He paused for a second then read in "Montgomery."

"What is the state flower of Alabama?" Again he paused. "The Camellia."

He switched the button on the microphone off and watched the tape stop. Then he pushed the rewind button on the machine and saw it spin itself backwards. He flicked it on again.

"*What is the capital of Alabama?*" a voice came back.

His mouth dropped open. He blinked.

That wasn't his voice. It didn't pop and squeak like that. It didn't see-saw from low to high.

"*Montgomery,*" the thing said, breaking into a shrill squawk at the middle.

Henry leaned closer, looking at the tape to see if it was really moving. The machine made a soft, airy sound, like somebody breathing past his teeth.

"*What is the state flower of Alabama?*"

He fumbled with the switch to cut it off, so he wouldn't have to hear "Camellia" come out.

He cocked his head to the side, staring vacantly into the room. "Camellia," he said. "Alabama."

See? I don't sound that way.

He flicked the On button with his thumb. "*Camellia,*" the tape squeaked back.

There was something wrong with the machine. There was something wrong with the tape. The girls must've used it so much that their voices were stamped inside somehow. After two, hard, coughs that hurt his throat, he swallowed. He practiced a few times, then tried the recorder again.

"What is the state tree of Alabama?" he said, pushing his tongue to the floor of his mouth as he groaned the words from his chest. He paused, then shoved out "Loblolly pine."

But when he played the questions back, it sounded like the same voice, only smothered with a pillow.

He was about to call out for Martha when he heard her come inside. He listened to the whine of the kitchen cabinet doors as she rummaged about, pots and cookie sheets clanking against each other. At length, she slammed the doors shut and peeked around the corner.

"Is it working all right?" She held three mason jars, one in each hand and the third trapped against her stomach by her forearm.

"There's something the matter with it," he said, holding the microphone out. Lying the jars on the sofa cushion, she squatted down next to him.

"What?" she asked, taking the microphone from his hand. "It won't record?"

"No. Listen. Listen to how I sound." He rewound the tape and cut it on at the machine. His gaze fixed on her face, waiting to see how the sound registered.

"It's working," she said, nodding in an annoyed way. She cut the machine off.

"*I* don't sound like that," answered Henry, annoyed back.

Martha looked down her nose at him as though she'd noticed something for the first time. She bit her lower lip and smiled.

"It's working fine, Henry." She patted him on the knee, which aggravated him all the more. "That's the way you speak. You just don't realize it."

Henry scooted around a bit, shifting his weight to his hip. His tail was going to sleep.

"Unh-uh. I know how I sound. It's too high to be me. It catches in the middle and—"

"That's because it's changing," said Martha, nodding one step ahead of him. "Don't tell me you hadn't noticed it?"

Henry shut his mouth with a clack of teeth.

"Well, *I* have," said Martha. "It happens whenever boys go through puberty. You know what 'puberty' means, don't you?"

Henry's gaze broke loose from her face. It wandered about the walls and floors, around to the bookcase that held the *S.* He nodded absently.

"I mean *really* know? Not Cox's way. Have you ever read anything on it? Because there's an article in the encyclo—"

"I know," answered Henry. A hot, flushed shame burned in his face. "I know."

Martha's hand moved off his knee back into her own lap. She sighed and turned the recorder on. A whisper of air preceded his voice.

"Loblolly pine."

The sound scraped across his ears. He caught a glimpse of a smile in Martha's face. She held the microphone out to him.

"It settles down eventually—your voice, I mean. It goes through changes, like now, and then it sticks on the voice you're going to have for the rest of your life." Her hand went onto his leg again, a firm grasp on the globe of his knee. "Don't be worried about this. If you—" She stopped, squeezing his knee to make him look up.

"Have you—do you—"

He scooted away, hunched over his book. He coughed to clear his voice.

"I know. I'm not an idiot. It's not broken then, so let me get back to—"

"There's nothing to be ashamed about," she soothed.

When he refused to give her the look she wanted, he felt her tighten. She whispered some oath that sounded like his father's name.

"You learned about this the wrong way, you know. I'm doing all I can to help you, but—I mean, there's a *sensible* way to learn about things."

"Who said I was ashamed? I'm not ashamed." He said it all into the book, his eyes barely askance. "I gotta study."

Martha sighed, then pulled herself up.

"I can't say anything right to you. If *Cox* said the very same thing, you'd—"

But she didn't finish for some reason, and Henry wouldn't look up to see why. After a moment, she collected her jars. He felt her staring into the top of his head, trying to decide what to do. She settled on telling him how he could always talk to her. Intelligent people should be able to discuss things, she said. Henry grudged her a nod.

When he finally heard the kitchen door slam shut, he loosened his shoulders and breathed a sigh. His legs had cramped at the hip, so he lay back and spread out on the floor. For a time, his gaze wandered about the ceiling.

A low voice. A man's voice.

His hand went to his face, feeling for anything new: the smallest nubbins of hair, the barest tickle of whisker. Nothing. Yet. His eyes fixed onto a seam in the ceiling, a join of sheet rock. He eased his hand down his pants, feeling about his groin for thickened strands, coarsening wire. The amount was about the same, but he knew the hair was turning a darker shade of brown, streaked with red. He could see it best when he was in the shower, drenched.

All at once, he sat up, scrambled onto all fours and crawled to the bookcase. Pulling out the S, he flipped to the right page. He read the article again.

A different kind of joy swept through him this time. It wasn't the relieved, freed-from-prison feeling when he'd first read it at the drugstore. It was a peaceful satisfaction. He smiled.

If you knew things, like he knew now, there was no need to be scared, the way he had been. If you knew things, you didn't have to wonder if you were bleeding from a vagina or not. He shook his head at himself, then closed the book and rubbed his hand over the creamy, green and white surface.

Martha was right. If you knew things—enough things—all you could get—then there was no stopping you. On top of that, nobody ever wondered what the use of smart people was. They didn't have to prove themselves to anybody. If you were smart, the rest had to prove something to *you*.

"Times have changed," he thought. He was struck with having thought it before, on a different occasion, in a different place. It bothered him for a moment, that he couldn't remember, but his mind moved on, enticed by the news.

He stared at the spines of the set, each volume bearing a letter, each letter surrounding a volume of words. And each word, if you knew what it meant, was yours to own and use to win geography bees—write comic books—or just to keep from scaring the shit out of yourself.

He scrambled back to the sofa and sat himself in front of the recorder again. He felt like opening every book in the place.

"What are the industries of the state of Alabama?" he asked the recorder.

He was as proud of his voice as he was that he knew, without looking, to answer "farming, crunched stone, textiles, and timber."

Henry stacked his clean clothes in a gray Samsonite suitcase, the one Big Mama had given Martha for a wedding present. When he had moved out to live with Cox, Martha had passed it down to him. Rolls of underwear and socks were caught inside the elastic netting of the top cover. Ten days worth of freshly laundered clothes lay on the bottom. Before he hauled it off the bed, he closed the latches and scrambled the numbers on the combination lock.

"Whatever you do," said Martha, her voice calling to him as he stumbled the heavy case down the hall, "don't let them bother you. Concentrate on what you're doing."

She stood at the front door, wide-eyed. One hand rested on the knob as though she were about to release him into a blizzard. The other hand held the crumpled top of an old grocery bag.

"Remember, you've got a lot on your mind right now—with the geography bee on Wednesday. So just concentrate."

The suitcase banged against his shin and knee until he got to the door. He set it down for a breath.

"And what'd I tell you about Tollet?"

Henry coughed, then picked up his suitcase. "Leave him alone when he's drunk."

She shook her head briskly, as though he had gotten it wrong, yet again. "To leave him alone *period*. Understand? He's getting crazy. If you mess with him, and let him tell you a bunch of trash, then you won't be able—"

"All right. Let me out. He's waiting."

She wouldn't move from the door. Her eyes jittered about. "Promise me you won't."

Henry sighed. He had to set the suitcase down to get another purchase on the handle. He hefted it again. "I promise. Now let me out."

Martha gave him a sideways hug, then handed him the grocery bag she held. He had thought it was food until he felt the weight.

"I left one tape inside the recorder," she said as she eased the door open. "—the one on Europe. And I put labels on all the others."

The truck waited at the curb. Cox might have been a toy driver snapped into his seat. Both hands lay on the wheel. He faced forward, staring out the windshield. When he noticed Henry coming, he slid off the seat and met him at the back.

Henry didn't look at his face, but he felt the way Cox took the suitcase from his hand—not a jerk or snatch, but not an easy glide either. Instead, the handle dropped into Cox's hand, with a little jolt, as if he'd caught it in mid-air, like "nothing that's touching you is gonna be touching me at the same time." Henry watched him hoist the case into the truck bed as easily as if it were a sack of dog food. They climbed into the cab and pulled away.

He hugged the grocery bag against his lap as they sped towards Wolfy. They never spoke much, he and Cox. But then they had never been away from each other for so long, either; not since he'd moved back home. A whole week away. He decided he must be growing up because he would have been much more homesick before. In fact, he had been a little homesick. Like always, Martha had made him confess it. Like always, he couldn't say why.

"What is it you like about it out there? What? I can't understand it. It's beyond me."

Henry could only stare at her, amazed as much as she was.

"Well, you won't always feel that way," she said. "After you get to Memphis, then you'll see. You'll forget all about it."

When they slowed at the green dumpster, and got onto the chert surface, he realized Cox wasn't going to talk about what had happened the week before, in the yard. The road curved around a newly turned field that sloped along a gentle hill rise. In the distance, Henry saw a dull green tractor heading along the slope, its driver leaning uphill in a crooked stance to throw his weight in favor of the balance. His stomach caught at the sight, at the thought of the tractor tipping, rolling, crushing. He glanced at Cox's sunken face, then brought his gaze to his lap. He sighed.

It was easier to think of geography questions than to worry about Cox. He had gained a command of the United States and Canada. He knew Europe, inside and out. In fact, he probably knew Spain,

South America, and Sweden better than *The World Book* people, thanks to the S. He was shaky on the Far East. He was better at Australia than Africa.

The provinces of Canada are British Columbia, Alberta, Saskatchewan, Manitoba, Ontario, Quebec, New Foundland, Nova Scotia, New Brunswick, Prince Edward Island, Yukon and Northwest Territories. His memory device was *BASMOQ + 3 Ns + PEI*—"pie" spelled wrong. For some reason, the other two were no problem: "Yukon and Northwest Territories" went at the end as naturally as "Amen" finished a hymn.

He would win the bee at school, he was sure. Then he would go on to the regional competition in Tupelo, and he would win that too. Although his own school wasn't very good, if he did well on some exams, and if he won the competition, Martha said the school in Memphis would let him in. And he wouldn't have to sleep there after all. He could go take that comic book class every day and come home every night to the farm.

He shoved his mind past the thought of Lois, who sprang into his head for a minute, calf-high boots and all. She ambushed him every once in a while—she and one of the beach girls—but he had better control of his mind now. And when he had something big on his mind, thoughts of the women weren't as powerful. Besides, when he got to Memphis, he would find him somebody that Cox hadn't messed with. And with his voice changing, soon he would know better how to handle himself. He would find a book on the subject when he got to Memphis.

The crackle of tires on gravel lifted his attention from his lap. They were already at the turnoff to their house. Cox slowed the truck, moving onto the sandy shoulder.

"Something in there you wanta pitch?" Cox asked. It was the first thing he had said, so his voice was strung with saliva. His gaze moved from Henry to the grocery bag.

"Oh. No. Not this time." His fingers moved tighter around the top, so wrinkled it was softer than cloth. "It's a tape recorder."

Cox knitted his brow. "A what?"

Henry nodded and shifted the bag to his far side, ashamed all of a sudden.

"She gave me a tape recorder to study with, so I can ask myself questions and give myself answers. It's a way to learn."

Cox's expression moved back, suspicious. "Asking questions to yourself and answering yourself, both?"

Well, not like *that*, Henry thought. He nodded anyway.

"Sounds like her, come to think of it," said Cox.

Henry turned his face away. He listened to his father breathe a heavy sigh and swivel about to check for cars. He eased the truck back onto the road once more.

▬▬▬▬

The Junior High School assembly squirmed and coughed its way through the first thirty minutes of the geography bee. Beyond the dazzle of stage footlights, Henry could distinguish only the outlines of bobbing heads. Three teachers sat on stage, behind a table positioned to one side. They had each prepared questions, and doled them to the six remaining students, who stood against the gold, crushed-velvet curtain.

For the occasion, Henry had dressed in his blue cowboy shirt, blue bell-bottoms, and brown Wallabies. He had exchanged the white gauze that had been taped to his brow in favor of flesh-colored Band-Aids—smaller and less noticeable. Three girls stood to his right: a short, redhead in a light blue dress and scuffed, red patent-leather shoes; Frances Bass, with black-rimmed glasses, her blonde hair staked in a pile on top of her head by a plastic rose; and a tall pretty girl—tan knees, thin arms, and thick brown hair that she would push behind her ear from time to time. They were all in another class, and, up until now, he had known only Frances's name, since she rode his bus. Against the other half of the curtain stood Antonio Armstrong, Dickie Mott, and Delores Davis, all from his homeroom. Antonio was running his hand along the inside of his belt, and swallowing with big, froggish gulps.

Too nervous to win, Henry thought.

Dickie, a fat boy in a turtleneck, wasn't nervous, but he was more the math-type, all and all. When the questions moved out of America, Dickie would miss.

Delores was about to screw up on the question just put to her by Mrs. Goza, the geography teacher. The girl's pock-marked face twisted in confusion.

"The Hawaiian Islands?" guessed Delores, after taking more time than she should have been allowed, according to Henry's watch.

Mrs. Goza shook her jowly face, disappointed. Her two hundred pounds compelled her to sit back from the table, but her short arms forced her to lean in for the slips of paper bearing the questions.

"That is incorrect," piped Mrs. Goza, winded from the effort to put the slip back.

As Antonio answered "West Indies," Henry's gaze escorted Delores to the row of losers' chairs. It was his turn again.

"Henry," said Mr. Jewell, the American history teacher, but more especially, the battle of Vicksburg teacher. Its study took up practically all of his class time, at the expense of the other 199 years and ten months.

"In what Mississippi city was the most significant battle in the War between the States—the Civil War, that is—fought?" The man stared over his bifocals at Henry.

Mrs. Goza turned to look, visibly confused as to what this had to do with geography. But since it was an easy answer, Henry blurted out "Vicksburg" before the man could be challenged. Mr. Jewel smiled at Henry. Henry smiled and looked at Dickie Mott. Dickie Mott didn't smile.

"Dickie, what is the capital of Buh-livia?" asked the girl's basketball coach, Miss Cash, a short, stocky woman with close-set eyes. She was always sweating, even outside in January. She had come unprepared, and had to be fed questions by Mrs. Goza. The old woman frowned at every transmission of paper, as though she were being forced to give bread in time of famine.

The capital of Bolivia. Henry whispered "La Paz"—Peace—to himself. But then he squelched the answer out of his mind, just in case there was something to ESP.

Dallas, he thought, loud and hard—say "Dallas."

Dickie coughed to buy time, then spoke. "Repeat the question, please."

Though it was allowed, Mrs. Goza didn't like repeating. It meant he was probably going to miss, and she took offense at any of her students missing. Henry had heard her complain to Martha that no other teacher's skills were subjected to such scrutiny. She wanted to know if Martha had thought up the idea of the bee—something she had never heard of outside spelling classes—just to evaluate her publicly.

". . . Mr. Porter and the whole school board's gonna sit out there thinking 'How come they don't know where Lake Pontchartrain is?'—and hold me responsible. . . ."

Nothing Martha said could make her feel better.

"Bolivia City?" answered Dickie. Mrs. Goza sighed frustration and shook her head. Dickie waddled off as the pretty girl, Rosemary, answered "La Paz." He smiled. That she would know that.

After a round without error, the redhead with the red shoes missed a question on the Rio Grande. Antonio had to sit down after he stumbled out the right answer to what mountain range separated Vermont from Canada, but took it back in favor of the wrong one. And Rosemary struggled with which city in Europe was known for its gondoliers. A twinge of grief cut through Henry's chest when she answered "Florence." She crossed in front of him, her eyes staring a few feet ahead of her saddle shoes. With a slender hand, she flicked a rope of hair behind her shoulder, the saddest thing Henry had ever seen.

But what was done was done. It was down to him and Frances, and Frances held no mystery. In fact, she had smiled when responding "Venice"—the answer that had escaped Rosemary. It was a mean smirk that crinkled her mouth into a tight, old lady smile. He would avenge the wrong. Besides, the rose on her head was stupid.

Before Mr. Jewel could ask another question, Mrs. Goza put a hand on his forearm. He leaned toward her for a whispered conference, then flipped his legal pad over with a slap. After sulking for a moment, he asked Henry what body of water separated England from France.

"The English Channel," Henry shot back. He snatched his chin up and threw in for good measure, "the narrowest part is a twenty-one-mile stretch between Dover and Calais."

Mrs. Goza was in the middle of handing Miss Cash another question. She stopped cold. The flicker of a vindicated grin passed over her lips, and she glanced into the audience for a credit-taking moment. All at once, Henry was flush with generosity. His heart was full and wide enough for everybody.

"Frances, where—is—the—lovely—Blue—Danoob—River?" Miss Cash stammered. Frances stared a hole through Henry, the rose aimed at him like a periscope.

"It runs from Germany all the way to the Soviet Union and empties into the Black Sea."

Miss Cash shot a look at Mrs. Goza, who nodded that it was right, despite the simple answer on the slip of paper. Miss Cash stuck the paper into the used box and mopped her glistening brow.

"What is the land around the tip of South America called?" asked Mrs. Goza.

Henry scanned the shadowed crowd, squinting to see it over the footlights. Everyone had settled into a watchful quiet; not so much mumbling, coughing, and sneezing now. There was a casual, pin-eyed curiosity about the room—a desire to see which it would be—this one or that. He knew that kind of interest himself. It was the kind he experienced whenever Cox picked which calves he wanted to auction, which he wanted to keep, and which he would take to the slaughterhouse. It was the slaughterhouse that could make Henry stop petting the cat, or swinging on the gate, or throwing rocks into the water tank—look up—see—which ones were marked to go.

"Tierra Del Fuego," he answered, his neck hair bristling. He was right.

"Give the ancient name of modern Istanbul."

"Constantinople," Frances said.

A pause for breath, the pistols had to be checked, the barrels oiled and reloaded.

"Henry, what is the name of the highest mountain in Japan?"

"Mt. Fuji."

"The largest lake in Africa, Frances?"

"Lake Victoria."

He could hear the barn gate screeching open—the rattle of the truck's muffler—a scurry of hooves on the oak-planked chute. That one and that one and that one. . . .

"Where would you find the koala bear?"

"Australia," he said.

"What is the state flower of Alabama?"

A long lull, the air filling with sand and smoke. Henry's mouth watered. His buttocks tightened. The muscles in his forearms flinched. He stared into the dark face of the one floodlight that had burned out—banged with the explosion of a rifle's shot.

"Repeat the question, please?" asked Frances. He didn't have to look. Her voice was frightened.

Mrs. Goza sighed and picked up the paper once more.

"The state flower of Alabama."

"I—I think it's—the azalea?"

"No," said Mrs. Goza. A slight rumble set up, but the woman silenced it by raising her huge, fleshy arm and snapping her fingers, once.

"Henry, do you know what the state flower of Alabama is?"

He kept his gaze on the darkened bulb, its frosted white face, powdery with black soot. At length, he gave Mrs. Goza a series of jerky nods. His wavering voice whispered the answer to him from the tape—from reel to reel and out the microphone in his hand.

"The Camellia."

"That," said Mrs. Goza, lowering her arm with a rustle, "is right."

The crowd fell into a round of polite applause, and the teachers scooted back from their table. Henry's gaze broke free at the sound of feet crossing the wooden floor. Frances moved slowly off the stage, through the chute, and into the crowded herd of people who hadn't known quite enough.

————

Martha though it might look bad—her being in the picture with Henry—so he stood between Mrs. Goza and the Vice Principal, Mr. Howard Harolds. The news photographer posed them so that both adults shook one of his hands. From the looks of it, Henry decided, they were having to hold him up—like a poster child during a fund-drive. After three shots from different angles, the assembly was excused before the photographer could take the *"Head of School Board Shakes Winner's Hand"* picture. Mr. Porter's morning meeting had run late, so he had yet to arrive with the prize donated by the board. Henry had no illusions about the prize being anything other than an educational tool.

With Mrs. Goza and Mr. Harolds drinking coffee backstage, he hoisted himself on top of the questioner's table and waited for Mr. Porter. Martha had gone to make a phone call, and the photographer had gone to the bathroom. Henry kicked his dangling feet back and forth, grinning.

So. He had won. He had beaten everybody. Whatever they would give him would testify to what he was. Next week, he would go over to Tupelo, to the regional geography bee, and beat all of them too. The state was next, then the whole country. At the thought, a surge of excitement broke over his body. He stilled his swinging feet for the shudder to pulse into his toes.

It was different from anything he had known, winning was. It not only made you feel good, it ranked you, made people move aside. The right doors opened, Martha said, for people like Henry. Nobody would dare question him now.

One of the series of wooden doors at the back of the auditorium opened. Silhouetted in the square of light stood Martha, her hand waving. The footlights hadn't been turned off yet, so Henry shielded his eyes to see her. For some reason, she didn't come in.

"Mr. Porter will be here in just a minute. I'm going to find the janitors, so they can help lift your prize onto the stage."

He nodded and waved back. The door closed again, leaving him in the cool, peaceful auditorium gloom. He sniffed, listened to the echo, then coughed to hear that as well.

Martha hadn't congratulated him yet, but she had told him she wouldn't make a big deal over it.

"Some petty, jealous types might think I've rigged the thing," she had said over the phone that morning, "and just because the contest was my idea. But you know I'll be proud of you. And when we get home, we'll have Barnes over and make tacos." Henry had grunted an "all right," careful not to interest Cox and Tollet, who sat at the breakfast table, eating cereal.

Other than the day Cox drove him home, Henry hadn't mentioned the contest to his father. He had spent most of the week before in his room, quizzing himself with the tape recorder. From time to time, he heard Tollet shuffle to his closed door, then pause at the constant repetition of Henry's voice, taped and real. It made Henry want to be someplace where he had earned himself a slot, a place where he didn't have to justify a thing to anybody. He wasn't talking to Tollet at all.

The auditorium door swooshed open again, vacuuming air from the hall. But instead of Martha, speeding down the sloped aisle was a small, anxious-looking man in a business suit. He traveled at such a clip that his arms made pumping motions. His feet spanked the tile.

They're gonna take it back, he thought. I did something, and they're gonna take it back.

The man stopped just below the stage, so that the white footlights hovered beneath his face. Henry couldn't make him out very well.

"You him?" the man said, more than asked.

"Uh—I'm the one that won."

The man snatched his head to the side. "Well, by God, you're him, then."

He walked over to the steps at the far left of the stage, took them two at a time, then sped across the floorboards as he re-stuffed his shirttail into his pants. Henry scooted back.

The man's face had a scalded look, with small eyes buried deep beneath his brow. His gray hair was cropped into a G.I. cut, but the bristles were too thin to hide the penny-sized moles on his scalp. His seersucker coat and pants swallowed him, so that he looked to be more wrapped than suited. When he got close, Henry sniffed the strong smells of peppermint and talcum powder.

"Ambrose Porter," said the man, his voice as high as Henry's. He took Henry's hand, crushed and released it. "Your daddy works for me." He nodded vigorously, as if there might be an argument. "Cox Tollet is your daddy."

"That's right," said Henry. He shifted back even further.

This couldn't be Mr. Porter. This man was too small, too high-voiced, too—not the kind of man Cox would respect. The real Mr. Porter was five inches taller than Cox and outweighed him by a good fifty pounds.

"What's all that on your head for?" said the man, squinting. "You in a car wreck?"

Henry frowned, touching the Band-Aids.

"Hey. Where'd you learn all that stuff?" asked Mr. Porter, hands on hips, gunslinger-style. "Here at *this* school?"

Henry shook his head. "No, sir. Not here. I read a lot. My ma—"

"I didn't think so. But you got a *gooood* head on your shoulders. A *gooood* head. That's gonna help." He winked, confidentially. "I got me a good head, too. But not for the same kinda things. Got me a head for figgers." He squinted sideways, as if he might be selling himself short. "Aaaand, I know how to get along, too. There's such a thing as street sense too, you know."

Henry nodded that he knew. He didn't know any such thing.

All of a sudden, a white Lifesaver appeared in Mr. Porter's teeth, caught between his uppers and lowers so that it stood perched and perfectly round. His tongue darted in and out of the hole.

"You gonna win next week in Tupelo?" He asked it through the Lifesaver, as if he were performing a trick.

Henry stared into the hole, fascinated by the pink flesh flitting in-and-out. The smell of peppermint was fierce. He answered the man with an absent nod.

Mr. Porter bounced his eyebrows. "Gooood. You got to have confidence in this world. You can't let 'em know you're scared."

Henry blinked, annoyed. His gaze moved from Mr. Porter's tongue to his eyes.

"I'm not scared," he said.

"'Course ya' are," said Mr. Porter. He flipped the Lifesaver inside to suck on. "Only natural. I'm scared myself. Most all the time. Just don't let it show."

The auditorium doors swung open again. But it still wasn't Martha. Instead, two old janitors came down the aisle, rolling a sheet-covered cart.

"Here it comes," said Mr. Porter, turning to point with his scrawny hand. He chomped on the candy, shattering it with a loud snapping sound that made Henry look.

The two men rolled the cart all the way to the bottom of the stage steps.

"We don't hafta lift it up there, do we?" asked one, his face a snarl. The other added an exasperated look in support.

"It ain't *that* heavy," said Mr. Porter. He tore off his suit coat like he was getting ready for a fight, slung it at the table, then hopped from the stage so fast the two men jumped.

"Come on. I'll help you. Grab ahold." He was already squatting underneath one edge of the cart before the men could gather themselves. Spurred, they each caught an edge. At Mr. Porter's count of three, they hoisted the cart up the steps.

As they rolled it over the boards, Henry leaned to the side to see beneath the sheet. He had hoped for maps—even better, topographical maps—pictures of the places he knew about—bumps and ridges he could run his fingers over.

"Madrid is the capital of Spain"—and there it would be—on the wall, proving him right.

But it probably wasn't maps. It was probably more books—things he already knew—already had a mastery of and couldn't be scared by. He gave Mr. Porter a slight grin. It was okay if they were books. He was satisfied.

"Where's your mama?" asked Mr. Porter, his breath spent. He glanced at his watch. "Where's the picture man?"

"He's in the bathroom," answered Henry.

Mr. Porter smiled into one cheek. "Well, that's natural. Perfectly natural. But still, I gotta get goin'. I gotta get back to work."

He snatched the cover off the cart, sending dust into the air. It danced in the stage lights.

"*World Book Encyclopedia!*" boomed Mr. Porter. "Latest version they come out with. Brand spanking new."

A chill blew over Henry. He leaned out, over his knees, squinting. At length, he lifted himself from the table to draw close.

They did indeed say *World Book Encyclopedia* on their spines, but they weren't green and white, like the ones at Martha's. They were blue and red. The letters were sunken and pale. The covers were smooth instead of bumpy. The C was divided at a different place. The P was divided as well. And worst of all, the S was no longer in one volume. Henry shrank back.

"I've—read these."

The sound of paper tearing caused Henry to glance around. Mr. Porter was unwinding his roll of Lifesavers. After he popped one of the little white circles into his mouth, he held the cylinder out to Henry, who refused.

"Not *these* you haven't," said Mr. Porter. "Your Mama told me. You read the old ones. These here are brand spanking new. They got stuff in 'em you don't have in yours."

Henry's head shot around. "What?"

Mr. Porter grinned, as though this was all to be expected. "These here have all the stuff that happened since yours was printed. And on top of that, these here come with a 'supplement' every year. See that'un on the end there? One that says *1975*? That's the *1975* supplement—right there."

Henry's stomach seized. "What do you mean I haven't read them? What's a 'supplement'?"

Mr. Porter smiled generously. The new Lifesaver appeared at his teeth, a white halo hung between picket fences.

"It's got all the stuff in it that happened that year. The stuff the set doesn't have because it hadn't happened yet: All the fires and wars and beauty pageants. All the accidents. Every year something new happens you don't know about, and they give it to you in a supplement."

Henry's gaze traveled back to the blue and red books. He felt betrayed.

"You'll never know it all," said Mr. Porter, "not if you live to be a hunnerd. But you can take a good run at it with all these supplements. Looka there," he said, pointing proudly, as if he had written the books himself.

"*1975*—right there. And next year, *1976*. Then here comes *1977*. New stuff in every last one of 'em."

Henry set his jaw, backed away. "Tollet said there's nothing new under the sun."

The Lifesaver flipped over as the man nodded, begrudging the point. "Maybe so. But it comes at you in different ways, so you can't recognize it. Leaps out *aaaand*—Gets ya!"

All at once, he stamped his foot and grabbed Henry in the stomach. The boy jumped sideways and let out a loud squeal. Mr. Porter only laughed.

"You'll like these here," he assured, nodding. "Wait 'n see. There's always something you'll need to know. No matter how smart you are, there'll always be a fella you gotta get up early just to lose to. There's some folks you got to run hard after, just to stay behind. Watch—"

He reached down and slipped out *1975*. He flipped through the pages and found something.

"What happened in the Orthodox Church this year?" he asked.

Henry went cold.

"You even know what the Orthodox church *is*?"

Henry went colder still.

Mr. Porter shook his head. "Me neither. But here's this feller, knocking on a door—gotta big crown on his head—like he just ate some Imperial margarine." He pointed to a picture of a man with a long beard and a crown, a big stick in his hand. It did look kind of like the Imperial margarine crown.

Mr. Porter pulled the book back to his chest, as though to keep Henry from peeping. He flipped a few more pages. After a minute, he asked Henry who it was that Mr. Ford had picked for a Vice President. Henry licked his drying lips.

"Don't know, do ya'? See! It was a Rockefeller. One I never heard of. Looka here."

He showed Henry a picture of the Rockefeller, wearing big, horn-rimmed eyeglasses.

Mr. Porter snapped the book shut with a victorious clap and stuck it back into the set.

"And that's just one book, too! They'll be another one comin' soon as you're done with it. It'll take ya' a year just to read this one."

He chomped the candy with the sound of boots on dry gravel. Henry flinched at the harsh noise. A knot formed in his throat.

The boy in the next bed, who would wait in the dark, always knowing more; stealing out across a dark, cold floor, to beat him with a carved, department store stick.

"It's got to stop some time," said Henry. If it didn't, Martha would have told him. She would have told him if there were more answers than you could know. She wouldn't let him think—

Mr. Porter barked a laugh as he emptied the candy roll into his hand and popped all of the circles into his mouth. He didn't even stop to suck this time, but pulverized the mints like grist beneath a millstone. The fresh, ripped smell shot up Henry's nose.

"No it don't, neither," said Mr. Porter. "Don't never stop. But you got a *goood* head on your shoulders. You'll get a good run at it, 'fore it's all over."

A press of air stole from the room as the doors swung open in back. He heard the photographer's voice, then Martha's heels following him down the tile. But Henry didn't glance her way. He didn't know where to rest his gaze anymore. It fell to the waist of his pants.

Martha came to the stage edge, then stopped abruptly.

"Oh. You've—already shown him," she said, disappointed. "What's the matter, Henry? You thanked Mr. Porter, didn't you?"

The man spoke for him. "'Course he did. He's crazy about 'em. He's just worried 'bout next time, that's all."

Henry straightened his shoulders, then struggled light into his eyes.

"Ya'll come on up here and take this pitcher," said Mr. Porter walking about. "I gotta go."

Henry broke the seal on his lips, drew breath, and took his place beside all that he had won.

━━━━━━

He sat in the tree swing in Martha's back yard, his heels clawing at the dirt as he wound the ropes into a tight braid. When the braid crawled down the rope and knotted at his chest, he hesitated. The force was loaded onto the side of his foot, the power scotched. Then he released—an unraveling—a spinning that turned the leaves and branches above him into a hissing pool.

Barnes, he would ask—Barnes, what did he see? The man at the drugstore who knew what you were—the one with the sick wife.

What did he look at? Your face? The way you worked your hands? Did you talk, and he heard something? Barnes—how could he know, when he'd never clapped eyes on you? What if you weren't smart enough to figure it out?

The swing uncoiled and recoiled in the other direction, braiding itself this time. He felt the force turn about, loading onto the other side. Then it began again, without need of him. Green and brown, rioting above him, a whirlpool.

Yours was easy—he *told* you—it's like a test, and he filled in the blank: "Barnes is ———."

But what if no one told? And what if you fill it in yourself because that's the best you can figure? But what if you're not right? How much time do you have? Does something fill it up if you're not fast enough? Does something seep in from the sides—and make you—be—something else?

Everything moved to the surface of his skin—leaving a funnel— the hollow around the stirring teaspoon. He remembered the hole in his chest—the times that he had sensed it—with the boy—and after he was done with Lois—the clean, clear cave that waited—the blank that was him.

Barnes—What if you don't like it? What if it makes you sick? Do you have to anyway?

Easier this time, as the rope switched and spun him slowly the first way again. He swallowed the acid that crept up his throat.

Should you go ahead and be something anyway, even if you know it's wrong—just so long as it's something that *you* picked?

That's what she had said, but—No. No. It's still the wrong thing, either way. It's still wrong.

One last turn, sputters and remnants, the swing lazily spending itself.

You don't know, do you, Barnes? She doesn't either. Nobody does.

"Henry, stop that," Martha called from the porch door. "You'll make yourself sick. Besides, the tacos are on the table. And Barnes is here."

The side of his foot dragged against the dirt, bouncing him to a halt. His head swam. Drunk. Sick as a drowned man pulled to the beach, beaten back to life. He lay his temple against the swing rope. The earth shook beneath his feet as he climbed up and wobbled himself inside.

Henry is ———?

Henry is ———.

Henry is.

And that was all.

It was a similar set up, just a different school. The people in Tupelo gave them chairs while they waited for their question, and there was a microphone to answer through. Henry had worn the same outfit as before, but right before the bee started, Martha had made him change into a white dress shirt and a red, clip-on tie she had brought with her. The collar sawed him beneath the chin each time he turned his head. With his hands clasped on his lap, he picked a spot to focus on—the first star on the American flag, which hung like a banner from the stage ceiling. The bee had only just begun. Nobody had missed yet.

"Margaret Morgan," said a man in a bow tie and high-water pants. He stood at a podium to one side. "The island in the Pacific on which you would find strangely carved stone heads?"

a house all stilled

Easter Island, answered Henry silently. The girl said the same, then returned to her seat after the sounding of a small gong. Despite the noise, Henry kept his eyes on the star, forcing himself to look at one of its rays, the topmost.

"John David East: The name of the area in the Atlantic Ocean known as a breeding ground for eels and. . . ."

The Sargasso Sea, Henry thought, pointing it in John David's direction. After the gong, the boy returned to his seat.

Henry had watched him come on stage that morning. He was big, two sizes bigger than he should have been, and with a bunched-together, stubbled face. He glowered, even when he answered "Sargasso Sea."

Who knows what somebody like him would do? thought Henry. Somebody smart and big, both. Cox with an education. How could you stay ahead of him? How could you stay even close enough behind?

"What is the name of the island off the coast of. . . ."

His head was hot. The flesh-colored Band-Aids made them hotter. Every place that had ever bled stung like it was rubbed with saltwater. Henry lifted a hand from his lap and fingered his brow.

The girl next to him rose from her seat, walked towards the microphone.

"What is. . . ."

His gaze fell from the star, found John David's grown, smirking face.

There wasn't going to be any peace in Memphis.

A picture flashed through his mind, him in a car, traveling north towards the city. Instead of trees, the road was lined with shelves and shelves of books, none of which he had read, miles and miles of things others knew that he didn't, things they would hold over him forever. The library of John David East.

The man at the microphone stared over his glasses at Henry. Coughs and sneezes passed through the crowd. Someone dropped a book. Henry rose and approached.

He looked for his mother and found her on the front row. Her teeth were gritted in a tight smile. She clutched the arms of her seat.

Her eyes all but trembled, straining for him—for him, but for something else too, something more—straining like something hungry strains, like something half-starved strains.

And she's read every book there ever was, he thought.

A drenching sadness wrung him through.

"Henry Tollet—"

A hot fever broke about his head, drumming at his brow like tapping fingers. He blushed, embarrassed. He thought of the boy in the woods, his stick, the pain that hung in his head like something alive.

Was he bleeding? He looked at his fingers. Only sweat.

"The mountain range that borders northern Spain."

The man was already shuffling his cards for the next question.

Henry shut his eyes, released his grip. The microphone's silver-dimpled head was too high for him. He had to raise his chin, as a dog would to howl.

"The Appalachians."

The words came out one syllable at a time, each like a stripe across his back.

After a moment, he heard a triangle ring gently offstage, a much prettier sound than the gong. He looked in its direction, preparing to follow.

"I'm sorry, that's incorrect. Let's all thank—" the man checked a list—"Henry Tollet—for coming here today, from Cellarsville Junior High School."

He turned from the microphone, escorted by the clatter of polite applause. A woman pointed him to a seat below the stage, a cold metal chair, the first in an empty row.

▬▬▬▬▬▬

When the bee was over, he left his consolation prize on his chair. It was a map of the United States, showing each state's capital and a tiny picture to illustrate an industry. Mississippi had a cotton boll, like always.

He looked for Martha in the crowd but couldn't find her. They hadn't spoken of where they would meet in case he lost. Of course, he hadn't known he was going to lose, not up until the second he had

decided to. The crowd milled about, congratulating the winner—
John David East—and all the runners up. Flashbulbs went off; prizes
were given. Henry shouldered his way out of the auditorium. A
bench in the front lobby seemed as good a waiting place as any.

In time, he spotted Martha's red pants suit at the back of the
crowd. Mrs. Goza was there too, her bulk shifting from one side to
the other as she walked. They stood talking for a while, apparently
unaware of him. Finally, they moved closer.

"Here I am," he said.

Martha turned, smiled, nodded. Then she went back to her
conversation. He expected her to be aggravated with him, but he
couldn't tell.

"You did fine, Henry," Mrs. Goza called, as she walked away. "It's
hard to think when you're nervous and scared."

In the car, Martha cut on the radio to drive home by. But she
could only get AM, and she didn't like the rock bands they played.
She cut it off again.

Henry glanced at her from time to time, expecting her to ask
him, politely, what the hell he had done. But she never did. Her face
was as empty as the car hood she stared over. The most she gave out
was a long, sighing breath whenever she glanced in her side view
mirror.

They took the long way, on a road that wound through the town
where Big Mama lived in the nursing home. And to his surprise, they
turned in at the Silver Era sign and drove up to the building. Out
front, a yellowed old man in mismatched pajamas sat in a wheelchair,
holding back the metal door.

"I'm going to run in here and visit Mother for a second," she
said, sighing as she turned the engine off. She clamped her eyes shut,
preparing to go in. He knew she hated to see her alone.

When she opened her eyes again, she stared at the center of the
steering wheel. She placed her fingers on the insignia there and
began to rub it softly. The interior filled with the buzz of the dash-
board clock. Henry tightened his thighs, folded his hands, waited.

"Someday," she said, glancing to her right, out the window, "you'll be able to go."

He gave her the nod she wanted. She didn't look at him. After a breath, she opened her door and climbed out onto the sidewalk. Without thinking, Henry did the same.

Martha glanced over, surprised. She hesitated, waiting for him to meet her.

"One day, you'll want to go," she repeated as they walked.

At the door, Henry stepped around the old man—his loose, sunken eyes, his hanging flesh.

No, I won't, Henry thought—sure of it, amazed by it.

I never will.

Chapter 12

A fifth of Old Granddad sat on the Formica counter, next to a bottle of blended scotch and a vase-shaped bottle of something Cox had never heard of: Calvados. The man at the store said the last would get you drunk the quickest. Quickness wasn't really a concern, but Cox went and bought it anyway. He pulled a fifth of Jack Daniels out of the sack, for good measure, then lined up the labels. He stood back to look at his work.

Soon, Tollet would stumble in, blink, catch the wall for balance. Even if he were suspicious of the bottles, he wouldn't resist. He'd be drawn to them like a cow to water—poisoned or not.

That'll do it, ole buddy, Cox thought, as he threw the bag away. You can drink prune juice and sing all day long in the Cloverdale choir. Shape notes or sacred harp or whatever else. I won't have to hear it.

He walked over to the screen door to look for Tollet. Soon, he would come from Felix's across the back pasture, just as Henry would in an hour or so. The sky was cloudy, threatening rain. A weak wind sent the green maple seeds spinning.

"He's not going," Martha had said last Sunday morning. "Not next fall, anyway."

He had just arrived to get Henry when she came out of the house. Her arms folded across her chest, she walked right up to his truck window and stopped. Her stare rested somewhere beyond his right shoulder.

"I don't think he could get in right now, anyway," she said, her voice trailing. "There's a waiting list, and he hasn't taken the entrance exam. They would have considered him as a special case if he'd shown something extra, like winning that contest."

She backed into the middle of the quiet street. One hand rested against her hip as she stared at her foot.

"He lost on purpose," she mumbled.

Cox nodded, though she couldn't see.

"I don't know why, or what happened. He says nothing did." Her gaze eased up her leg, waded through the space between them, then locked onto his face. Her head tilted to the side.

"I guess you're satisfied? You've got him broke to ride."

Cox's mouth dropped open. His grip twisted on the steering wheel. Satisfied?

"Well," she muttered, her eyes tight, "nothing's changed. If he can't go, thanks to *you*, Tollet can't stay, either, thanks to *you*. Nothing's changed. Nothing."

She ground the sand on the asphalt with her foot, then walked off.

As she entered the house, she passed Henry coming out. With the Samsonite banging him in the shin, he lugged the case down to the truck. To Cox, he looked older than ever. Not in size, but in age. Henry's face was as grave as a man at the end of his life, staring just past that end, into—what? As he struggled the case into the flat-bed, Cox studied the boy in the rearview mirror. Was that what Henry was thinking about whenever he was so far below the surface?

A week had passed since Cox had asked himself that question, and he still couldn't answer it. He'll be coming soon, Cox thought, eyeing the pasture. It was a peculiar green and blue, deeper than usual. He remembered, though, some time when it had been this color. Or did he?

His stomach twisted. It was just the sky. It was the hidden sun that made it look that way.

He walked out the screen door, down the porch steps, and across the yard to the barn. It was late afternoon, and he had to feed the steers. When he came to the barn, he saw them standing in a muddy corner of the lot, watching nothing.

Lately, he had thought of being alone in the house. Henry would be staying at Martha's more and more. And with Tollet in the nursing home, Cox would have the house to himself. He planned to keep Lois in one bed, somebody else in another, and roll the projector all day long—maybe four projectors—one for each wall. A minute wouldn't pass without a pizza in the oven, warming. And who could say a thing about it? Who would care?

He took a black plastic bucket from inside the tack room door and moved to the barrel full of sweet feed. When he took off the drum's top, the smell of molasses-covered oats rose about his face. His mouth watered. Sometimes it was all he could do to keep from digging his hand deep into the pile of cool, moist feed, then drizzling a handful onto his tongue, just to see. He scooped some into his palm, lifted it to his nose, inhaled, and dropped it into the bucket.

Two coffee cans full of feed, a half can of calf manna. He stepped over to the other barrel.

But now those plans were lost. He hadn't counted on Henry coming back for good, but back he was, and stranger than before. Cox couldn't look at him for long.

He lost his grip on the scoop, scattering feed pellets over the concrete floor.

One thing he wouldn't have, one thing he couldn't deal with, was the two of them together: a drunk and a freak. It could only get worse: Tollet slobbering out lies—maybe even changing his will one day—and Henry lapping up whatever he said like first milk, just so he could sit, stare, and sink. Or worse yet, Tollet might choose, for spite, to tell the truth. To tell the boy awful things. And then what would become of him?

Ever since the time in the yard, whenever Henry broke loose, came untethered, it made Cox's heart shift over. He felt like he had been trapped inside a still, dark box, with one thing dying and one thing trying to die.

Cox leaned over the barrel. He sucked in a long breath, pushing out the walls of his chest. Slowly, he blew the air through his clenched teeth.

If Henry wasn't going, Tollet was. Martha didn't even need to threaten him. He wanted it himself now as much as she did.

With a sweep of his arm, he grabbed the bucket from the floor and carried it out to the steers. They were turned in opposite directions, facing each other, as though in conversation. He felt them watching as he took their feed over to the trough, then spread it from one end to the other.

Come and get it, he thought. A few more pounds, then off to the scales.

As he left, he heard the sucking sound their hooves made in the mud, each stirring to follow its nose and stomach.

———

An hour passed, and the old man still hadn't come back from Felix's. So Cox took the opportunity to call the lawyer, which he needed to do without Tollet around. He had to know how you started the process. How much evidence did you need to put somebody away? What did it take? Whatever he cooked up with the whisky and with Shreva eventually had to be put on white paper, stamped, and filed. So how much did you have to have to fill the paper?

Using the kitchen phone, he dialed Clark's office.

Macby, Brown, and Babcock.

"Yeah, this is Cox Tollet calling for—" he stopped to remember the woman's name.

"I don't know. Miz Babcock, I think. Clark told—"

Please hold, the secretary said.

An instrumental version of "Do You Know The Way To San Jose?" started in mid-song.

Cox flattened his lips against his teeth. He didn't like being handed off to this woman, but at least he wouldn't have to deal with Clark's fat-assed self. He leaned against the wall and let the phone sink to his shoulder.

The bottles stood like candles on the counter, ready to burn down Tollet's throat. Curious, Cox slid the pint of foreign stuff across the counter. A knuckle's worth went into a juice glass. He sniffed it; the skin next to his eyes crinkled. A thimble full washed onto his tongue.

A flat, woolish taste. He spit thick, brown phlegm back into the glass. With his index finger, he broke the string of saliva between his lip and the brim.

Sweet feed would taste better, he thought, sliding the bottle away.

It might have been Tollet's love for the stuff that made him resent it. If it hadn't caused so much trouble, Cox might like it as much as he did tobacco, pizza, Lois, and movies. After all, it was just another flavor, another itch. But this itch caused problems. Time for it to stop. Time to scratch it out. Finally, time. He pushed the glass away too.

One thing was sure. He had never done *that* to Henry.

The lawyer still hadn't picked up the phone. The receiver rested like a parrot on his shoulder, easing Muzak into his ear: "Let it Be." "Winchester Cathedral." "Moon River."

His eyes slid closed. Despite himself, the burnt taste pulled at his mind, calling things from it, into it.

When Cox had found out the truth, it came in an unexpected way. Then, when he had finally understood, it had slowly ironed itself into his blood, like the cancer that had eaten his mother from the inside. Slow and inside, so that it took the pain in her eyes to tell you it was there at all. But before that—before that, he had just been confused.

And mad, sometimes, when he watched Tollet stumble in, his boot heel crunching toys left on the floor, the unmendable sound of wood snapping. Mad when Tollet clambered over to vomit in the kitchen sink. Shocked, sometimes, when Tollet stumbled in to eat straight from stove pots. Sometimes he would stick his soggy, soiled hand into Cox's hair and scratch his head with it. Even tortured, sometimes, when he woke to find himself abandoned inside a freezing truck—the seats tight and cracking from the cold. Buckets of black paint might have been dumped over the night sky—dead dark, but for a string of yellow lights on a sagging porch, far ahead. There was the noise of a whiny Victrola, spinning. And a rustling, tumbling, grunting sound that pinned him to the seat, too frightened to move.

When his eyes grew used to the night, he dared to look out the window. Another car. Inside it, a man—only his back, or Cox could have told who—ramming his paw down an ugly woman's shirt—and her laughing, toothless gums—her throwing a hard elbow against the glass, nearly shattering it.

But then—and sometimes as soon as the next day—the anger, shock, torture would melt away. Because Tollet would come in from the back room, singing. He might smile at Cox's mother, yell out, happy that she had made cat-head-sized biscuits—he might place his strong, carved hand—the shade of ashwood—across the nape of her neck, where her wavy, iron-colored hair escaped from the bun.

And then, then he would dress for church and wear a tie. No one had ever looked so clean as he in a white shirt, in a red tie with blue stars with a tie tack that bore a treble clef; all of him was scrubbed to a sheen. The other—what Cox had seen—was a dream in the face of this. It couldn't have been—because, look!—look at the white, starched cleanness; sea-green eyes; ashwood hand on his mother's neck, placed so gently it makes her turn. Look! See?

And before they left, while they waited for her to pin her hat on, he would sit Cox in a big chair by the front window, and he would preach. Love sounded good from his mouth. Love never came so open-armed, so true. It made Cox heartsick to hear. He would squirm in the seat as Tollet's voice stroked him.

"And the Lord said," his eyes wet, lifting an ashwood hand out for Cox's shoulder. Cox would shrink from the touch, curl into the corner of the chair, afraid he would die of love.

"Forgive them, father. For they know not what they do."

After that, there could be no altar too high—no sacrifice too great—no life too precious to give. After that, he wanted grace after grace, just so he could give it all back again.

He was seven—eight—nine?

Years passed.

Long stretches of love, but always—marked—dirtied—by Tollet's stumbling, coughing, vomiting.

And then, one day, with the same hand he held at Cox's shoul-der, the very same hand, he had fumbled at the door, staggered inside, fallen sideways onto his chair. His eyes were a soup, but they fluttered to bring Cox close; and when close, he told him: I am a hero—of the great war—in France—at Darmontiers.

And Cox, who had begun to edge back, came forward again. And he had thought: Yes, you are. I knew it all along.

"There was a girl. A mad'mazelle, they called her—the 'Mad'-mazelle Armantears'." His smile curled into his eyes. "Hadn't seen her in years and years. Lilly Marleen."

Cox moved closer, his stomach resting against the chair arm.

She was small, rose-mouthed, Tollet had said. And coal-black hair tied with a blood-red knot. Everyone knew her, but I was the only one.

And Cox had turned, to look for his mother, to see if she could hear. Outside at the well? Away to the barn? Gone, at any rate. He pulled closer.

Strange to be told this secret—to want this secret.

From then on, whenever his mother was away, Tollet spoke of the girl—of the war—whenever he came home, stumbling. Cox urged it, insisted on it, prompted him to show the ribbons he had won, stored away in a metal box.

Tollet had bent on wobbly hands and knees to pull the box from beneath the bed. Not only ribbons, but also stripes, and a blue pin, chipped, that read "first place" on the front. Tollet tottered on his knees:

"Only the A number 1 soldier got this here."

Cox didn't dare touch it.

The country was beautiful, he had said, his hand waving at a scene of purple grapes, wheat fields, oak-lined roads, red flowers with yellow middles.

Lilly took him to Armantears, and they climbed up a tower—Alfie's tower—and saw all the way to England.

He would have married her, Cox learned, his eyes as wet as Tollet's, had she not caught the Spanish fever. He had shot twenty Germans when she died—and gotten the A1 medal.

Tollet had married in his forties because "it took twenty years to find a woman that could make me set her down."

And Cox looked down the hall, to his mother's bed. Be proud of that too, he told himself, that she is that kind of woman.

His gaze came back to his father—to the hands, holding old ribbons.

And what altar was too high? What sacrifice too great?

So when the teacher wanted a story, what else could he tell? What else was *worth* telling?

A graphite pencil, smudges on his fingers from the writing—the smell of burnt rubber from erasing—changes, to do it justice. Clever, guarded, he altered it to his "father's friend," and waited, sleepless, for the next day.

In a near-dusk schoolroom, he stood before them to read. Their feet would stop wagging—their throats stop itching—their eyes stop gazing out the window as soon as they heard his father's story.

"Lilly Marleen—from Armantears—who lived next to Alfie's tower and saw England."

He wasn't half-way through before there came a stinging laugh. His gaze shot up. If a gun had blasted, sent a bullet past his head, he could not have been more surprised.

Not the others—who sat as awed as he had been—but the teacher, a woman he had thought pretty. She asked him where he had gotten the story. Cox, burning, told her.

"That's a song," she said. "Two songs, in fact. From the first World War."

Her head never stopped shaking, her mouth never stopped smiling.

"All the doughboys sang that song. Your father must have been joking."

His mouth dried; he fought his tongue to form the word.

Liar.

"What did you say?"

"I said 'Liar.'"

And she was never pretty again after she pulled out the encyclopedia, after she showed him the town in France. And the way it was spelled, correctly— "Amentiers." And "Eiffel," instead of "Alfie."

And then she called in the old janitor, and made Cox stand up front while she asked him about the songs—songs too dirty to sing out loud.

The old bastard knew them. He even hummed them, though he couldn't call the words: "LA—la—La—la—Tra—la—La—la—DO—DI—DOO. . . ."

Then, over time, it all came unspun, unraveled—blow after blow after blow:

Tollet hadn't gotten any further than boot camp in Maben. He had picked up the clap from a girl over there; got discharged. Ribbons from the Houlka air show—a pin from the Clay County Fair for a pie-eating contest. No rose-mouthed woman—no dead Germans—no tower over a sea.

Coldness shimmered along the span of his bones, locking them in ice.

No neckties. No singing. No Jesus.

No forgiving—not even if he "knew not what he did."

And most of all—nothing—*ever*—from "way back when." Never that. If it couldn't cut you open or ram against your knee, if you couldn't pour it down your throat and piss it, or stick it in your mouth and swallow it, or rub yourself into it until you burst with hot milk—then shut up. By God, shut up.

"Mr. Tollet, this is Trula Babcock. I'm sorry to keep you waiting so long." Her smoky voice came over the line, too close. He jumped, clutching at the counter.

"I understand you need help with your father?"

"Yes," said Cox. He stretched the phone cord as he walked to the middle of the room.

There was Tollet, still a hundred yards off, stumbling over the blue-green field. And there, just beyond him, coming out of the woods, was the blur of Henry's white shirt, his red jacket.

He had time. "Yes. That's right."

———

He arranged for the Babcock woman to come out a week from Friday. By that time, Tollet would be well on his way down a tear, and Cox would have his story straight with Shreva. He wouldn't have to worry about Henry, since that would be his weekend at Martha's. He would even fix Felix, telling him not to expect Tollet, since he was "sick with the flu."

Before he left for work the next morning, Cox looked in on the old man, to check his progress. The room was a sweat bath, steaming with stench. The window shades were pulled down beyond the sill. Cox had to flip on the lights to see.

Tollet didn't move. Open-mouthed, unshaven, he was swaddled inside the bedspread like a mummy. The sheets had come away from every mattress corner. Flattened pillows lay about.

Cox clapped his hands to make sure Tollet could still move. The old man flinched, grunted, rolled over. Cox cut off the lights and shut the door.

That week, he filled out orders, waited on customers, and cussed his sorry help for being sorry. The days passed quickly. Even Friday afternoon, which he saved for paperwork, wasn't as bad as usual. He took a figure from a receipt, carried it over and stuck it in the right line on the ledger. His eyes brightened as he worked, and at one point he had to stifle a chuckle.

It was damn funny, the way Tollet tried to disguise his whisky-stealing. One day, just before he came in the door, Cox hung up the phone, rushed to switch the TV on, then flopped into his recliner. A baseball game rose to the screen and steadied by the time Tollet was inside.

The old man was sneezing from his allergies, so he shuffled past the counter full of new bottles and headed straight for the bathroom. The toilet paper roller spun a couple of times, followed by a hard nose-blow. But when he was done, instead of coming back out, Tollet slammed the door and dropped the commode seat with a bang.

Cox was disappointed. He would have to wait for his reaction, since it was Tollet's habit to sleep for a while, then get up to cook supper. But then he heard him shuffling towards the living room again. His house shoes swept at the floor, sanding it, then stopped.

Tollet didn't say a word. The baseball announcer spoke of two balls, one strike, no one on base, the Yankees down 3-1 in the sixth. It was the kind of odd, half-quiet that Cox knew from childhood— whenever he heard boots tromping on oak steps. Tollet reversed himself and shuffled down the hall to his room. He gently closed himself inside.

Later, Cox thought to stick the bottles underneath the counter. It was less obvious that way, though he didn't suppose Tollet could dream what he had in mind. Even if he could, it wouldn't keep the old man from breaking into them. Sure enough, every time Cox checked, each brand was half an inch lower.

"D'you see me in the paper with your boy?"

Cox's head jerked up from the ledger. He had heard somebody walk up, but assumed it was one of the stock boys with yet another question for him. But here was Mr. Porter instead, on the other side of the counter, leaning on his elbows. The man, dressed in a maroon suit and a blue tie, was so close that Cox had to back off a step.

"Well—of course," said Cox. He shoved his pencil behind his ear. "I sure did. I was mighty proud of him."

Mr. Porter gave him an open-mouthed smile. A white lifesaver clacked between his teeth like a hockey puck.

"How come you wasn't at the contest?"

Cox felt a sharp pain at the small of his back. He put a hand to it.

"Well, I couldn't get off," he shrugged. "There was so much to do here—"

"You coulda asked me. Coulda worked it out," said Mr. Porter. His eyes narrowed. He leaned further over the counter.

Cox shrugged again. It was such a useless little gesture that he was embarrassed. "I know. But I didn't wanta worry you."

"Unh-hunh," said Mr. Porter. He nodded slowly, squinting at Cox like he had something on his face. "How's he like them *World Books?*"

Cox blushed. "Oh, he loves them. Reads 'em all the time."

"Unh-*hunh*," grunted Mr. Porter. "Well things musta changed a lot then."

He chomped down on the candy so fiercely that Cox's cheek twitched. He was about to say "yes they have," but he didn't know what in the hell Mr. Porter was talking about. And what was worse, Mr. Porter knew he didn't know. When the man finally left the store, he took what was left of Cox's good mood with him.

He worked an hour later than necessary, to avoid going home, then decided to drive by the gas station on the way. But Lois was out running errands, something it had never occurred to him she would do. And on top of that, the chicken place was closed due to a death in the family. Cox turned the truck onto the Wolfy road.

It was one thing for Mr. Porter to keep tabs on him, he brooded. It was another thing entirely to have his affairs messed with. Up until now, Mr. Porter just accepted whatever answers Cox gave him. But for some reason, he had taken to meddling behind the answers.

His chest tightened.

He needed people to let him be, to get off his back. Too many folks rooting around in his head, digging about in his business. The sooner he got rid of them, if only one at a time, the better.

So instead of driving on, Cox turned down a road a few miles from his house. He had planned to see Shreva the following afternoon, but now was as good a time as any. Besides, he had to pay her the seventy-five dollars up front.

Though the road was a shortcut, it was a bad one, and it got worse as he drove. The honeysuckle flourished from the late spring rains, crowding the fencerows that hugged the road. Huge gullies had opened down one side, eroding the dirt and gravel into the ditch. At one point, the road crumbled beneath Cox's left tires and sent him jarring against the door. But before the truck could get stuck, he gained traction by wrenching the wheel to the right. After another mile, he dead-ended into pavement.

It was a road that skirted several communities, then led back to Cellarsville. Cox turned to the left, drove a few hundred yards, then pulled off beside a row of dumpsters. Besides garbage bags, soggy cereal boxes, tree branches, milk jugs, and coffee grinds that littered the place, a broken sofa frame stuck out from one dumpster's top. A rusted, doorless clothes dryer sat beside it. A row of trucks and cars, each worse than the next, was strung along the roadside.

Cox turned the engine off, got out, and headed for a spot between a pair of young pines. Whenever he had driven this road before, he had seen people climbing out from between the trees, so he knew a path was there. He passed the last dumpster holding his breath, then ducked beneath the pine tree branches and set out for Shreva's.

The path ran between two small, tree-covered hills. Some stretches of dirt were scraped clean, worn and stamped to a shine.

Along others, bushes stood in the way, some thorny, some smooth-leafed; trash trees—black gums, redbuds—shoved wiry arms into the path, so that Cox had to duck or squat to get by. Every once in a while, he'd come across a cleared-out spot with what passed for a house on it. Folks stared, cautiously nodded; he did too.

As he walked, he wondered if this wasn't the way Henry came home every day. The road he had just left was where the bus picked up the Wolfy children, but he wasn't sure at what spot. For all Cox knew, Henry waited for the bus beside those dumpsters in the mornings and was met by them every afternoon. He shoved the thought out of his head.

"Say you've seen him lying passed out on the porch when you come by," he would tell Shreva. "Say sometimes you see him wandering around in the yard like he doesn't know where he is. Say he heads for the road sometimes."

There was some truth in all of it. Some.

He figured if Shreva just happened by on Friday while the lawyer was there, it would look better—unrehearsed.

"Tell her you don't always come up to the house, 'cause you hear him singing songs—and know he's drunk—and decide maybe you'd better not."

He stopped to check his bearings. At the join of another little hill, full of pink and white dogwoods, blooming, the path broke in two. One way traveled in the direction of the lower hills, the other headed towards Shreva's. Cox eyed the ridge, gauging where he thought his own house stood, a mile or two east. That meant Shreva's was to the left. He turned, finding the threads of the path beneath leaves shredded from last winter. With a nod, he moved on.

"Tell her it's getting worse and worse. Tell her *that* for sure."

Because it was. At least since Tollet was drinking all this new kind of hard liquor, it was. Anybody could see, and they would surely get a chance to. Cox smiled. It was funny, trapping flies and catching mice.

Then he thought on, despite himself. Green eyes, ashwood hands, tenor voice. His smile faded. If he could get all these things out of his mind, he could go on living.

"Tell her you're afraid," he'd demand. "Tell her he pukes in the grass. He stomps down the flowers. Wets his britches and wipes his hands on—"

Shreva's voice shot over the hill rise, a taut, shrill screech. Cox's gaze rose from the tips of his boots.

If it were anybody else, he would have thought she was in trouble. But that was the tone Shreva saved for her children. Then another, lower voice—a man's—responded. Cox couldn't make the words out for the echo that they caused. All at once, Shreva hollered again, madder than Cox had ever heard. What she yelled sounded like a name, or a curse. Then her trailer door slammed. The vibrations pealed through the trees, then shimmered into quiet once more.

For a woman stuck back here in a trailer, he thought, she's always got company.

Cox picked up his pace. By his estimation, he was about fifty yards off, around the next bend. The ground grew muddy at the seam of the hills, so he hopped his way to the dry spots. As he was about to lunge over a large, oily puddle, he saw someone walking over the hill. No more than the back of a head and a shoulder, but enough to tell it was a long-haired old man.

Probably Shreva's next husband, Cox thought. Can't get 'em any younger anymore.

Though his jump was well placed, the ground was soggy on the other side of the puddle. His toe sank into the mud and wet his sock.

"Shit and damn," he yelled.

The trailer door swung open, Shreva screeching as she came out.

"I told you to—"

She eased her neck out, searching. She had on fringed shorts and a man's T-shirt, and held what looked like a hoe handle. With the door open, two little boys escaped past her legs and ran into the woods.

"What?" Cox asked.

Shreva jumped back against the door, her face a fury. She jerked the stick up to a cocked position, its tip making a tiny circle in the air.

Cox came the rest of the way.

"That's a fine way to meet somebody bringing you seventy-five dollars."

She glanced off, looking up the hill again, her face unsure, unset. The only sunlit ground left in the hollow was at the top of the facing hill. The trees' shadows drew railroad ties down the slope, across the trailer, over half her face.

"I thought—" she began. She stopped to draw her tongue across her lips as though to lick the thought back inside her mouth. "I didn't know you was comin'."

Cox drew his wallet out and glanced up the hillside himself. One sharp sunbeam stabbed his eyes, hurting his brain. He turned back.

Musta got in a fight with her boyfriend, he thought. He fingered the bills.

Shreva took three twenties, a ten and a five from his hand, propped the stick against the door jam, and began to count the money.

"Now, listen," said Cox. "Get this straight in your head. There's a woman lawyer coming to my house at four o'clock next Friday. A week from today. Understand?"

"Go on," Shreva said, mumbling numbers.

"I'm gonna keep her there about an hour, just talking. Then you show up at quarter 'til five—don't be late—quarter 'til five—playing like you want to sell me some eggs, like always. And I'll come out to buy 'em."

Done counting, Shreva backed her lips off her teeth.

"I oughta tell her some other things," she said.

"Shut up."

"Like how you wouldn't spit on my head if my hair was on fire, not 'til you needed something—"

"You want this money or not?"

"Looks like I *got* this money." She crammed the bills into her pocket.

"You want the rest of it, then?" he yelled.

Her answer was a snort. Cox resettled his heels in and continued.

"All right. So I'll introduce you to this woman—and then, all of a sudden, I'll say—'Miz Shands knows what I'm talking about, don't you Miz Shands?' and you'll say yes, you do. You'll say at different times you've seen him wandering towards the road drunk—laying out on the porch drunk—singing songs without words—"

"What?" said Shreva, her brow twisted.

Cox shrugged, his tongue hesitating on his teeth. "Yeah. He does that."

Shreva's face twisted further, as if she had her limits. He let out a pestered sigh.

"Never mind, just say it. Do you need me to write all this down?"

"I can write!" she screeched.

"Then you write it down!" he yelled back. The boom of his voice drove a flock of birds from the pines.

"Just don't screw it up. You be there on Friday, ready to talk. Hear?"

She put one hand on the door knob and re-seated her grip on the stick.

"You be ready to turn loose of some money," she said, her voice rising to a wail. "Hear?"

She slammed the door in his face.

━━━━━━

Before the next Friday rolled around, Cox worked late nights making sure the house was spotless—all except for Tollet's room. It was hard not to bite the old man's head off when he tramped in clay mud and slopped up the counters. He was prone to miss the commode a lot too. But rather than leave it to Tollet to clean, Cox went behind him.

When the day came, he used two cans of Lysol to freshen the air, laid out a red doormat that spelled "Welcome" in little rubber bumps, and stuffed his projector and box of reels in the trunk of his car. Then he checked one last time on Tollet. The old man was burrowing around the bed like an earthworm in a dirt pile.

With an hour to go, it was time to shower and shave. He dressed in his best khakis, a white dress shirt—with the sleeves rolled down and buttoned—put on a red tie, and slipped on some polished black wing tips. His hair was too short for Vitalis, but he dabbed some on his scalp for the smell. Women liked that, he thought. He brushed his teeth, slapped a palm full of Hi Karate on his face, and went out on the porch to wait.

The sky was more white than it was blue, and the muggy air made his shirt stick to his shoulder blades. Left over from yesterday's

shower, the clouds stretched, thinned, and evaporated above the facing hill. Cox thrust his hands deep into his pocket, then stood looking out over his property, listening as cars wound through the hills,
like tops spinning about a tin plate.

At length, his attention fell to his sorrel brood mares, both grazing in the pasture fenced with page-wire beside the house. They were
Tennessee Walking Horses, but neither one of them had good blood-
lines. He had lost money on every colt they had. Still, horses were
something Tollet had never raised. Cox's gaze unhinged from the
mares and wandered back to the road.

They had raised beef cattle and corn, but little else. If Tollet
hadn't been a pretty good mechanic when he was sober, and had his
mother not made cobblers and hot rolls for the school cafeteria, they
might not have gotten by. Everything was for sale. Always. Not just
the cows and the corn. An acre or two, close to the creek—the trees
for lumber—the truck. Even the furniture was liable to be traded in.
Once, when things were tight, they had swapped the bird dog—a
lemon-spotted setter bitch, named Lou—for three Dominecker hens.

"Don't get too used to that," they would say, warnings in their
faces. After a while, Cox got to where he would say it to himself.

He cleared his throat at the sound of tires crunching on chert. As
though to clear his face, he swiped a hand over his smooth, shaven
flesh, pulling the skin down to his jaw. By the time the woman's Pontiac nosed against the mimosa tree, he wore a broad smile.

"Come on in," he called.

He neared her car and the door swung open, bouncing on its
hinges. A high-heeled black shoe, stuffed with a fat foot, clopped to
the ground. Above the shoe and foot was a calf the size of a cured
ham. She struggled to get out from behind the wheel.

Cox took his hands from his pockets. "Let me—help you," he
said, clasping a doughy arm.

She was so big, she nearly pulled him back inside with her. After a
clumsy moment, she tussled her way loose and got to her feet, winded.

"Rain musta shrunk my car," she winked, unembarrassed. With
sharp pulls at her big black dress, she straightened her appearance.
She reached back into the car for a gray briefcase.

Cox nodded, too impressed by her size to answer. She was tall enough to look him in the eye, level. Her face was broad and rouged, and she wore white-rimmed glasses with rhinestones in each corner. Her frosted hair reached to her jaw, then curled up at the ends. Her dress looked to be all one piece, with head and arm holes cut out.

"They don't make 'em like they used to," offered Cox, shutting the Pontiac's door.

"Shoot!" She rolled her eyes and chuckled. "Me or the car?"

Cox smiled again.

"Trula Babcock." She shook his hand without trying to break it.

He raised his eyebrows. "Cox Tollet. Pleased to meet you."

In no great hurry, she turned to the pasture and lifted her arm to shade her eyes.

"My husband raises those," she said, nodding to the horses. "Loses a helluvalota money. But he says they keep him from having heart attacks."

Cox drove his tongue into his cheek. Owning the horses struck him as silly all of a sudden.

"I guess I oughta get rid of 'em," he mumbled. "They don't do any good."

Trula shook her head briskly, then started walking.

"Don't. You might have a heart attack."

Cox grinned, then followed her up the steps.

She said after a week like hers, any place to sit was good as the next. They settled down in the living room, her on the sofa and him in his chair. Cox said he didn't mind her kicking her shoes off, and was glad when she asked for a beer instead of a cold drink. It turned out that she had bought a lawn mower from his dealership, and it seemed to her that Cox was the salesman. The mower had been slung off the back of a moving pick-up truck once. She still blamed her husband for not closing the tailgate, and he still blamed her, but the lawn mower still ran, so they were satisfied. Cox smiled, as pleased as if he had built the mower himself. They needed to get down to business, but there was plenty of time.

Besides, the more she talked, the more familiar she looked. He had known a girl like her in school—somebody who, to his wonder, didn't take anything seriously. You couldn't hurt her with jokes about her size, because she poked fun as much as anybody. In the end, he had wound up liking her, though he never would have told.

"Who were you before you married?" he asked, squinting.

She took a sip of beer, swallowed and nodded. "Trula Squires. Grew up in Bon Aqua. My daddy was the sheriff—"

"You're daddy was Jim Doss Squires—" said Cox, awe in his voice. His mouth opened as large as his eyes. "He arrested me once."

Trula smiled as if she knew it. "He arrested lots of people. But he was a good—"

Cox waved his hands. "No—no—no. You don't have to apologize. I was sixteen and I was chasing a boy down the sidewalk with a folding chair. Your daddy nearly ran his car up through a storefront to stop me. Hopped out, took two steps, and kicked me right in the—"

He paused when he noticed Trula's eyes mist over. She wiped a knuckle across her lids.

"He was always doing that. God bless him." She sniffed, smiling over tears. "Why were you chasing a boy with a folding chair?"

Cox blinked, looked down at his shoes. "I don't know anymore."

He blinked again, surprised that he had picked another part of the story to remember.

"All I recall is your Daddy telling me I needed to learn some manners—then kicking me again—big ole' ten-and-a-half steel-toe boots, lifted me off the sidewalk where I was lying."

He winced at the thought, moving his hand over his ribs, feeling the old pain. A grin broke over his face.

"Spent the night in jail. Gave me a cup of coffee the next morning and a fried pie."

"Peach or Apple?" asked Trula, she edged forward on the sofa, her face open as a child's.

"Apple," Cox remembered.

"Mama made it!" shouted Trula. "Mama made apple and the colored woman that worked for her made peach. Her and DeLouise went round and round about whose pie was best."

"Then it was your mama's pie," said Cox. "He told me not to come there acting like that again. I better get me a job and a wife—and do right—or he'd kick my heart up in my mouth."

"God bless him," said Trula, her voice catching. She fiddled with the hem of her dress as she fought for composure.

Cox's face fell. He didn't know what to do, so he found himself talking.

"I guess he's dead then?"

She tried to say "Yes," but wound up nodding, swallowing, and sniffing at the same time. Finally, she managed to get a hold on her voice.

"Been dead. Eleven years. Think I'd get used to that, wouldn't you? But here I am cryin'." She wiped her big, wet hands on the knees of her stockings, then laughed. "Anyhow, I guess you did what he said, didn't you?"

Cox tilted his head, rolled his shoulders. "More or less. I got a job. Got married."

"And had you some children," said Trula, one more sniff and wipe. She swiveled about to bring her briefcase closer. "I never was that lucky, having children, that is. Anyhow, I guess that's why we're here, isn't it?" she said, unlatching the top. "About your children and—your Daddy?"

Cox set his beer down. It was time, but somehow he wasn't ready. He nodded, then picked the can up again.

"He drinks too much."

"That's what you said." She took out a legal pad, shut the case's top and used it for a table.

"But you know, you can't put somebody away just because of that. It might not suit you, but he has the right to manage his own business, if he can."

Cox set the beer down. He rubbed his hands on his thighs as if he were cold. Though he had been unaware of noises while they were talking, now he heard Tollet rolling over on the bedsprings. If he kept moving, she would ask what that sound was. Of course, that was exactly what he had wanted her to do: to ask—to see. That was what he had wanted.

"Well. It's more. He's out of his head most of the time." He straightened his legs out and snatched at his trousers. His joints were cramping. "He—threatens to build a bar on this place."

Trula nodded. Her gaze followed his fidgeting.

"Well. He can if he wants to. It's his property. But unless his mind is gone, or he's in such a state that he does irresponsible things, there's not much you can do."

A sinking feeling pulled at his stomach. He was forgetting what he'd rehearsed and had to fight to bring it to mind.

"He talks about—he sings songs—and talks about places that don't exist anymore." He jerked his head in the direction of Camille. "Back there—back in all those trees. And I'm scared he might try and go back there sometime, like he talks about. He might go back there."

Trula batted her eyes, then made a note on her legal pad. She started to speak before she was finished writing.

"All right. Now you mentioned you could get me some record of his inability to—"

Cox's head shot around. He stared down the hall where Tollet lay.

He was flopping around on the bed now, like a child jumping on a trampoline. God help him if he started to sing, because then she would ask. But then, he had wanted her to ask.

"Mr. Tollet?"

"I'm sorry. What?"

"I asked what your father's name was, so I can get somebody to come out and observe him."

Cox scowled. He picked up the beer and rolled it between his palms. "Observe him?"

"We'll have to have somebody do a psychological study. Somebody who doesn't have anything to gain. The court won't accept it, otherwise."

He hadn't counted on that. His fingers drummed on his knee caps.

"His name's Jack Tollet."

She made a few notes. Cox bit his lip and asked, "They won't just take our word for it?"

She said No, then cocked her head and raised her chin. "Whose word besides yours?"

"Hey," came Shreva's voice.

Cox jumped. He couldn't make himself turn around, but watched Trula lean out a few inches, so that she could see through the screen door. Her face changed from surprised to curious.

"Umm," stumbled Cox. "Umm—well—who is—who is it that'll come observe him?"

Trula's gaze drifted, then came back. "Oh. Somebody the court appoints. Somebody—"

"Hey, in there!" shouted Shreva. From the sound of her voice, Cox could tell she was walking across the yard.

"Somebody from Cellarsville?" he asked. He squirmed in his chair. Trula leaned out.

"Mmmhmm. I think—" she stopped, her gaze hung. She lifted her arm to point out the door. "You know there's a woman with a cardboard box out on your porch?"

Cox nodded briskly. "Don't pay her any attention."

BAM—BAM—BAM. The screen door banged in its frame.

"Hey!" Shreva yelled.

"All right!" shouted Cox. He leapt from his chair and bounded to the door. She was peering in, one hand pressed against the screen.

Cox reached for his billfold. Suddenly, he didn't trust his plan, let alone for it to work. Not now that they needed an observation.

Just pay her, he thought. Pay her the seventy-five dollars and get the hell rid of her.

His breath caught in his throat as he heard the first, faint strains—notes—of a hymn. It caught again as he realized he had left his billfold on his dresser.

"I don't have—time right now," he said, opening the screen an inch. He rifled through his pocket for a couple of dollars and shoved them through to Shreva. Then he cut his eyes back and forth between Shreva and the fence, motioning for her to leave.

"Just set the eggs on the porch. I got company. We'll settle it all later."

Shreva took the money, studied it, then eased her head up. She glanced over his shoulder at Trula and gave Cox a hard look.

"You said you'd pay me that back money you owe me." It was loud enough for the next three houses to hear.

Cox snarled and shook his head.

"You owe me close on a hunnerd dollars, Mr. Tollet. Lord knows, I been patient."

His palm slapped the door jam as he swung around. Storming towards the bedroom, he called over his shoulder: "I'll get it right now. Then you gotta get goin'."

He passed Tollet's door on the way, holding his breath against any sounds he might hear. The old man was humming, but in a voice too low for any but Cox's ear.

"Who're you?" he heard Shreva ask. He tripped over a box in his bedroom, hurrying to get to the dresser.

"Name's Trula Babcock." She answered in an uneasy way, as though she had noticed something. Before Cox found the billfold, he heard Trula get up and walk across the room.

"I'm Miz Shands. Do bidness with Mr. Tollet—sometimes." A moment passed, then she added, "You come to check on his crazy daddy?"

Cox winced and sped into the living room again, trying not to run.

Trula stood inside the screen, her arms crossed as she studied the woman on the other side of the mesh. Shreva might have been an animal at the zoo.

"Here you go," said Cox, scooting between them. He edged the door open and stuck the money out the hole. Shreva took it, then smiled in a way that made his blood curdle.

"How'd you know that?" asked Trula. "That I came about his daddy, I mean." She didn't look at Cox.

"Miz Shands comes by here every other day," he offered. "I might have mentioned it."

"His daddy sure is crazy," said Shreva. She didn't look at Cox either. He stood helplessly to the side, his fingers drumming against his thighs.

"I never seen him any way but drunk—in the house, on the porch, walking towards the highway. Isn't that right, Mr. Tollet?"

Cox's head nodded and shook at the same time.

Trula backed away a step.

Shreva came closer. Her face nearly touched the screen.

"Always has on filthy clothes, too," she said. "Vomick all over him. And wet britches." She cut her eyes at Cox. "Awful to see somebody th ataway. A shame, shame, shame."

Cox's neck hair bristled.

"Don't I know you?" asked Trula, studying Shreva. "Aren't you the one that ran your car into the post office last year?"

Shreva shook her head. "That was my sister."

Then, as if she were sliding a checker over a board, she stepped to the side and spoke again. "I seen him mowin' the yard naked before. I seen him wear a—"

Cox stamped his foot, hard; blood was in his eyes.

Trula moved further away. She squinted at Shreva.

"Aren't you the one that ran over all those dogs last year, on the same street?"

Shreva shook her head again. "That was my other sister." She eased her tongue along the edge of her bottom lip. Her eyes danced and her voice came out low.

"Listen. Listen. I hear him singing."

"Go on!" Cox said, louder than he'd meant. Both women watched his face flush.

"We gotta get back to work here. You go on and do the rest of your rounds."

Was the singing louder?

"Ain't you gonna show him to her?" She squared her eyes on Trula.

Cox looked at the woman, whose face seemed to set the question before him. He didn't like her expression—colder than before, as if she had been disappointed. He had lost control. He was trapped now.

Except for the sound of their steps, the house was quiet as he led her down the hall to Tollet's room. Unable to open the door himself, she did it for him. The hinges creaked liked something that had been shut too long.

The sounds weren't even notes yet. They stayed in some place between humming and whimpering, lingering on one plaintive key.

The music, which wasn't music, rode out on a wave of soured smells—clammy, sweat-soaked sheets—dank air, breathed and rebreathed—unwashed flesh, clay-stuck clothes—grease—hair—the rot of spilt bourbon.

Instead, he kept his gaze on the opposite wall, staring at an outlet that was missing its cover. In time, the door closed, and Trula backed away. He moved aside to let her pass.

"Maybe he'd be better off," she said. "Better off—after all."

She collected her things as she spoke, careful not to look him in the face. They didn't even swap gazes at the door.

After she left, Cox glanced out onto the back porch. Shreva had gone, and the yellow sun was slipping below the hill's black fringe, like a coin sinking into the pocket of an old winter coat.

Chapter 13

Henry slouched low on the sofa, his body parallel with the floor. Only his head was vertical, propped against the back cushion. He drummed his fingers on his stomach and watched the steam rise off the pots boiling on the stove.

Before Tollet went to lie down, he had sloshed water over pinto beans, black beans, butterbeans, and snap beans in four different pots. For some reason he was cooking everything they had stored in the freezer. He would likely forget and burn them into asphalt.

Henry changed the beat of his drum, alternating fingers so that they thumped his stomach one at a time.

He hated Saturday afternoon the most, nothing but baseball and wrestling on television. He had tape recorded cartoons all morning, but they weren't as good without the pictures, so he had gotten tired of listening. The little black box sat on the sofa, next to wads of crumpled paper, his failed attempts to draw a real-looking Superman. He couldn't draw eyes well, or noses and mouths. All that was left to do was sleep. He swung his legs up onto the sofa, closed his eyes, and tried to rest before Cox got home.

He had grown to hate being alone with him. Although he felt the same with Martha, he didn't notice it so much at her house, since other people were around. She stared at him in her confused way, like he was a crack in the plaster she didn't know how to fix, but he could count on her attention moving to Barnes or the girls.

At home, it was Cox and only Cox. Tollet had been drinking so much lately he hardly sat up anymore. And Cox seemed to take every inch, all the room, while ignoring he was there. It was worse than Martha's looks. She made him feel guilty. Cox made him feel like he was disappearing.

He flipped onto his stomach and tried to think about cold water running through his brain. That was what he did whenever he couldn't sleep. He imagined it washing out all the mess in his mind, like dirt flushed from rocks. When it worked, he would ease in and out of consciousness. But before he slept, he could always make out voices, like people talking to him from behind the rocks—conversations between Cox and Tollet and Martha. He couldn't always understand what they were saying, but it always seemed to be about him.

His lids slipped open, his eyes so close to the cushion that they crossed.

He didn't want to hear them, their voices ringing down a well. That's what he felt like: a bored-out space—a blank, a hollow. And what Cox had couldn't fill it, and what Martha had couldn't fill it. And it wasn't like Barnes had said, either. There was no opportunity, no opening, rising from a mistake, nothing that would tell him what to do. He *was* the mistake.

He was about to get up when Tollet came out of his room. It had been a long time since they had talked. He had been mad at him for a while. Then, just when he was over it, Tollet had gone on an endless drunk. Henry sat up, picked out the least crumpled piece of paper, smoothed it on his knee, and pretended to draw.

Tollet shuffled over to the kitchen. Dressed in a brown striped pajama top, some ratty suit-pants, and his slippers, he suddenly lost his balance in the middle of the room, like something had pulled him back by the shirttail. He rolled about on the balls of his feet, then regained momentum by leaning forward for the last few steps. Instead of turning off the beans, Tollet caught ahold of the counter and made his way, hand-over-hand, to the sink. Gently, he lowered himself so that he was level with the bottom cabinets. He pulled out a bottle, labored to stand, then uncapped and drained the liquor. He was very still for a moment, like a man being held, as the whiskey washed through. His shoulders rose. He swayed back an inch. Then he threw the bottle in the trash and turned, as if he had just brushed his teeth.

Henry cast his eyes down to his drawing. Tollet noticed him and edged backwards towards the stove. He peered into the pots, his face low enough for the steam to bathe it. Then he lowered the heat under the eyes, so that the steam tapered.

"Don't—" he started to speak, but got strangled. He cleared his voice and began again. "Don't wanta scorch 'em."

Henry nodded. "I was watching."

Out of the corner of his eye, he saw the old man send a scrawny arm out like a walking stick, feeling his way to the counter. When he arrived, he breathed a heavy sigh.

"Whatcha doin'?"

"Drawing."

Tollet nodded. "For school?"

Henry shook his head. "For me."

Tollet nodded in a bigger way, as if he should have known.

"What's that there?"

Henry glanced at the tape recorder, then back to his drawing. Superman's nose was turning out better than it had when he was concentrating.

"I was tape recording things with it this morning."

Tollet lifted himself up to his full height.

"Like what?" His voice was serious.

Henry looked up from the paper. The man's face was hot and his eyes were sharp. "Cartoons," said Henry. "Just cartoons."

For a moment, the old man stared at his hands, one lying on top of the other. The stove eyes clicked behind him, cooling. At length, he lost interest and shuffled back to his bedroom. The bedsprings wrenched up and down.

When he had finished, Henry was still dissatisfied with his eyes and noses. He crumpled the paper into a ball, gathered his scraps and threw them all away. Then he walked back to his room and pulled on his boots.

On Saturdays, he got to feed the stock for Cox. He had postponed doing it all day, to give himself something to look forward to. But there was nothing else now.

Summer was coming hard, crowding spring. He was already sweating by the time he opened the feed room door. The cat, lounging on the loft stairs, jumped up and ran to him, stroking herself against his pants leg.

The thick, brewed smell of molasses and oats rose up from the metal barrel. He dug the coffee can into the feed, filling it to the brim. Then he poured it out again, just to see the dust rise. All summer long he would hear this sifting sound, smell this sugary smell. With only one more week of school, the idea of summer had begun to sicken him. Days that yawned on and on, filled with nothing but wet heat and stinging light that refused to give up, and stretched farther and deeper into the evenings. He had never been given enough jobs to pass the time, since Cox said he was too small. But this was the summer he was to learn how to drive the tractor, if he was tall enough.

Henry backed up and looked himself over. Then he stretched his right arm out to the side and studied his tricep and bicep.

He was bigger this year, even bigger than at Christmas. He would point that out to Cox—remind him of his promise—if that were still possible. But there was a new strangeness to his father now. After he had come back from Martha's, Henry had stumbled across Cox several times—in the living room, shoulder against the window—in the feed lot, hammer in hand—standing and staring. It had spooked Henry so much that he had tried to ease away without notice, like Cox was a sleepwalker he didn't want to disturb.

He dumped four coffee cans full of feed into a bucket, scattered some calf manna pellets over the top, then shooed the cat away from his pants leg.

He took the bucket outside to the brood mares in the side pasture and made two piles in the trough, one at each end. She could only eat one pile at a time, but the biggest mare put her ears back at the other and ran her away. Henry climbed the fence and swung the bucket at her head. She backed off, and the other mare got a few bites. The peace would only last until he was out of sight.

At first, Henry thought Cox was mad about Martha. Maybe Cox thought that since she and Barnes had decided to get married, she would cause some kind of new trouble for him. But when he had mentioned their news, Cox's color had drawn back into his face. Tollet began a coughing fit.

Whatever Cox had on his mind, Martha or something else, it was Tollet that jolted him awake again, sent him scurrying. He had noticed it on his first day back. Cox wouldn't be alone in the same room with Tollet. If he was eating at the table when the old man stumbled in, Cox took a plate to his recliner and finished his meal in front of the television, with the volume full blast. He wouldn't move until it was time for bed. Each morning, he folded his breakfast— either a slew of biscuits, a stack of pancakes, or a pile of Pop-Tarts— inside a paper napkin and carried it with him out the door. Tollet was too soaked to notice.

Still, Henry had seen it. So it wasn't just him that Cox was trying to ignore. He was just the only one Cox was successful at ignoring. Tollet seemed to give him more trouble.

With the teasing pony's feed in one bucket and the saddle mare's feed in the other, he made his way down the barn hall to their stalls. The mare had cataracts on both eyes now, but she knew he was coming. She neighed over and over, hurrying him on. He swung her door open and was met by the sweet manure-and-straw smell of a stall that needed cleaning. After he dumped the feed into her trough, she buried her grizzled nose into the pile and spread it around.

Milk might have pooled and dried inside her eyes. He had given up trying to pet her since all it did was make her spook. He closed her door and moved down to the next.

Shut inside a stall, the teasing pony jerked his flax-maned neck about when Henry entered. He was in the middle of pissing a hot yellow stream into the straw, the hard sound of hose water on dry brick. The pony was as mean as he was short. Henry used to think it was because he never got outside, or because his hooves needed trimming. They curled up on the end like clown shoes. But since Lois, and the S, he knew what "teasing" meant, and why the pony went crazy when Cox shoved a mare's butt up to the opened top half of his stall. His nose would twitch, and he would practically climb the door. He wasn't so much mean as he was crazy; like Cox was crazy; like Henry had almost been.

She still came, Lois—but less and less. Now someone else came, taller and younger and with tanned knees—but his mind was too full of other things at present to dwell on her.

The cattle were in the pasture, except for the two pink-eyed steers. They had both healed up, but for some reason, Cox had moved them back into a stall last week. While he was feeding the pony, he had listened for them at the end of the hall—for their gentle shifting from one foot to the other, their low calls to him, at the food he brought.

After he dashed four cans full of feed into a bucket, he set off to the farthest part of the barn to feed them. Once mad with fear, beating their blind, bandaged faces against the fence, they were gentle now. The darkness that their disease had brought them to somehow had stilled them. They would let him touch their ears, stroke their necks, stare into their deep, brown-black eyes as they ate patiently from the trough.

The cat, back for his ankles, followed along, nearly tripping him as she wound about his legs. He glanced down at her, standing in a spring-loaded position next to the stall door. She was interested in a faint scratching noise inside.

Must be a rat in there, Henry thought, easing open the latch.

It was dark and hot at this end of the barn, a place where big rats scurried from one beam to the next, to feed their squeaking babies, hidden in unseen holes. It was because of this corner of the barn that Cox let the cat stay. It was because of this corner that he had taken her kits.

The door swung open and the cat dashed into the dark, scaling the feed trough after the sound, chasing its trail. Henry watched her disappear, then followed inside.

He had one foot over the threshold, the bucket lifted to empty the feed, when he noticed the quiet. It was hotter here and darker than it had been. Uneasy, he peered further in.

His hands seized around the metal handle. He looked about, from corner to corner. Nothing was there.

The bucket clanked to the ground. He ran through the hall, to the outdoors—darkness, shadow, then a hard, mean daylight, the sun's heat spanking his back, catching him up like a hand, lifting him over the fence, into the yard, across the grass to the open door. He didn't know he was yelling until he saw Tollet's face.

"Wait!—Hold it!—Hold it!" The old man stumbled from the back hall, his arms out.

With a jerk, Henry stopped just inside the door.

"Hush, hush!" Tollet yelled, still coming. His eyes swelled, fixed onto Henry's head in strange way. The boy's arm shot from his side, swiped his brow. He looked at his hands, but they were only covered with sweat and dirt.

"Godamighty," said Tollet, pulling him onto a chair. "Whatza matter with you?"

They sat facing each other, Tollet studying Henry's face, Henry listening to his breathing fall as he stared out the door. In time, he spoke.

"The stall's—empty!"

"What stall?"

"The steers'!"

Tollet took a long breath. He leaned against the back of his chair, his face unclenched.

"Is *that* all? Slaughterhouse come for 'em yesterday mornin.' You knew they would."

Henry looked out towards the lot where the calves had stood ankle-deep in mud. He pictured their heads turning, eyes newly healed—soft and black and sleepy—bending in the dark towards the smell of whatever approached. Feed? Hay? Water? A man. Two men. A truck. A sledgehammer. One, then the other, first feed—then a sledgehammer—and not the sense to know the difference. So eyes healed for what?

Tollet struggled up from his seat and went to the stove. He slid the pots off the burners and turned the eyes down.

"That's why I'm cooking up all these beans we had froze. Gotta make room in the freezer."

No matter how much he swallowed, he still needed to swallow. He put his fingers to his scalp. It felt numb, burned.

"What's the matter?" asked Tollet. "Why you lookin' thataway?"

All at once, Henry felt a rising within his chest—a groan or yell. But before it reached sound, it smothered to death in his throat. His mouth opened and closed, a useless motion. His eyes filled with hot water.

Tollet's jaw set. He studied the boy for a moment before nodding to him, then motioned to his room with a toss of his head.

"Follow me," he said. "Get up and follow me."

Henry found himself rising, trailing the old man down the hall, towards the next sight or smell, the next darkness or lack, whatever lay at the end. He was as mute as if his cords had been cut. He stared at the heels of the old man's shoes, scratching and scraping the hard-wood, leading him into the damp, sopping room, hot as summer dirt—shades pulled past the sill—dank sheets and pillows thrown about the shadowed floor.

"I know what you need," said Tollet, in a murmur. "I know what'll fix you."

Henry minded the whispering, thought it odd, didn't care that it was odd. He took his old place, below Tollet's chair, and waited for whatever would be given. It was as though he were turning inside out—his bones and flesh and blood sifting into the air—fewer, scanter—less and less—his arms, his legs, his head.

"Don't worry," said Tollet. "My Daddy gimme this for colds and coughs." He gave a soft, delighted little laugh. "Works on what you got, too. And you got it bad. I know."

From behind his chair, hidden, Tollet pulled a sleeve of glass, half clear-half caramel.

"Works on most everything."

In the night-light's used glow, Henry watched the man roll the bottle between his palms, like he was kindling fire. And when the top came off, and the caramel slid down his throat, fire was just what he felt. A rolling ball of lava mingled inside his skin, blended with blood, already thin as mist. It scourged and chased what was left of him, down the bottomless hole. He didn't even cough.

From then on, Tollet invited him in every afternoon, like a guest he was surprised at having, but was glad to have. Henry stayed there until just before Cox came home. The old man wouldn't let him have much—just enough to loosen him, to unbuckle the straps in his head, and the ones that tied his tongue down.

"Don't wanta let 'im know," said Tollet, his green eyes darting towards Cox's room. "Long as you don't *act* stupid—he'll just smell you, and think it's me."

Henry didn't care. Not about Cox, or Martha, or anybody. He didn't even care what Tollet wanted with him. Maybe the old man thought of him like he did Felix: a drinking buddy. Maybe he thought of him like he did Royce and Marcel: somebody to do bad with. It didn't matter anymore. It gave him a time to look forward to.

"It's not the taste," Tollet said, handing him a glass. The whisky poured from the bottleneck in cheerful gulps. "Not at first, anyhow. It's—what it does."

And he was right. Terrible as it tasted, it laid a warm blanket over Henry's brains. The brown water scoured through the rocks in his head. He forgot to worry about what had happened, or was happening, or would happen. No matter how bad, those things wouldn't fret him. Sooner or later, they all lost hold, slipped into the current, over and again. In time, the water was so dark that all he could see was the water: afternoons of dark water. And through them all, Tollet weaved his little pictures—harmless stories—almost liquid themselves. Henry wondered why he had ever been scared of them. The tales swept by, under the water.

"Me and Marcel—or me and Royce—don't remember who," said Tollet, not bothering to lean forward. Henry was sprawled on his back, listening as the stories passed over his head. They painted pictures onto the gray ceiling, all clouds and smoke.

"Hung that goat from the barn joist. Royce said—'Jack shove him—shove him out the loft.' But I was tired by then. Sweaty from carryin' him up, pullin' him by the horns all the way."

A picture swam across the ceiling to meet the words, to rise from them. Tollet—the Tollet from tattered black and white photographs—

bony and slick-headed, a sharp smile digging creases into his face. He was perched on his haunches, in somebody's loft. Theirs? Yes, theirs.

Tollet laughed. "'You come help me'—I whispered at him—'I carried the sonuvabitch up here—now you come hang 'im.'"

Henry saw the goat's white head jerk, turn—dumb white eyes, flashing. Not a sledgehammer, this time. A rope, this time.

Why, Tollet? Why'd you hang the goat? Henry thought.

He watched Royce—or Marcel—he always pictured the same person—whether Royce or Marcel—scale the ladder—shove the goat out the hole—scraping of hooves across dry boards.

"Why?" Tollet repeated, confused.

Henry turned his head. He must have spoken the question, though he hadn't heard his voice.

"'Cause it was her husband's goat," said Tollet. "And Royce said this was a way to 'get it.' See? See? I'd already done got his 'cat'—her hangin' from the porch eaves."

Henry blinked at him. So it was the same man—his "goat," his "cat."

Tollet breathed in a phlegm-strangled way. "'Course, she had to leave that boy—had to move off. I've thought I seen him 'round, from time to time, with that bad eye of his."

He stopped, shook his head. "But her—she had to move off."

A long time passed. Henry looked over to see that Tollet was far beyond the story now. He was already drifting out to another one, which swam up to meet him.

"When time come, I told Cox to do the same thing. But it— worried him. And I couldn't—" Tollet's eyes grew tight, as if he'd been pricked. His gaze came back to the boy.

Henry lay as still as he could manage, as though trying to be passed over, unnoticed. He felt himself leaving with a creeping numbness. He had begun to bleed into the air, melt into the darkness that huddled in the corners, beneath the bed.

"—I'd done got his cat," Tollet began again, his voice straining for brightness, "and now here I was gettin' his 'goat.' See?"

Henry watched the goat sway from the rope's end, its feet twitching. A long neck; a strange angle. The only thing that wasn't black and white was the faint, pink tip of its tongue.

"But *why'd* you want his cat?" he asked, with a cracked voice. "*Why'd* you want his goat?"

The sound of liquor washed down the bottleneck. The old man moved against his cushioned chair. He looked like he was being held and tied.

"'S all we *had*, see? All we *had*—was what we made up. And after a while—boys you know—we just—" he shrugged. "Just natural—to come on to meanness." He cocked his head, as though to look at the words. "Feed chickens—fix a fender—stir up a l'il trouble. Gets to be—" he shrugged again, "Natural. Then, that's all you do."

Henry rolled onto his stomach, his cheek against the cold floor. His eyes slid shut.

He stopped taking supper at the table. Cox ate at the TV now, so he didn't care. In a few days, Henry was feeding himself like Tollet did, standing up: a piece of bread, a slice of ham, some cereal from the box. Then he would go to his room and sleep.

Sleep was easy now. It wound around his head as he lay there, heavier than the quilts, the layers of patched pattern, sewn by his grandmother, whoever she was.

Martha called to ask why he had skipped the last two days of school. He enjoyed the lie he told—sickness, need of rest. She would bring his report card to him, she had said—all As.

Good, he thought. Goooood.

With school over, and Cox gone to work, he had the whole day to give to Tollet's room. And now he wanted it more and more. It was a different a kind of wanting. Instead of the red hot itch in his crotch that built and sparked and exploded—instead of the cool blue flame of what he knew and what he would never be afraid of—instead of those things, lies that promised what they could not give—this was a smoldering that never died. It could not lie because it was past, and dead things promised nothing. It was black, like ashes were black. But beneath the black. . . .

Mid-afternoon of a broiling day. As he fed the horses, he noticed the stock under the hackberries lining the fencerow. They stood in a file, nose to tail, clinging to stay inside the scant shade. They looked as though they were holding their breath in the heat, trying to stand it until all was over. It was a sight that made him tired to see.

He came inside, to the wall unit air conditioners, roaring full blast. They blew iced air through the house, like a sickness, spreading. And once he was in Tollet's room, the cold grew even colder. For some reason, Tollet had filled the glass higher this time, and handed it to him like a gift.

The day crept on, into late afternoon. He slept and woke and slept, no longer cold.

"You don't know nothin' 'bout this here," the old man started.

Henry lay face down on the floor, his head turned to see the dust beneath the dresser.

"But oncet, me and Marcel 'n Royce and Lewis and—that boy—from Van Vleet—that boy from Van Vleet. . . ."

Tollet blew a few desperate puffs, searching for the name.

Henry's mind was foggy, but it was sharper than Tollet's. The old man had gotten lost, started to sink beneath the waves. If he couldn't remember, the story would fade out, and he might start to cry.

"Leo," said Henry. He moved his arms to lay them against his body. The near empty glass sat beside him on the floor, like a dog, watching.

"Leo!" said Tollet, grabbing the name. He chuckled to himself for a moment, glad of his safety. Henry turned his head to the other side. He stared at Tollet's slippered feet.

"The six of us—"

"Five," said Henry.

"Five—of us caught that boy comin' out the sawmill. Him lookin' down at his paycheck—eyes turned in on it, like the number wasn't right—and Royce caught him across the throat with his forearm. Knocked him onto that dust."

Tollet wrestled about in his chair, showing the struggle. Henry had heard it many times—this same boy, ambushed outside a sawmill. It was the same boy whose wife—"cat"—Tollet had rammed on the porch, hanging from the eaves—the same boy whose goat he had taken to the loft and hung from the barn joist.

"And we drug him off—now, we was so bad drunk by that time we couldn'ta drug him far—but to the—the—"

"To the well house," said Henry. And he saw it: wood and stone, sunk low into the ground.

"To the well house," Tollet whispered. At this point the man's voice would drop. Something about it started to worry him.

"And Royce had 'im by the mouth to keep 'im from hollerin'—'n—'n—that sonuvabitch bit Royce on the inside of his ring finger—bit hard!"

And Royce got mad, Henry told himself. And threw him down on the well house floor. With his bit hand, he balled a fist and drove it again and again into the same socket of the same eye—kick and squirm and scream—no matter. The same socket of the same eye—like a drill, mining. It brought up a slick, bright red, over and again. A red oil. And even Tollet couldn't laugh at that. The old man told it fast, before he could stop himself.

"And him screamin'—and us runnin' out—and me behind Royce—watchin' him dry his knuckles on his pants leg—wiping that mess—on his britches leg—and kept on runnin'. . . ."

Henry nodded, swiping his cheek across the floor. His gaze left the old man's slippers, traveled up his legs to his face. Tollet stared as the memory swarmed his head.

He had heard this story. He knew this tale. It didn't scare him. That part wasn't even worth telling. What Henry wanted to know, Tollet would never say. He decided to press him once more.

"But—Why'dja—" He had to fight his tongue; it was stuck to the inside of his teeth. "Why'dja hang *his* goat?"

Still, he failed to break Tollet's stare loose. The boy slurped the spit to the back of his mouth and swallowed. He spoke again, desperate.

"Why'dja—want—*his* cat?"

Tollet warmed, his face turning towards the question. His eyes were cold. One cheek rose, creating an odd sneer on his mouth.

"'Cause—he was the kind. He was the kind—you could *do* that to."

The look dug into Henry's chest like the jagged nail of a bony finger, puncturing his heart. He climbed to his elbows, then to his knees. Then he kept climbing, fighting to rise. He turned his ankle and fell back into the same spot.

To his right, the dog was watching him. To the left was the wall. In time, he drained what was left from the glass and clamped his eyes shut. Croupy breath rattled around his lungs.

"I—hate—him. *Hate* 'im." He pulled a deep breath. "Her too."

Tollet sat still.

"I hate 'em all." He opened his eyes to lasso every last thing, to let nothing escape.

The old man leaned forward, but Henry scooted back. His hatred rolled like a barrel through his chest. His mouth shut with a clack of teeth. He aimed his face at Tollet.

You too, he thought. And I can hang more than goats.

"Sit still," Tollet whispered, a dry hiss. "I can fix that."

He reached for the bottle. It rested beside his chair leg like a tiny soldier. He kept his gaze on Henry, staring as though he recognized something in his face, as though he had just now realized who the boy was, after all this time. He held the bottle out, a gift he had saved for this reunion. Henry took it.

"Just sit still," Tollet whispered. His voice rolled about in a marvelous way. He nodded, then smiled.

"Stay here. With me." He felt about the air, like he was grazing his fingers over old furniture—the bed he had been born in, the bed where he would die. "This here's—safe."

Henry lifted the bottle to his lips, threw it back. The brown water washed in eddies through the coils of his brain. In time, he heard Tollet speak again.

"'Member what I toldja'?" he asked. "It won't get no better."

He cut his eyes at the window, its shade pulled nearly to the floor. "N'matter what they say. N'matter what you do. So just—sit still. Don't move."

Henry batted his eyes, neither yes, nor no. He lifted the bottle.

In time, his gaze wandered from place to place—from a broken spider's web in the corner, to his own frayed shoelaces, then to Tollet's face: head back, mouth open, lids shut in a black sleep.

Henry's eyes fogged. The room had been varnished—Tollet, his chair—everything—sealed in a thick, clear lacquer. Or was it his eyes? Like the steers' eyes?

A goat. Pink tongue.

He leaned forward, sent a shaky hand out to his grandfather's pants leg. It was too dark to see. Too much brown water. The air was cold again, and the dark made him suffocate. He needed light, to see.

His hand floated clear of him, reached for the shade. But it fell somewhere short, so that he fumbled with a curtain's hem.

Then, somehow, he found himself inside a box, inside a tight chest. His head banged against the lid—covered with dirt?—beneath water? The air, cold, grew thin. His lungs pulled at it, but yanked back like a string, snagged. He yanked again. His chest spasmed, dry heaves.

Somewhere, somebody was singing. A thin song, full of holes, without words, but with a thing like words.

Fa—Sol—Fa—Sol. . . .

He scratched his way up the box's lid, his knees bouncing against its boards as he climbed towards what was above him—or was it outside? An angle of light, creeping around the lid's sides—lines of yellow and red—reached in, to draw him out. He clawed at the lid and coughed some hard, yieldless coughs.

The sound of hinges—the lid opening—a door.

All at once, a hand grabbed the collar of his shirt, lifted him clear of the ground. The brown water cleared and he saw, with a mixed joy, his father's face. But it was wrenched—warped.

"Goddamn it!" he heard. "Goddamn it!"

His hot breath roused Henry—set him squirming—fighting to get free; all joy faded. Then he found he was flying through the air, Cox slinging him onto the bed. He bounced off the mattress, slid to the floor.

He managed to stand, foundered out of the room, his hands meeting this wall, that wall. Before he left, he glimpsed Cox bending over Tollet. The old man had slumped out of his seat, curled into a ball beside the chair.

"Goddamn you!" Cox screamed.

Henry knocked through the dim hall, towards the next room. The box was his house, and the lid was its roof, and the only light he could find was a weak, cool light—emptying through the screen door, like water pulled towards a drain. Outside, he found the reason.

On the far hill, the sun had been caught—dragged down—by the trees' dark arms. Its red face was being smothered, silently, by a thousand black fingers.

He steadied himself against a porch post, then wove his way across the yard, through the pasture, wandering in the direction of the light's quiet, formal slaughter in the evening sky.

Chapter 14

Cox couldn't dial the right number. Whenever he got past 255-23 . . . he had to stop. It wouldn't come. He couldn't make it come.

Shit—I lived there—*lived* there. Dial it all the time. It used to be mine. . . .

The house reeked of beans and steamed water. The air conditioning poured out the screen—he hadn't had time to shut the door. How could he? When he had heard the goddamn singing the minute—the very minute he came in—and a knocking to go with it, like somebody beating on a box. And strangled coughs.

The sight of them! Stinking—sopping—rolling around on the floor. Henry—having a fit against the wall—a toy gone crazy, trying to crawl up the curtains.

255-23—4?—4.

No. Not four.

"Goddamn!"

He laid his forehead against the wall and stopped to think. The receiver dropped, clanked to the floor, bounced, hit his toe.

He had ripped the shade off the window, crumpled it inside his fist like a sheet of paper, yanked it clean from the roller. The sun blasted through like a canon.

4.

His eyes opened, glanced sideways.

Where was Henry?

He had cracked the bottle against the dresser's edge—regretted it when the whisky flew all over him—splattered his face. God, the smell. He swiped his nose across his shirt sleeve.

With a match, he would have lit the whole thing. With a hose, he would have drowned the place.

"Henry?" he called.

He looked out the door to see—the sun was gone and the land had turned blue—gray—shoe polish black.

Think. Think! 2345 . . . 2346.

He had ripped Tollet from the floor—dragged him to the bathroom—stuck his head in the toilet without seeing whether the piss had been flushed or not. Tollet had sputtered, screamed, cried. He had been hunched against the tub when Cox left him. Left him for the phone.

2345?

The phone book. No. He would not—would not—look up his own wife's goddamn number in the goddamn phone book. Surely to God he wouldn't. It had been his, after all.

2345. He scooped the receiver from the floor—dialed—stood for the rings, one after the goddamn other.

"Martha?"

"*What?*" A man's voice.

"Put Martha—"

"*I'm sorry, you got the wrooooong number,*" the man said.

Cox's fumbled to hang up, missed the cradle, hung up again.

"Henry? Henry!"

He had seen him stumble out of the room—drunk. Drunk!

In the barn, probably. Like always. Skulking off. On the bottom. Like always. But a different bottom, and a different kind of drowning. If he'd only known this was going on while he was away.

To see him like that—climbing a wall—a dog gone crazy acted like that—tried to climb things he couldn't. A colt, weaned, did such things, insane for its mother.

2346—no answer.

2347—the fire department.

Try them all. Every goddamn one. Numbers.

No sound from Tollet. Not dead, though. He hadn't killed him. No. It would be the other way around. *He* would kill them all, Tollet would. He would live past all of them—stand, stagger, wobble—he would tromp over their dead bodies looking for a drink.

Cox rubbed his head from brow to crown, slid his hand down to knead the ropes in his neck.

The phone book was on the counter.

The pages turned like flimsy wings, tearing at the tops—along the bind. Her name would be . . . would be. . . .

"Mrs. Cox Tollet?" "Mrs. Martha Tollet?" "Martha Tollet?" "M. Tollet?"

It was there—beneath his own: Tollet, M. Macby—255-2354.

Yes. One number wrong. That was all he had been off—one number, the wrong way.

One at a time, under his finger, he rolled the dial around to the catch.

Clickclickclickclickclick.

Another—clickclickclicklclick.

Static. A gargle of rings, pauses, rings.

"*Hello?*"

Her soft, lotioned voice. Cream. Froth.

"*Hello?*"

But, if he spoke, his voice would turn hers from soft to hard, from fresh to stale. It always did. So no words this time. Or just enough to make her stay. A groan—like a word, or enough like a word to have her ask.

"*Mother? Henry? What's wrong?*"

He shuddered at the thought of her hands, how she had placed them on either side of his neck, cool against the bone. She would fold him in, like a child to a full breast.

The skin of his face tightened, his tongue doubled, rolled.

"*I'm hanging up.*"

"It's me."

Then all they had ever done to each other poured into the silence, began to sour and ruin the time. He caught his breath as he waited for her voice to change.

"*What do you want?*"

"I—"

"*What?*"

His mind slid, fell from the shelf of his skull.

"*What?*"

Everything. Always wrapped and taken—given to others—what was his—given to others—before he had ever even. . . .

"*Are you—drunk?*"

"No. No!"

She sighed. He felt his skin go cold, move beneath his clothes.

"*Leave me alone, Cox.*"

He sighed, to get it back.

"No."

"*It's over now. All over.*"

No.

"*Goodbye.*"

Static. A long time of nothing.

On the dusty, hardwood floor, with empty hands. Only his hands, and the slurred, shredded voice of his father, breathing shape notes into the air, like a sickness, like a death rattle, come to claim. He closed his eyes and listened to the hums rising from the back of the house.

Before he even had a chance.

Chapter 15

The sun was gone. The moon's pearly face grew into the violet sky like a diver rising towards the surface of the sea.

Henry gathered a long breath. Before him stood the first line of trees, their heights staggered as they climbed the hill. He scanned the woods from one side to the other, then stared at the farthest thing he could see—a line of firs at the crest, grazing the heavy, sagging night. The more distant the trees, the flatter they seemed, like black felt glued to purple paper. For no better reason than that he was facing that way, he walked towards the woods, beneath the green-black branches.

How long it had taken to get through the field, he did not know. But as he had crossed, his mind came back to him, like a sponge opening to cold water. He had never lost consciousness—never fell—even at his drunkest. Using them as handholds, he had made his way from fence post to fence post—the lattice of page wire in between—the whole row, a line, pulling him to his senses—eyes, ears, skin, quickening.

He reached a cluster of cedars and leaned against one of the shredded, papery trunks.

The churn of a drill bit bored through his stomach—an auger, scraping out a widening pit. He stared at the ground, feeling the trace of the auger's path, the curve it would take—grazing, slicing, splitting his heart. His gorge rose. He bent over his knees and vomited into the grass. His throat and mouth burned. He wiped his lips on the back of his hand and walked on.

His feet took him along a path he could travel sightless. He waded through spent leaves, beneath the sound of newly born insects, screaming their way into the treetops. On a level lower than the rest, but more constant, there was the sound of some distant saw, some engine straining to start. The sharp-smelling cedars, their brushes stirring in the slight breeze, seemed to bring him scents of new grass, birds, and from a place nearby, smoke. Beneath the trees, the ground was a heavy gray-black, with scattered patches of moon-gloss standing out like islands.

He wondered if he could keep walking when he didn't know the way anymore, after he had reached a place he hadn't been. He saw himself, ageless, in friendless towns, stared at by half-hating faces. Or maybe not noticed at all—ignored and stepped around—like a hole dug, but unused.

His legs moved under him heavily, his hips swinging at the sockets, his feet sent out on missions to take his weight. Moving just to move, walking just to go, towards nothing and no one.

It was something that should make him cry, he knew—something that should throw him under the first truck he saw, like he had heard of people doing. But he was, even then, being scattered like feed—or more like something pulled loose—his parts unglued, snapped free.

He stopped at a clear, wet-smelling place near Shreva's trailer. It was a sunken spot, covered by dense trees, so dark that even the bugs hadn't found it yet, a place as still as a room where the only candle has been smothered.

Minutes passed. His stomach and ribs broiled, the drill-bit churning.

His eyes shifted about the trees. Footsteps, breaking sticks, grinding leaves.

His nostrils flared for something above the smell of smoke and sprouted grass. His skin shrank. He felt like he was being reached for, approached—from both outside and in—two things coming towards a meeting place, an exchange at the desert of his heart. But before it could happen, he saw the boy.

He was lit with the backsplash from the light he carried—an old, odd light—fierce with glare—a light that dangled from a handle.

Henry couldn't see his face, only part of his body, his elbow and side, the turn of his hips. Still, he knew him.

There was nothing left to do, no place else to go. So he followed at a distance, one at which leaves and grass muffled his own soft steps.

At length, his mind unbuckled. His movement, step-shift-step, was all he knew. He floated through the dark, up and along the ridge, down and along the creek bed, following the circle of light. On and on it went. There was nothing else in the world—no other time than this black, wet time that swept him in its water, in the wake of a drifting flame.

At some point, he noticed his breath heaving in his lungs. Miles they had come, off the path, in a direction he had never thought to go, over hills he had never walked. His shoes were filled with water he hadn't seen until he felt it, his cheeks and arms scratched by trees he had not noticed until they whipped his flesh. All was wrapped and layered, near to dark, close to black.

Then, after one hill more, a row of yellow lights bloomed in the distance—tall thin rectangles, side-by-side—the panes of windows—arches at their tops. The boy's light traveled towards them, with Henry in its tow.

He knew at once that it was where the boy lived. The beam faded, jogged and jittered—up steps? A door opened and closed. A familiar sound in a strange place. It moved his mind like gears in ratchets. He blinked. The evening's cool washed his face.

Through low brush that caught at his clothes, he waded towards the house. It was long and narrow, more windows than walls. In the moonlight he could see a dome-topped box on the roof. It had an opening on all four sides, but whatever had rested inside was gone. It wasn't the chimney, because a stovepipe jutted through the tin, smoke belching from its top.

He found the outline of a small, falling-down fence. A caved-in mailbox lay on the ground.

There had not been mail in years, Henry knew. Nobody—not the town or school or government—would care about what was this far back, tucked away.

No further, he told himself. There was nowhere else to go. The only place left to walk was up the steps and into the lighted house.

The wind from the cedars blew across his face, ran fingers through his hair, a clear perfume born on the cool breeze. It braced him, tensed his muscles. Before he could move, a door opened again—not from the front this time, but the back. He looked over the house and saw the round glow nodding through the far dark.

Henry gathered himself to follow, like a dog trailing his master. But as he started to round the house corner, there came a slight creaking sound, like the lid of an old chest. A blade of light came out to lay across him. He stopped.

In the front door was a black silhouette, one hand on the knob. Henry looked away, towards the woods. He couldn't follow the boy now. His light bobbed over what might be a hill rise, shimmered against what might be trees, then disappeared. He watched its last place for a moment, then drifted his gaze towards the man at the door.

"Who're you?" The sound was old, cracked, dry.

Henry didn't answer. The question slid off his mind like a pebble bouncing down a cliff.

"Come here."

His eyes grew used to the light. The doors were double, the man standing in the open one. He rustled through high grass and pulled himself onto the buckled porch by a roof post.

As he came, the man slowly backed into the house's redness. His features grew clear. By the time Henry crossed the threshold, the man had backed into full light.

He was dressed in a worn black overcoat that reached to his knees, each chipped button in its own hole. The sash was pulled tight about his waist. A few inches of brown pants showed beneath the hem of his coat before ducking into the tops of black, galoshes. He was as old as Tollet: scrawny, stooped, folded at the shoulders like him. His skin was more taut, though, and though the top of his head was bald, thick white hair fell from above his ears to his collarbones. But for the caved-in sink of his left eye socket, his face was the same as the boy's, with the stick and the light.

"I asked who you was."

He stood among slat-back chairs and tables, cluttered with boxes full of soup cans, knives and forks, old magazines, yellow newspaper. Army blankets hung clumsily from tacks over the windows. By the high-pitched ceiling, and the length of the one room, Henry could tell the house used to be something else. The place smelled of the ground, and of smoke from the green firewood that popped in the corner stove.

"I got lost," Henry said. He wasn't sure what he had been asked. He stared into the vacant socket rather than the fierce black eye.

"Where's Wolfy?"

The man snatched his head to the left, his hair sweeping about like a girl's. "Thataway."

Henry nodded, then rolled his lips inside his mouth, licked them.

"Where am I, then?" he asked. He just wanted to hear it said.

"Camille."

He looked at the stove, its fire so loud it might've been its business to heat the world. Sweat cropped along his forearms, waist, the small of his back. Nearly summer, and a stove roaring.

"Who're you?" Henry asked.

The man's eye widened. His mouth opened slightly.

"Shands."

Henry's blood simmered beneath his brow, back, ribs. A bloom of sweat spilt from his scalp, drizzled down his temple.

"Well? I asked who *you* was," The old man took his hands from his coat pockets and made a helpless gesture, a flit of his wrists, then returned them.

"You're in *my* house. You gotta say."

Henry pivoted to see behind him. A cot covered with dirty sheets and green army blankets sat against the wall, next to an open cedar chifforobe. Hanging inside were clay-stained pants, flannel shirts, and the red plastic poncho. He wanted to walk over, to look close, but the man asked him again who he was.

"Who is he?" Henry asked back. He motioned to the clothes with a backward nod.

The old man's face fell. It took a frightened cast. He looked like a prisoner caught with a shovel in his cell.

"My boy."

Henry took a step toward him, then stepped back. A mean heat flared in his belly, licked at his skin.

"How come I never saw him before? At school—or—"

"He don't go. They don't know 'bout 'im." He stopped. "He's turned a man now, anyhow." The man nodded briskly, as though to convince himself. "I need 'im more'n they do."

Henry swallowed. His throat was dry as hemp rope.

"Where's your wife?"

The man's face clouded. "Ain't got one." He bit his lip. Then he said, as though he had to tell the truth about it: "One run off. One run me off."

Henry felt a surge in his chest, like thirst.

"Where's his mama, then?" he asked. He rolled the balls of his fingers over the tops of his thumbs.

"What?"

"I said 'Where's his mama?'"

Shands glanced at the floor, then up and over in the direction of Wolfy.

"She lives thataway. In a trailer." He stared at the wall, as though he could see through the boards and the dark hills beyond them. "I took him with me when he come."

Henry sighed, wrung through with heat. He wiped his face with his hands, smearing the salty sweat onto his lips. Traces of old scab came off beneath the pressure. He was on fire.

"What happened to your head?"

He took his hands from his face. He couldn't think straight. He looked at his fingers.

"He—your boy," he managed. "Beat me."

The man passed the gaze of his eye over Henry's body, a site finding its mark. He took a step back.

"You're a Tollet."

Henry fluttered his lids for an answer. He mopped his throbbing brow with his forearm.

"Did *he* tell you?" he asked, nodding at the poncho.

Shands bunched his mouth, shook his head.

Henry stared hard into his eye, then into his socket. He could make him tell, he knew. He could make him tell just by staying there until he told. The man shuffled about in a useless delay. At length, he spoke.

"Heard his mama ask him to do it." He stopped for a breath. Henry trained his eyes on him, careful not to blink or flinch, to give him no place to go.

"She come 'cross late one evening." His face fell. "She gets a gov'ment check, for bein'—my widow." He said the rest to the floor.

"Half of it's mine. We trade money—groceries—chickens."

He shook his head. He had said too much, for no reason, to a strange boy who had no business in his house, no claim to the truth. He had said too much; too much truth. Suddenly, his head came up, his black eye flashing.

"But she come here, and knocked on that door—'rap-rap-rap'— like she owned it. And him sitting there, pulling shoes on—he hopped up from that bed—"

The man stopped to point a crooked finger at the cot, as though Henry needed to know where it was to understand—"one shoe in his hand, one on his foot, and come towards her like a—fool. Like a child."

He gasped at what he described. "Him grown, but still actin'—" he broke off, composed himself, and pointed at Henry's head. "That's what she wanted, so that's what he done."

Henry squirmed. He pulled his shirt away from his slathered ribs. "Why'd he do it?" he asked, amazed.

The man flashed an aggravated look, as though Henry had no right to misunderstand.

The boy lowered his eyes, cowed his head. "Why'd she want it, then?" he asked.

Shands cut the words with his teeth. "To get something from y'all, I guess."

Henry shook his head. "How come you let him?"

The old man took his hand from his pocket, grazed shaking fingers beneath the round of his left cheek, as though to wipe it clean. His good eye flickered.

"To get something from y'all, I guess."

The roar quickened Henry's blood, his guts turning against him. If he were dying, it would be like this; if he were being killed, it would feel this way. But he had more to ask. His voice came out in a fury.

"Why didn't he take my money? I had money. If that's what she wanted? I had it to take."

The man shook his head. "I don't know. I wish he had."

"I screamed it out—Daddy made me scream it out—I had money." His mind raced. "*She* knew I had it! She musta told him—"

"She did. She wanted him to. I don't know."

Tears boiled in his eyes, snot ran onto his lip.

"Why'd he look at me that way?"

The man turned his face away.

"Why—" Henry swallowed hard, a rock in his throat, "—did he stop?"

The man shook his head fiercely, scattering his hair about his shoulders.

"I don't *know*." His stare rolled about the place, as if it were suddenly unfamiliar. Then he leveled his eye at Henry and shouted. "I don't know why he does what he does."

The stove wood sent red sparks shooting from the iron door. Henry tottered on his feet.

He shifted his weight so that he could look back at the red plastic cover hanging in the chifforobe. Then he glanced through the open door, at the tired light that spilled over the porch.

"Where'd he go?"

The old man took a long breath, nearly too tired to tell. "He feeds a dog back in there. Gets scraps from what people throwed out, 'n feeds 'im."

Henry heard him shake his head, his hair rustling.

"I told him he'd wind up gittin' bit, but he won't listen." He paused, as if to unhitch one thought and buckle another. When he spoke again, his voice was quieter, distracted.

"He'll come back in a while. He never goes too far off, with me needin' him so much now." The man nodded, assuring himself that it was so. "He'll come back."

Henry grunted. He was dazed with weakness, more drunk than he knew. It made him want to laugh.

"You so sure?"

The old man looked past him, unbothered. "Yes. He's that kind."

The night grew loud outside the door; it pulled at Henry; there was no reason to stay.

"Don't tell," the man called after him, his voice knotted in a plead. "Don't tell 'bout us! We won't get the checks if you do!"

But Henry was already out the door, down from the porch, over the rottening fence. He shook his head that he would not tell, though by then he was well out of sight.

———

He saw a hill, climbed it, then circled down again; another hill, a third. His hands grabbed at saplings like an old man reaching for canes. He wasn't sure of the way, but he knew the direction.

Another hill, the smell of cedars, the carol of bugs. A pain grew in his chest, a blossom of what he had felt before.

Another creek, or the same one again. The pain had a new color this time, a bright red edge that forced tears from his eyes.

If he could see the boy's bobbing light, he would run him down. He would have the right questions by the time he saw him. This time he would talk, and Henry would understand.

Was this a hill he knew? A bend of path he had felt? It seemed so. No matter. At the crest he would see, and the crest was close.

The pain leapt—the jagged end of a jagged stake. It rocked him to a stop. He held his arms out to the dark, as if to fend off blows, and a hand went up to touch the pain. His eyes closed in its favor, submitted.

Now. Now, his heart was being thrust through his rib cage. He shivered and dropped, the moist groundwater seeping through his pants' knees. The heels of his hands met in a clasp, pressed down on his breastbone, to hide the sound. His heart was an apple, pushed through the mesh of a screen door.

If he could have found him, he could have faced him. His face would have told him all.

Henry climbed to his feet again, to get to the top of the hill. The only air was there, the only relief. But when he finally reached the crest, felt its curve under the soles of his feet, it betrayed him. The ripe, steady suffering buckled his legs, drove his eyes fast. His mouth opened, shut, his teeth clacked.

The straining of meat through a sieve—a mad pumping in the bony case of his chest. He would die. Here. Among cedars, under the hot, close smell of birds. And a great company of pain would be with him, as real as a person.

Again, he saw the red, chapped mouth, the sounds it had made, two taps of rain water—

He was going back to his father. In spite of. Anyway. No matter. Because he was that kind.

Everything rose inside him—pulled out by hooks and anchors: what he had wanted, what he had thought he had wanted, what they had wanted, what they thought they had wanted—scratching and knocking out into the open—a house, exploded.

His eyes opened to see what he had smelled in his nostrils, tasted on his tongue.

Though it was a hill and a pasture away—he would die within the light of home.

On a bit further, so they would at least know he had been coming back—that he had been on his way—towards them, and what had made him. It was important that they know. It was all that was worth doing.

But as he walked, the pain faded—shimmered lightly through his chest into the cool night air. He stopped and felt for the wet, mangled pulp, the butchered mess. Instead, his heart beat beneath his palm with steady, sharp thumps, loud as metal rings.

Henry stood still, listening to the meter of old, old music. His breathing rose and fell in currents—cool to warm, salt to fresh. He dragged in sweet gulps of cedar-cooled breeze, each black breath filling the hollow inside him.

In time, he began his descent; nervously at first, feeling his way from place to place, then with increasing speed and strength, as though he were bearing in his arms, down the hillside, the first and last of some much-needed thing.

Chapter 16

Cox stared through the panes until his eyes shifted focus, found his own reflection—slick and shadowed—staring back at him. He withdrew; moved on.

Wandering from window to window, jingling the truck keys in his pocket, he argued with himself as to whether he should go or not. As he made his rounds, he turned on all the lights and lamps, indoors and out.

Let Martha have her steer, Cox thought. Let her have him, for all the good he can do. I never wanted her in the first place.

In fact, he would be at Lois's right now, screwing her raw, if Henry hadn't wandered away. But he couldn't leave. Not yet, anyhow. Not with him still gone.

He walked to the back door screen and stared out at the barn. It was quiet, but he was sure the boy was there. Probably sitting in the loft, studying his lap. Cox mulled over whether to go get him and end the whole thing. It had been hours now. He lay a hand on the mesh to open the door, then thought again.

He'll come in after a while, he told himself. He stared into the loft door, searching for some movement in the dark. His palm eased off the screen. It gave a gentle squeal and popped closed.

He'll come in, soon as he's hungry enough.

But time passed, and Cox himself grew hungry. He stood in front of the open refrigerator door and ate, on the spot, most of what was left inside: a cold hamburger patty, a plug of dried cheddar cheese, wilted red celery, dill pickles, some tuna fish that had browned, and two bites out of a bruised peach. He switched the TV on and turned it up loud, so that he could hear the noise of a baseball game without watching. Then he sat in his chair and waited.

It wasn't just Henry that kept him there. He was also waiting for Tollet to come to. Between mouthfuls, he decided to go back to the old man's room and cut on his bedside lamp, so that he would wake up thirsty, but not scared. Then he came back to the TV and sat.

Cox swallowed. Before, when he had held Tollet's head under the water, he had come too close.

The thought brought him out of his seat. He switched the set off and walked back to the kitchen. Pulling the last fifth from the cabinet—Wild Turkey—he tore off the seal and carried the bottle to Tollet's bedside table.

More time passed. He moved from chair to counter to chair. His keys rattled like muffled bells. At length, he went back to the kitchen, folded two pieces of bread around the next to the last hamburger—Henry might want one—kicked the door shut, and carried the sandwich and a beer back to his room.

He stopped to look out the hall window, to see if the boy was coming. Nothing, except that the moonlight was thicker than before, glazing the barn lot and the fence around it.

Cox shook himself and continued down the hall.

The projector was out all the time now, sitting on a card table beside his bed. He had dragged his over-size dresser against the window, so that there was more white space on the wall. That way, he could turn the lens a few notches and make the picture grow. The women became giants, their heads touching his ceiling as they loomed over the bed.

Cox laid the sandwich on the card table, placed his beer on the floor, and sat down to rifle through his cigar box full of films. Two new ones were on order—one about Jungle women, another about a car wash. Neither had come in the mail yet.

He picked up the reel that starred his favorite—the brown-haired, mousy, secretary-type with a hard body and wildcat eyes. But he shook his head and laid it down again. He didn't want to see that one tonight. His second favorite, a hard-core job from Mexico, wasn't doing much for him lately; no surprises anymore. Its failure to stir him was worrisome, so he shuffled it to the bottom of the stack. He flipped the tapes over one by one, considering, rejecting—too tame—too old.

He found his third-best favorite, which took place in a lake, on a bass boat. But the tape had broken a few weeks back. The woman had been leaning over a casting chair when a small, yellow sun appeared on the screen, growing like an A-bomb as it ate through the celluloid. He had rushed to stop the projector, but the strip was already burned in two. Though he had patched it once, the patch had caused the film to hang against the projector bulb.

He sniffed hard, swallowed his snot, then stared at the film's soldered edges. The thought of the red casting chair made him pick the reel up and string the ribbon out to see if he could fix it better.

After a few bites of sandwich, ketchup oozing from the sides, he crawled across the waterbed and pulled some scotch tape off his dresser top. With a strip stuck to his index finger, he tried to rejoin the two ribbons of film.

Pictures flashed through Cox's head—Martha's mouth as she had talked to him—the actress in the casting chair, her bra falling to the indoor-outdoor carpet on the bass boat floor—Henry's head bumping, his fingers scratching, at the wall—the way he had felt so light, like a baby—light enough to scare him when he had lifted him from the floor by his collar—light enough to hurt if he had yanked too hard. And Tollet.

Cox pinched the bridge of his nose.

It was too dark for such close work. His eyes ached. So he crawled over the bed again and lifted the only lamp from the dresser top. Setting it on the floor, he plugged it in and swung the shade sideways for light.

Though he folded the adhesive around the film once, it stuck in an awkward way. It would only snap and tear again. But when he tried to pull it loose, the film tore under the pressure. He cussed, grunted. Aggravation made him want to throw the thing down—like he had seen one of the girls—Lucy or Betsy?—do once, long ago, with a little string-laced shoe she had been unable to tie.

He steadied himself with a breath, then pulled off another piece of tape. He tried again, his tongue digging into the corner of his mouth.

Tollet turned over on his bed. Cox heard the springs creak, wildly. He waited, listened: faint movements, probably the quiet lift and drop of the bottle. The first strains of notes—fa—sol—la—then silence. It had started, but there was a ways to go yet. He still had time for a movie. He just had to keep an ear out.

Resettling over his work, he squinted at his hands. In the harsher light, he was able to make out which frame was torn—the tiny rainbow square of the bass boat, the brown water, the woman's hand coming into the picture.

Cox's fingers seemed huge, twisting the tape around the tiny film. They looked too big even to try. Feathers rumbled in his stomach, a rush of nerves. It was as if there was only so much time left, and he had to hurry. He didn't know why, but he felt the sharp, all-at-once awareness of a man about to be lunged for. Like an old memory, a bad dream, in which he was dragged across a dust-covered floor—hands scratching for purchase—he, himself, the last thing taken—given to a black mouth that lay beyond the edge.

Cox shot his gaze around the room as though something had been let loose on the floor. The dresser, covered with work clothes, barred the window; the waterbed, the card table, the projector—all the same. The door to the room was closed. But the light coming from the lamp on the floor cast a vast, dense circle on the ceiling, a circle that funneled down to the shadowy bottom, where Cox sat.

Just as quickly as it had come, the nervous feeling left him. And, with a jar, he felt the opposite thing: time had slowed, even stopped. He had ages to do his work.

He noticed how massive his hands were, nervously fussing, twisting and re-twisting the slight ribbon of celluloid. It was cheap and tore easily.

Ages to do it.

He blushed, as though a trick had been played, as though someone were prancing him about like a doll. His jaw eased open, his mouth gummy with drying spit.

And he had let them do it to him. He had let them hoax him, trick him. Take, take, take. Until there was nothing left but this—this fumbling.

Rage rumbled in his chest, rolled to the tops of his ears. His eyes narrowed, pulled tight.

And *him*—with the nerve to lie there, quiet. Now, of all times, to be quiet. For all Cox knew, he was listening, waiting for the next thing to steal, figuring out the next string to pull.

Cox had to show them, every one of them. He had to be able to stand up to the lawyer, or the court, or whoever it was that could end this and say: See? Listen! Hear? *That*—all my life. All my life."

He was tired of waiting.

It took two strides to cross the room. The door flew open, banged against the wall. A few strides more to Henry's room, where he found the recorder on the boy's desk. He took the microphone, studying the switches as he moved down the dark hall.

When he first turned into Tollet's room, he thought for a moment that he had reentered his own. The bed was piled with clothes and sheets, a dim shadowy light came from the wall outlet. But no. There was Tollet, lying on his back. He was partly propped up, his head on the bed board, his chest and shoulders on top of a folded pillow. His pajama top had come loose in his tossings, exposing his sunken ribs, his fallen, hairless chest. The whisky bottle lay against his thigh, his left hand holding it loosely. His eyes were hooded, dreary, but from his lips poured the full, rounded notes of a song.

"Sol—la—meeeee . . . ," and it stopped.

"Sol—mee—laaaaa. . . ."

Cox stole around the wall, eased close to the bed, kneeling at its side. Quietly, carefully. He had to keep everything as it was, drive it deeper. He turned off the bedside lamp, so that the room was spread with a diffuse light.

His hands shook as he fumbled with the recorder's buttons. Once before he had come here, to do this—once before, while his father lay drunk—to catch this shame. But he had not been able to make the thing work. The box refused him. He had pushed "record" over and over, but it would never set the wheels spinning like it did for Henry. He had flicked the button on the microphone, and held it close to his father's groaning mouth, but it had never caught a word, not a note. He couldn't prove that it had happened. Afterwards, when he had played the tape for himself, all he heard was the empty sound of steady wind, the flow of water. Another trick.

"Now," whispered Tollet. "This one."

His bleary eyes struggled to find something—his place on a phantom page—and he began.

"Fa—so—la—la—"

Cox budded with sweat. He couldn't miss this—it was what he needed to bring the house down. He pushed a button and waited. A shudder passed through the cross of his shoulders at the sound of his son's voice.

"*What is the capital of Alabama?*"

He jerked to his left. His gaze shot up to Tollet, who blinked, but kept singing—

"—sol la me fa. . . ."

"*Montgomery,*" Henry said again.

He had forgotten to change tapes. Quickly, he pressed what he thought was the "stop" button, but a squeal came out instead—a screech, like blowing against plastic.

"What? What?" said Tollet.

Cox jumped. The old man's gaze rolled over to him. The eyes were clearer than Cox had expected. He wasn't as drunk as usual. In fact, he was swimming up, towards sense.

Cox rose on his knees, leaned close to his father's withered ear. He swallowed, licked his lips.

"Sing," he whispered, his breath hot. "Sing for me."

Tollet blinked. He made something like a sleepy, pleased nod. A breath, then— "Sol—faaa—mee—sol. . . ."

Cox lifted the box close to his face, his eyes paining to find the right switch. He pushed "record" as hard as he could, mashing it with his thumb. But nothing happened. He shook the box hard, strangling it, then grabbed up the dangling microphone. He flicked the button on its side, as Henry had.

"*What is the state flower of Alabama?*"

"Shit!" He found the stop button—the only one that worked.

Tollet shuffled about. Cox felt his stare, and locked gazes with his father, who had breached the surface now. Cox had to be careful, to soothe him back down. He leaned closer.

"Sing, Daddy," he whispered. He heard his voice, a boy's from years ago, asking the same.

Tollet's lids batted once, a slow drag. His mouth fumbled for the tune. But instead of notes, he let out a scratched groan. His brow clouded.

"Sing?" the old man asked. "Sing—what?"

Cox's mind worked to find the tune—a dark, minor-keyed song that had always scared him. He had loved it.

"'Come Humble Sinner, In Whose Breast,'" he whispered.

Tollet's face held still, sank beneath confusion. Cox saw it was somehow stirring the old man, sobering his cluttered brain.

"What?" he said, rising on his pillow.

"Just start—" urged Cox. He wanted to yell. "Start in the middle."

"No, No." shook Tollet. He rose further, catching at the sides of his open shirt. He looked suffocated, smothered. "I don't know it—I don't know it—"

Another trick. Another lie. Cox bit his lip, trying to stop himself. It was no use.

"Yes, you do!" he snapped. "By God, you do, too!"

His eyes flashed. He walked closer on his knees, rocking on the caps, his teeth in a tight grit.

Tollet shrank back.

"La—Fa La La Sol Mi—Fa Fa —Fa Fa Sol La La Fa La."

Cox's voice rose and fell in a murmuring sway, then faded into hums—a drone that melted on the plane of his tongue.

Tollet's gaze unmoored as he sang. His face softened at the memory. When Cox saw it, he stopped.

"Now go on," he ordered. "Finish it."

The old man smiled a feeble smile, but when his eyes found Cox, they were bleeding with fire.

"That," said Tollet, stoked. "I'd forgot that. Used to sing that—" and with a cut of his eyes, he motioned to the hill, and beyond the hill. "—back there. I'd forgot it. You reminded me."

Cox slid backwards, onto his heels, into the shadows. The old man leaned out, towards him.

"You 'membered for me," said Tollet. His voice was dizzy, but stronger. His blazing eyes broke through a film and rose towards sense. "You was there. All along. See? See?"

Cox shuffled back further, turned his head down to study the box.

"Just—sing," he said.

"You 'membered."

"Shut up. Sing."

Tollet attempted to rise. He swung his legs around and sat on the side of the bed.

Cox winced. That he could have this strength. He tried to walk backwards on his knees, but he was hemmed in by the wall. He couldn't back far enough away.

"All day singin'—back there," said Tollet, his breath, reedy. "Singin'—and dinner on the grounds. And you, and your mama, and—"

He wobbled about, nearly falling forward. He caught himself with a clasp at the mattress' edge. His gaze shot up, driving at Cox.

"And me—'n somebody—'n somebody else—sang that song—what you just sung."

Cox shrank onto his heels. A pain grew in his stomach.

"Sing it again, son," said Tollet. Cox blinked at the soured breath. "Start—I'll follow."

Cox shook his head. It weighed so much.

"Start," Tollet repeated. "I'll follow—"

"Shut up," muttered Cox.

"I heard you!" said Tollet, his eyes flashed.

He shook his head and kept shaking it.

Lies. Lies. Cox wrapped himself in the word, pulling it over him like a blanket.

But between the lies, a horrible shudder broke through his mind, waves of dark and light: the ribbons and the war and the woman who never was. But—also—and now, more than ever, brighter than ever: the men—slick-headed, tenor-voiced—holding parchment paper—a long brown church. And behind the paper, rising like a sun or a moon, his father's young, scrubbed face, his father's mouth, making shapes, calling notes, singing harps—the form of a love that could both kill and raise. The memory fastened in his mind—a picture hung from thick wire, on a iron nail's head.

Cox's skin went numb under his father's stare. What was he holding? What was in his hands? Truck—drum—a small black box? He pushed at the buttons—a confused squeal.

"*The Camellia,*" it said, and he screamed for his son.

"Henry? Come help me!"

"Go on! Start!" called Tollet—his face, voice, eager.

"Shut up!" Cox shouted. "Lyin'!"

Tollet shuffled closer still.

"It's true!" said Tollet, shaking his head. "How come you know it—if it ain't true?

"Lyin' sonuvabitch," he said, his voice taking old roads, falling into old grooves.

Tollet flinched, his eyes filling with yellow, sullied water. His breath rattled like a box of sticks.

"Say you know," he ordered, in a young man's voice. Low, hard, but clear—Cox had forgotten the timbre and tone. But now it rose over him, where he knelt. "Say you know."

"Henry—Come here!"

Now, the worst came near his heart, like a knife, turned sideways, sliding in to prize and prize and prize beneath his skin—splitting flesh from meat.

For if they were lies—the loss of lies was no loss. But if they were true—if only just a part—if only just a little; then God, the waste. God, the loss.

"Henry? Henry?" he cried, with a last reach.

The box slipped from his hands, cracking on wood.

All was hunger, and need, and a dark hole growing.

"Henry! Henry!"

With a rush—birds on the rise—the screen door pushed opened: the high, tuning sound of hinges, beginning their song.

Beats on carpet, wood, carpet: the drummed rhythm of feet meeting floor.

Cox closed his eyes at the approach—towards him, for him.

"Here I am," came his son's voice, filling the door. "It's all right. I'm here."

And his voice was shapes—notes—plucks upon harp strings— spreading through the dark, thirsty porches of his father's ears.

A *House All Stilled* was designed and typeset on a Macintosh computer system using QuarkXPress software. The text is set in Goudy and the chapter openings are set in Helvetica Neue. This book was designed by Cheryl Carrington, typeset by Kimberly Scarbrough, and manufactured by Thomson-Shore, Inc.